"Ms. McBride has excelled in this book . . . the pages will fly by and make you hate to turn the last page."
—MyShelf.com

"Will make you believe in heroes . . . Ms. McBride does a fine job of capturing small-town Southern charm . . . a heart-warming story."
— *Contemporary Romance Reviews*

"McBride has scored a bull's-eye with the sizzling chemistry between her two protagonists . . . a fun, flirty, and feel-good read."
— *Heartstrings*

"A very enjoyable story . . . an exciting story line with exceptional characters."
— *The Romance Reader's Connection*

## . . . and *STILL MR. & MRS.*

"Outrageously fun . . . thoroughly enjoyable."
— *Publishers Weekly*

"McBride deftly spins the estranged lovers through the hoops of passion and danger."
—NORA ROBERTS

"This lighthearted presidential adventure rings true with a compelling mix of comedy and heart-tugging emotion."
—CHRISTINA SKYE

"Mary McBride serves up a book that is both filled with action and packed with emotion . . . witty and invigorating reading."
—*Romantic Times*

# SAY IT AGAIN, SAM

ALSO BY MARY MCBRIDE

*Ms. Simon Says*
*My Hero*
*Still Mr. & Mrs.*

# SAY IT AGAIN, SAM

## Mary McBride

NEW YORK    BOSTON

Copyright © 2004 by Mary Vogt Myers

*Cover design by Diane Luger*
*Cover art by Michael Racz*
*Book design by Giorgetta Bell McRee*

Warner Books

Time Warner Book Group
1271 Avenue of the Americas
New York, NY 10020
Visit our Web site at www.twbookmark.com

Printed in the United States of America

First Paperback Printing: December 2004

10 9 8 7 6 5 4 3 2 1

*For Kimberly Hartstein,*
*My favorite long-haired lady*

# SAY IT
# AGAIN,
# SAM

# CHAPTER ONE

On a map, the township of Shelbyville, Michigan, re-
sembled a startled face. Blue Lake and Pretty Lake, each
very nearly round, formed a pair of staring eyes, set wide
by the dense woods between them. The pinched lobes of
Little Glory Lake sufficed for a nose, and just below it,
Heart Lake was carved out like an open, astonished
mouth.

Or, if you didn't have much imagination, Shelbyville
township looked like five lakes and a hell of a lot of trees
just above the forty-third parallel and a few miles east of
Mecklin, the county seat.

The population of Shelbyville was 1,245 souls, give or
take a soul or two. In June, July, and August, though, that
figure swelled, almost doubling with the influx of tourists,
or what the townspeople called "the summer folks." And
the summer folks tended to get in a lot more trouble than
the residents.

It was summer now, and Constable Sam Mendenhall
was responding to an early-morning call about more trouble. He walked into the post office carrying the coffee he'd

picked up at the Gas Mart, wondering why the postmistress had summoned him instead of the feds.

"What's up, Thelma?" he asked the elderly postmistress.

"Somebody stole my flag."

Sam took a thoughtful sip of the steaming brew, hiding his exasperation behind the paper cup. From her urgent tone on the telephone, he'd been expecting an actual burglary. He thought her cash drawer had been cleaned out, or that someone had made off with her stamps.

"It was a brand-new one, too. I just got it a couple weeks ago." She slapped a liver-spotted hand on the countertop. "Damn it all. In over fifty years, I haven't missed a single day — not one! — of running my flag up the flagpole out there. A lot longer than you've been alive, Sam Mendenhall, I'll have you know." She shook a crooked finger in his face.

Obviously Thelma didn't think he was taking this seriously enough. The last thing he wanted to do was to insult her. He'd known Thelma Watt his entire life. She had been Shelbyville's postmistress for more than half a century, which meant she knew more about the local population than they knew about themselves.

Just by handling the mail, Thelma knew who was getting ahead, who was falling behind, who was simply holding on. She knew whose children wrote home once they'd left the nest, whose sweethearts abruptly quit their correspondence, whose hearts had been broken by lined paper and a ballpoint pen.

His, for instance.

Hell.

Sam didn't doubt for a second that the old gal had read every postcard that passed through this building and held every interesting envelope up to the light. He wondered how many of those cards and letters had been his.

"Any idea who might have taken the flag?" he asked her now.

She glared across her counter, looking down her nose at him — a pretty amazing feat since he was six-two to her diminutive five one.

"Of course I know who took it," she snapped. "The same criminal who's been taking all the other things around town. Who else would it be?"

She was probably right, Sam decided. There'd been a lot of weird stuff going on lately. Things just went missing. Weird things. The curtains in Carol Dunlap's sun porch. Every single jar of peanut butter at the grocery store. A Detroit Tigers coffee mug that Jim Bickford had been sipping from one minute, then the next minute — pfft — it was gone. Last week, after graduation ceremonies at the high school, somebody noticed an empty space in the trophy case where the bronzed pigskin for the state football champs of 1968 should've been.

There was more. Sam had a list in the glove compartment of his Jeep.

Now he'd be adding Thelma's flag.

As crime waves went, this one seemed fairly innocuous. But still . . . Plenty of people were spooked, and Thelma was downright mad.

"How did it happen?" he asked her. "Somebody break in, or did they take it down from the pole?"

"I never had time to get it up there. I took it outside at seven-fifteen, just like always, hooked it on to the lanyard, but then the phone rang before I could run it up the pole. When I got back outside, the durn thing was gone."

"Who was on the phone?" Sam asked.

"Nobody." The elderly woman blinked. "Are you thinking that call was some sort of diversion?"

He shrugged. In fact, he was thinking it was probably just a wrong number, or that the octogenarian postmistress moved so slowly that the caller had hung up before Thelma reached the phone.

"I'll see what I can find out," he told her.

"You do that."

He was already on his way to the door when she called him back.

"Wait a minute, Sam. Mercy. I was so upset about my flag that I almost forgot to tell you. Beth Simon's coming back from California. Her mail's already being forwarded here."

"Oh."

It was all he could think of to say. His mind was suddenly a complete blank. His heart had given one hard kick, then seemed to quit beating entirely. He felt like an idiot and probably looked like one, too.

Thelma's head was cocked to one side, and there was an expectant expression on her face. Sam couldn't decide if the slant of her mouth was sympathetic or snide. What was it she wanted him to say?

*Oh, goodie. That's great. Glad to hear it. Good old Beth. I can't wait to see the woman who dumped me sixteen years ago.*

He drained the rest of his coffee, crumpled the paper cup in his fist, then lobbed it into the tall trash can against the far wall.

"I'll let you know what I find out about the flag, Thelma," he said, then turned and walked out the door before the woman could say another word.

☆

Poor Sam. Thelma had meant to warn him a bit more gently, perhaps even accompany the warning with some sage advice; but she'd been so discombobulated by the stolen flag that she'd simply blurted out the news about Beth, and the fellow had just stood there, looking like she'd punched him in the gut.

Not that she would have expected any other reaction, considering the history of those two.

She reached beneath the counter for the rubber-banded packet of mail that had arrived yesterday from San Francisco, CA 94117. There was a MasterCard statement as thick as a ham sandwich, a bill from San Francisco General Hospital, and a subscription renewal to *Victorian Times*. After more than half a century in the post office, Thelma could tell an awful lot from a few pieces of mail.

Obviously things hadn't worked out for little Beth Simon in California. She was broke, or at least heavily in debt. That no-good boyfriend of hers, the one she'd gone to California with, had undoubtedly hit her again, this time hard enough to send her to the emergency room. She was headed back here, to her family's big old Victorian house on Heart Lake.

On second thought, it was probably good that Thelma hadn't fully apprised Sam. After all, the U.S. mail was privileged information, not meant for passing on to third parties.

He'd find out for himself soon enough.

And for mercy's sake, she hoped he also found out who made off with her flag.

☆

Sam sat in his jeep, staring at the little spiral notebook and its growing list of oddities. There didn't seem to be a

pattern. At least none that he could discern. The only thing
that seemed to make any sense was that it was some kind
of scavenger hunt. The culprits were likely to be some of
the summer kids with too little supervision and too much
time on their hands. Still, a bit of petty theft was preferable
to drugs, booze, drag racing, or any other crazy stunts that
kids could pull.

He wasn't going to lose sleep over it. With any luck,
he'd catch one of the young perps in the act, give him or
her a stern talking to, then turn the little bastard over to
Thelma for whatever punishment she deemed appropriate.

Thelma. He'd managed to block out what she'd told
him for a full five minutes, but now her words hit him
again like a slap across the face.

*Beth Simon's coming back from California.*

The woman might just as well have said a giant asteroid
was going to hit Shelbyville, its date and time still to be determined. If she'd meant to inflict damage on him, the old
crone could've just reached for the ancient revolver she kept
illegally beneath her counter and put a bullet right between
his eyes. Her words had had just about the same effect.

He didn't want to think about Beth. It seemed as if he'd
spent the first half of his life thinking of nothing and no
one else, then spent the second half of his life trying to forget her. Not that he'd had much success.

Returning his attention to the list of missing objects,
Sam tried to forget her again by concentrating on the mysterious thief. What sort of idiot would steal the curtains
right off their rods in a person's house? They weren't even
good ones, Carol Dunlap had said, but water-stained and
bleached out by the sun. *Crappy* had been her exact description, and she was glad for an excuse to replace them,
even as she was mystified by their disappearance.

· The missing football trophy and the flag at least made sense. Especially the flag. Sam could understand a kid playing a prank on the postmistress. She could be terrifying. Sam had been a pretty fearless kid, but Thelma Watt had made him stutter once or twice. He remembered one time when he and Beth . . .

No. He didn't want to remember.

"Hey, Sheriff."

Sam turned his head toward the sidewalk to meet the steady gaze of a little boy who was maybe seven or eight years old. "I'm not the sheriff," he said. "I'm the constable."

Actually he was more like a rent-a-cop. His salary, such as it was, was paid partly by the Heart Lake Residents' Association and partly by the Shelbyville Chamber of Commerce. He didn't wear a uniform. He didn't carry a weapon. His powers of arrest were comparable to those of any citizen. By and large his duties entailed patrolling vacant summer cottages, annoying teenagers, and making sure that all the drunks at the Penalty Box got safely home without killing themselves or anybody else. Now he was apparently in charge of errant curtains, coffee cups, and flags.

"My dad says you're not so tough," the kid said, his little freckled face twisting in belligerence.

"Oh, yeah? Who's your dad?"

"Joe Dolan."

Well, that explained it. Sam pictured the freckle-faced boy he'd gone to school with. Joe Dolan was built like a fireplug and had even less personality, if that was possible. He was a lazy, flat-footed wrestler, a face-mask-grabbing defensive end, and an avid bully. Like all those of that ilk, he picked on the kids who were smaller, lighter, less apt to defend themselves. From kindergarten through their senior year, Joe had steered clear of Sam. Apparently he was still steering clear of him because in the year or so that Sam had been back, he hadn't seen Joe Dolan once.

"What's your dad up to these days?" he asked as if he truly cared.

"Nothin'," the boy said. "He's got a bad back."

It probably matched his bad attitude, Sam thought.

"My dad says you were a Green Beret."

"Something like that," Sam replied.

"He says that's no big deal."

Sam shrugged. He wasn't going to argue with an elf in a striped T-shirt and red canvas Keds.

The elf sneered. "I bet you don't even wear a gun."

"Don't need one," Sam said in a voice faintly reminiscent of Gary Cooper in *High Noon*.

"How tall are you?" Joe's offspring demanded.

"Six-two. How tall are you?"

The boy lifted his shoulders, then let them drop. He probably didn't even know how tall he was, or maybe he figured it wasn't cool to proclaim he was all of four-foot-two or -three. "What do you weigh?"

"Depends," Sam said.

"Oh, yeah? On what?"

"On whether or not I've eaten a little boy for breakfast."

The kid's eyes bulged like little green crabapples, and it was all Sam could do not to laugh.

Just then a fire engine red Miata sped past him, doing at least sixty down Shelbyville's main drag, where the posted speed limit was a stodgy twenty-five. Sam turned the key in the ignition, reached under the seat for his red light, and slapped it on the hood of the Jeep.

"See ya, kid," he said, and took off in pursuit.

☆

It took about two minutes — and two miles down the road — for Sam to feel less like Gary Cooper and more like one of the Keystone Kops.

His ancient, Army surplus jeep could barely keep up with the speeding Miata. The red light he'd slapped on the hood broke loose when he hit a pothole in the road. Little wonder since the rinky-dink, battery-powered implement was only attached by a flimsy rubber suction cup. And for lack of a siren, Constable Sam Mendenhall was forced to honk his horn like some maniac.

Meanwhile the guy behind the wheel of the Miata wasn't slowing down a bit. When Sam was able to pull up close enough, he could see the baseball cap on the guy's head, and he was pretty sure that the son of a bitch gave him the finger just before turning off onto Eighteen Mile Road. Man, he couldn't wait to run this asshole to the ground.

That happened thirty seconds later when the little red sports car's right rear tire blew, sending the car veering into the oncoming lane for a couple hundred feet before the driver was able to get control and maneuver off the black-top onto the weedy shoulder of the road.

Sam pulled over and killed his engine. He hoped it was Joe Dolan in the Miata. He was going to pull him through the driver's window by his earlobes and dropkick him all the way back to town.

"You could've killed somebody, asshole," he shouted, striding toward the red car, slapping its rear fender before he reached the driver's door.

"I know. Oh, God."

The female voice floated through the open window. Well, it wasn't Joe Dolan unless he'd had a sex change operation. Sam's anger ratcheted down a notch. Maybe he was a sexist pig, but he didn't treat women the way he treated men. Never had. Never would. Not in this life.

"Are you okay?" he asked.

"Just a little shaky," she said. "That was really stupid of me. I'm sorry."

As she spoke, she took one hand off the wheel and reached up to pull the baseball cap from her head. Blond curls — a torrent of them — cascaded onto her shoulders. And then she turned and blinked up at him with those perfect-day-in-June blue eyes.

Jesus. He couldn't breathe.

"Sam?"

"Hello, Beth."

# CHAPTER TWO

A few minutes later, Beth Simon was fairly certain she was having an out-of-body experience. What else could it be? Although her actual body was leaning casually against the hood of the car with her arms crossed and her lips moving and making small talk with Sam, her consciousness seemed to be hovering somewhere overhead, gazing down in amazement while offering snide remarks about the little drama unfolding below.

Beth hadn't seen Sam Mendenhall in over sixteen years, not since the rat bastard had dumped her and married somebody else. She hadn't wanted to see him again — *ever* — and yet here she was smiling and chitchatting and sounding oh-so-sweet and sincere.

*It's so good to see you.*

When Beth uttered those words, the evil twin above her made a strangled noise.

*So, how've you been, Sam?*

*Horrible, I hope.* Her alter ego stopped strangling and began to rant. *I hope you've been absolutely miserable. Suffering from migraines and allergies and incurable*

*postnasal drip. Plagued by boils. Chronically unemployed.
Homeless. Helpless. Utterly hopeless. Incontinent. Impotent!*

*You're looking good, Sam.*

*Good?* The voice above her snorted. Sam Mendenhall
looked great! In sixteen years, the lanky boy she'd loved
had filled out very nicely. Very nicely indeed. He seemed
taller by an inch or two and more muscular. Strong. Solid.
In a word — a hunk.

Nobody had ever looked better in faded jeans and a
black polo shirt that molded to the contours of his broad
shoulders and the sculpted muscles of his chest. His brown
hair was the shade Beth remembered, only now it was
touched with a faint ripple of silver at the temples. His
hazel eyes seemed a deeper green, and they were edged by
crow's-feet that told of a million facial expressions that
Beth had never had the pleasure of seeing. His mouth
was . . .

*Stop staring,* her evil twin commanded from on high.

Was she staring? Or drooling? Dear God, she hoped not.
What had Sam just said?

"Pardon me?" Beth asked.

"I said pop your trunk lid so I can get your spare."

"Oh, you don't have to . . ."

The Sam she used to know so long ago would have argued with her or spent however long he needed to explain.
This guy just muttered a curse and promptly reached
through the Miata's open window and popped the trunk
himself.

"Well, if you insist," she said to his broad back, as he
moved toward the rear of the car.

"I insist," he growled.

Beth reached through the window and grabbed the cell
phone from its holder on the dashboard, then punched in

her sister's number in Chicago. While she waited for Shelby to pick up, Beth walked a short distance away from the car.

It was a beautiful day. At least it had been until just a few minutes ago. There was nothing like a buttery June sun in a clear blue Michigan sky with a cool breeze playing in the treetops. There were no buildings along this stretch of road — just fields — so every now and then you could catch a silvery glimmer of Heart Lake through the foliage.

This was Beth's favorite place in the whole wide world. After the long and grueling three-day drive from San Francisco, she'd stomped on the gas coming through Shelbyville, more eager than ever to get to the big house at the lake. And now — dammit — she'd probably have to leave.

Shelby picked up. Without greeting or preamble, Beth bit a long-distance chunk out of her sister's ass.

"You told me Sam wasn't here. You swore to me, Shelby. You crossed your heart. I think you even mentioned something about a stack of Bibles. How could you do that?"

The stunned silence on the other end of the line was a dead giveaway. Ms. Shelby Simon, famous advice columnist and Big Fat Liar, was scrambling for an answer.

"I am *so* angry," Beth went on. "What the hell am I going to do now? Where can I go? I can't stay here."

"Well . . ."

"Don't you dare give me advice," Beth snapped.

"I was just . . ."

"Well, don't. Don't just anything. Just . . . Just shut up."

"Hey! You called me, Beth. Remember?"

"Yeah. I know. And now I'm hanging up."

"But . . ."

Beth stabbed the OFF button, wishing she were using a big old black telephone whose receiver she could slam into its cradle. Twice! Cell phones simply didn't cut it when a person was throwing a fit.

For lack of a phone to slam, she walked a few paces, reached down for a rock, and pitched it as hard as she could across the road and into the field. Her little act of violence didn't make her feel any better, though. In fact, the sudden pain in her hand reminded her that acts of violence — punching someone, for instance — often resulted in more suffering for the puncher than the punchee.

It wasn't like her to slug people, as she had slugged her business partner and former boyfriend, Danny Eiler, a few weeks ago in San Francisco, injuring herself in the process while leaving him unscathed. It wasn't like her to lose her temper and hang up on people as she had just done with the Big Fat Liar. There'd even been a moment while chatting with Sam that she'd wanted to kick him in the shins or to smush half a grapefruit in his ever-so-handsome face.

What was happening to her?

She'd always been kind and gentle and agreeable, forever willing to compromise to settle any dispute. She was diligent and thoughtful. She was steady and reliable. Ask anyone. Beth Simon wasn't the sort to rock the boat. Could a thirty-three-year-old woman suddenly become a sociopath? she wondered.

Probably not, she decided. It was just that she'd been under so much stress lately, trying to make the final break from Danny, trying to convince herself that returning to Michigan was a step forward in her life rather than two steps back.

And then — Bam! — Sam.

Beth dragged in a long breath. Get a grip, she told herself. Be cool. At least be civil.

Turning to walk back to her car, Beth saw a white convertible approaching. When the car came alongside the disabled Miata, its driver hit the brakes. That was when Beth noticed that the vehicle was crammed with teenage girls — five of them to be exact, two in front, three in back, all giggling like . . . well . . . like teenage girls.

"Hi, Sam," they called out in what sounded like a single, simpering voice.

Sam stood up, smiling as he wiped his greasy hands on his jeans. "Ladies," he replied, the word rumbling sensuously in his throat. The giggles in the car increased. There was considerable sighing.

Beth rolled her eyes. Oh, this was just great. The former love of her life was now apparently the Hunk of Heart Lake, setting young hearts afire with a blazing grin and a voice as deep as God's.

"We're going to Blue Lake for some serious, kick-ass water-skiing, Sam," one of the girls said. "Wanna come?" Her invitation was followed by a backseat chorus of *Please, oh please*.

"Maybe some other time," he told them.

By now, Beth was standing only a foot or so away from The Hunk.

"Oh, go on, Sam," she said. "I'll call the Gas Mart and have somebody come finish changing the tire. You don't want to disappoint your . . . um . . . fans."

He pitched her a dark glare, then squatted to resume work on the tire.

"Sorry, girls," Beth said with a smile and a little shrug.

The young blonde behind the wheel glared at Beth. "Yeah. Right. I'll just bet you're sorry," she said before she floored the accelerator, laying several feet of rubber in the convertible's wake.

Beth watched the car speed north with its youthful and flirtatious cargo of long, shiny, windblown hair and tan, supple flesh. Fans of Sam, one and all. She remembered the feeling.

She wasn't the sort of woman who obsessed about her age, and she could never understand all those over-the-hill parties with their black balloons and black crepe paper and goofy, depressing gifts. Her own thirtieth birthday three years ago hadn't bothered her a bit. She'd felt like a grown-up at last.

But now all of a sudden she felt old, absolutely ancient, as if she'd gone from a relatively young, moderately buff thirty-three to a wrinkled and crotchety ninety-three, all in the past few minutes.

Gazing down at the top of Sam's head while he tightened the last of the bolts on her wheel, Beth found herself searching for more gray hairs among the brown ones and any telltale signs of a receding hairline or incipient baldness. He'd be thirty-five now, two years ahead of her going over the proverbial hill.

Not that it showed. His hairline was right where she'd last seen it sixteen years ago. The line of his jaw was firm as granite. His biceps didn't show a hint of flab. She searched his beltline for evidence of love handles, if not the beginnings of a potbelly. There was nothing there but muscle.

Physically, he was perfect. Too bad she couldn't say the same for his character.

"There you go," Sam said, standing up once more. He pointed to the spare. "That'll get you to the house, at least, but it's just temporary, Beth. You'll need to get a new tire as soon as possible."

She looked up into those deep green eyes and thought how easy it would be to drown in them all over again, how tempting it would be to forget what went wrong and go back to the time when loving Sam was a simple thing, the only thing, the center of her life. She thought about their last moments together before he'd left for basic training.

Funny. Sixteen years ago they had driven down this very road from Heart Lake to Shelbyville, where Sam was due to catch an early-morning bus for Detroit. Neither one of them had slept the night before. Undoubtedly, they'd made love, but that wasn't what Beth remembered. Her most vivid memory of that night was Sam cradling her on his lap. For hours, he'd practically rocked her like a child while he stroked her hair and whispered.

*Come with me, Bethie.*

*Marry me.*

"I will," she said now, meaning she'd see to the tire while she wondered what might have been if she'd said those same words sixteen years ago.

Sam nodded rather stiffly, then began to replace all the bags and boxes he'd removed from the trunk of the Miata in order to get to the spare.

"You don't have to do that, Sam. I can take it from here."

Sam ignored her, picking up her crammed, two-ton suitcase as if it were packed with feathers, and wedging it easily in the trunk. Since she couldn't dissuade him, Beth stood idly by and watched him.

He moved purposefully and without hesitation, unfazed by the amount of boxed-up junk on the pavement and the limited space in the trunk, packing it far more efficiently than Beth herself had done when leaving San Francisco.

With his ropy forearms and his mouth flattened in concentration, he moved with a kind of masculine grace that made it difficult for Beth to look away even as she felt the beginnings of longing deep inside her, a hunger that had nothing whatsoever to do with food or the fact that she hadn't eaten breakfast this morning because she'd been so anxious to get on the road.

When her cell phone suddenly chimed, she was incredibly grateful for the distraction. And when the little caller ID window displayed Shelby's number with its Chicago area code, Beth answered it anyway.

"What?" she barked instead of hello.

"So, tell me," Shelby said almost in a whisper, as if she knew that Sam was standing nearby. "What's going on up there?"

"It's not a good time," Beth said through clenched teeth.

"You're with Sam? Right now?"

"That would be the case. Yes."

Her sister was quiet a moment on the other end of the line, as if she were carefully considering her next words. As if for the first time in her life she was thinking before she spoke. "Give it a chance, Bethie," she said. "It might work out this time. For what it's worth, Mick spent some time with Sam last year and really liked him."

Whether or not Lieutenant Mick Callahan, Shelby's new husband, liked Sam didn't seem to be relevant.

"Okay. Fine," Beth replied.

"It was my fault, sweetie. There. I've said it. I can't believe I'm admitting it, but I was wrong. And I'm so sorry. I shouldn't have talked you out of eloping with him all those years ago."

It was probably the first time in her life that Shelby Simon Callahan had ever made such an admission. Under different circumstances, Beth might've let out a giant whoop or popped the cork on a bottle of champagne, but right now her sister's apologetic words carried little consolation and even less satisfaction. Hearing them, Beth simply rolled her eyes.

"I'll have to call you back, Shelby," she said, noticing that Sam was shoving the last of her luggage in the Miata's trunk.

"I was wrong, Beth," her sister said again.

"Yeah. Yeah." Beth broke the connection just as Sam slammed the trunk lid.

He brushed his hands on his jeans, drawing Beth's gaze downward, where the faded denim conformed to the muscles of his thighs.

"There you go," he said. "All set."

She forced her gaze upward to meet his. "Thank you, Sam."

"No problem. Get that tire replaced in the next few days, okay?"

She nodded.

"And lay off the accelerator going through town," he said.

"I know. I know."

"It was good seeing you, Beth." He started walking toward his vehicle, parked several yards behind hers.

This was it? That's all there was? After all these years? Beth felt a flutter of panic in her throat. "Sam! Wait!"

He turned, his eyes narrowed and his whole expression suddenly pinched with impatience. "Yeah?"

"Well, I . . . I want to repay you for the favor. For the tire."

"Don't worry about it."

"Why don't you come to the house for dinner tonight?"

Oh, God. No sooner had Beth said the words than she wished she could take them back.

Once again her evil twin materialized overhead, smacking her forehead, groaning, *I can't believe you just did that*.

Beth couldn't believe it either.

It was as if she'd lapsed into autopilot, extending her customary invitation to a meal. She was a great cook, if she did say so herself, and that was how she thanked people who did nice things for her — with *coq au vin,* with *bouillabaisse,* with roast chicken and rosemary potatoes to die for. But not Sam. She wasn't *that* grateful. Or that stupid.

Since she couldn't erase the invitation, she wished a bolt of lightning would strike from the clear blue sky and reduce her to a sizzling little patch of DNA on the pavement.

Then, when lightning didn't strike, she found herself silently praying, *Say no. Please say no*.

Sam was quiet, so she assumed, if the man had any sense at all, he was formulating a plausible excuse. Hey, a flat-out *no way* or an *I'd rather eat dirt* would've been fine with her.

"Sure," he said finally, without much enthusiasm. "What time?"

Beth, practically speechless, pulled a number out of the air. "Eight."

Sam nodded, just as the sound of a cell phone shrilled from his parked jeep. He ignored it, though, and continued to stare at her, his lips slightly parted as if there were something else he wanted to say.

Beth could only hope it was to tell her that, on second thought, he couldn't come to dinner because of a previous engagement, whether it was true or not.

The phone shrieked insistently at his back until Sam finally grimaced, and muttered, "I better get that."

"I guess so."

"See you at eight, then."

"Eight," Beth echoed, vaguely hoping that the world would end at seven-forty-five.

☆

Sam slung a hip onto the jeep's front seat and practically ripped the bleeping cell phone from the dash.

"Yeah," he growled.

"Well, you don't have to bite my head off, for heaven's sake. What did you eat for breakfast, Sam? Nails?"

It was Blanche Kroll, Shelbyville's town clerk and longtime busybody. Between her and Thelma Watt, the postmistress, no secret was secure within a ten-mile radius of the town. Because the constable had no official office, Sam worked out of an old battered desk in a corner of the little cinder-block town hall where Blanche held sway.

"Something else has gone missing," she told him now.

"Thelma's flag," Sam said as he watched Beth maneuver the Miata back onto the road and head north at a reasonable speed. The turnoff to the Simon house was only three-quarters of a mile ahead.

"Something *else*," Blanche snapped.

She sounded like a snake about to strike, and Sam held the phone away from his ear a moment before listening again. He caught her in midsentence.

". . . took the darn thing right off the windowsill."

"What thing?" Sam asked.

"The apple pie she'd just baked and set in the window to cool. She no more'n turned around, and it was gone."

Sam got the gist of the crime. "What time did this happen?" he asked.

"About fifteen minutes ago."

"Okay. I'll swing by, take a look around, and talk to Lorna."

"No, don't do that, Sam," Blanche said. "She's too embarrassed."

"About losing a pie?"

"Not that. But something else went missing at the same time."

"What?"

"The brassiere that was drying on the line in the backyard."

He almost laughed. First a flag, then an apple pie and a bra. Their mysterious thief seemed to be a starving, patriotic cross-dresser.

"Poor Lorna's mortified," Blanche said. "You've seen her, Sam. She's . . . well . . . she's . . ."

"Well endowed," Sam suggested, glimpsing a brief and top-heavy mental image of the victim.

With a sigh, Blanche seemed to concur. "Just go over there and take a look around outside. Maybe there are footprints or something."

Sam doubted that since it hadn't rained for at least two weeks, but he agreed to snoop around anyway, for all the good a footprint would do. What then? Call the Mecklin County cops to cast the print of a hot pie and huge bra thief? They'd laugh him out of the county.

"Oh, and Sam?" Blanche said. "I guess you heard about Beth Simon coming back."

"Yep."

"Wonder how long she plans to stay out there at the lake?"

"Dunno."

He was sounding like Gary Cooper again, he thought.

Grim and clipped. *Yep. Nope. Dunno.* He and Beth weren't anybody's business but their own. But he knew damn well that was wishful thinking in a town like Shelbyville, where everyone's personal business was grist for the local mill. With the exception of his service with Delta Force, everyone in town knew pretty much everything about him. Hell, for all he knew, his secretive Army career was common knowledge, too.

"I'm on my way to Lorna's. I should be there in five minutes," he said, then quickly ended the call before Blanche could say anything else.

Sam sat there a few minutes, staring at the spot on the shoulder of the road where the red Miata had been, thinking about Beth instead of business, wishing she hadn't come back, wondering why she'd invited him to dinner and why he'd accepted the invitation and what sort of trouble tonight would bring.

As for the trouble in town, Sam didn't have a clue, and it occurred to him, as it often did, that he didn't know how to do this job.

He knew how to break into and hot-wire any vehicle — from a Beetle to a Bentley — with the aid of three simple tools.

He knew the interior configuration of every aircraft from a DC-3 to a 777.

He knew how to breach any door, using anything from a lockpick to C-4, and how to storm the room behind it, taking out the bad guys while leaving the good guys unharmed.

He knew how to lie in the woods, in the mountains, in the desert, anywhere, behind a sniper scope for forty-eight hours or more, without moving, without company, without food, without losing his sanity or his cool.

He knew at least a hundred ways to kill another human being and a thousand ways to keep from being killed.

But, other than catching the son of a bitch red-handed, he didn't know how to apprehend the pie snatcher.

And, other than leaving town this minute, he didn't have a clue how to defend his heart from a certain blue-eyed blonde.

# CHAPTER THREE

Beth pulled into the driveway, turned off the engine, then sat there a while, trying to forget everything but the wonderful fact that she was back at Heart Lake and it couldn't have been more aptly named, for her heart indeed belonged here.

God, it was good to be home.

She lowered all the Miata's windows to let the cool breeze from the lake blow through the car. Leaning her head back, with her eyes closed, she inhaled deeply of evergreen and eternal June.

She didn't need to look at the house to *see* it. The three-story Victorian Italianate structure sat proudly on the crest of the sloping lawn against a backdrop of shimmering aspens and soft white pines. Her great-great-grandfather, Orvis Shelby, Sr., had built the mansion in the 1870s with the staggering profits from his lumber business. Both the house and the fortune had been handed down through the generations, but by the time they reached Beth's mother, the fortune was long gone and only the house remained, the latter in a sorry state of disrepair, like Queen Victoria in tatters.

Although her mother had migrated south to Chicago after she married Harry Simon, she brought her girls, Shelby and Beth, back to the old house in Michigan every summer.

Of everyone in her family, it was Beth who truly loved the house at Heart Lake, who appreciated it not just for its history or its inhabitants but for its architectural beauty. As far back as she could remember, she'd been fascinated by every nook and cranny, every curve and knob, every seam and finely fitted joint.

Given her love of architecture, it had always struck her family as odd that she hadn't chosen it as a profession. But it wasn't architecture per se that had captured Beth's interest, but *Victorian* architecture. The buildings she adored hadn't even been built in the past century. Thanks to Frank Lloyd Wright and others, the world had gone all sleek and modern, leaving the lovely *grandes dames* of the Victorian age to chip and peel and molder. Anyway, architecture was out as a career because her math skills were . . . Dismal was a polite, if not quite generous, description.

So, instead of becoming a designer of homes, Beth had become a savior of homes. A renovator. A revivalist. That was her favorite job description even though it made people think she roamed from town to town, preaching in tents.

After college, she'd worked with several interior designers in Chicago, but opportunities to use her expertise on a large scale were few and far between. Then, three years ago, her parents had given Beth the chance of a lifetime by turning the house at Heart Lake over to her for a total, rugs-to-rafters renovation, after which they would let Beth operate it as a bed-and-breakfast.

Before even lifting a paintbrush, she'd spent several months doing research on the history of the place, rummaging through local libraries and scouring every archival source.

Mostly she patiently paged through the dozens of family photo albums and boxes of correspondence stored in the attic. The oldest photograph she was able to locate was taken sometime in the 1880s and showed clearly that the house had been painted in a multitude of colors, as was the custom in those years. Unfortunately, the sepia tones of the picture didn't give her a clue what those colors had been before her great-grandparents slapped a coat of white paint on every exterior surface.

In the end, Beth had painted the house to suit her very own Victorian sensibilities. She chose a pale Confederate gray with accents of midnight blue, rich burgundy, a deep ocher, and just a smidgen of gold. She'd paid equal attention to each detail of the interior. In fact, she'd done such a bang-up job that once her parents saw the results, they had reneged on their deal, deciding to live there year-round, obliterating Beth's plans for a bed-and-breakfast.

As much as Linda and Harry Simon had loved the house, though, it became impossible to run Linda's increasingly successful designer knitwear business from rural Michigan. So six months ago, they'd moved back to Chicago and once more given their younger daughter *carte blanche* with the property. The bed-and-breakfast deal was back on.

She opened her eyes to view the house and its wonderful colors and was gratified to see that they'd withstood three Michigan winters. The place looked great.

Plucking her keys from the ignition, Beth jumped out of the car and raced up the hill. She bounded up the stairs of the wraparound front porch, then, before putting her key in the lock, she kissed the front door with a loud *Mwah*.

The door creaked open several inches.

Whoa.

Beth took two steps backward. The hair on the back of her neck stood up.

Images from every scary movie she'd ever seen tumbled through her brain. That hadn't been just any old door noise. It had been a Wes Craven creak. An Alfred Freaking Hitchcock creak. Nerve-jolting and scary as hell. If this were a movie, it was her cue, wasn't it, to step across the threshold on wobbly legs, to blink in the dark interior, and to call out in a shaky voice *Is anybody there?*

Fat chance.

With her intuition screaming that something was really, really wrong, she leapt off the porch, ran down the lawn to her car, closed all the windows, and locked the doors. Convinced that an intruder was in the house, she grabbed her cell phone and started to punch 911, but then remembered that emergency calls went to the county sheriff in Mecklin, a good ten miles away. So instead she called Blanche at the Shelbyville Town Hall, whose number she knew by heart after dozens of permit calls during the renovation. With any luck, somebody would be hanging around who might be able to zip out to the lake and help her check out the house. Preferably with a gun or a baseball bat.

The calmness of her own voice surprised her when she said, "Blanche, it's Beth Simon. I'm at the house on Heart Lake, and I think there's an intruder inside."

The town clerk responded instantly. "Okay, honey. Listen. You just sit tight now. I'll call Sam."

Beth — so impressed by her own levelheadedness under frightening circumstances — lost it.

"No! Don't call Sam!"

Why would Blanche call Sam? What did Sam have to do with this? Or anything? He was the last person she wanted to see right now, for heaven's sake.

"Well, Beth, if you've got a problem out there, Sam's . . ."

"Not Sam," she insisted. "Isn't there somebody hanging around your office? Maybe Coach Tillman? Doesn't he come by for coffee every day? What about Bob Drew? Or that guy at the Gas Mart? The muscle-bound one? With the Mohawk? What's his name? Nate? Tate?"

"I'm calling Sam," the woman said in a kind of take-no-prisoners tone. "He's the constable."

"Oh, don't," Beth moaned.

When there was no reply, she had the distinct feeling that she'd been put on hold if not actually hung up on.

"Blanche?"

The line was as good as dead. Beth tossed the phone onto the passenger seat. Dammit. She wished she'd never called for help. She wished she'd just walked into the house and gotten clunked on the head, or raced to her car and driven right back to San Francisco. She wished . . .

Wait a minute! Sam was the constable?

It suddenly dawned on her that this morning, when he'd pursued her along Eighteen Mile Road, it had actually been for speeding. It wasn't personal. It had nothing to do with their past. He'd pursued her not because of a broken promise or a broken heart but because she was breaking the law. He was a cop, and she was a criminal. End of story.

Except, of course, it wasn't the end of the story because she'd invited Sam to dinner. In his capacity as town constable, he probably figured she was trying to bribe him.

"Beth Simon, you are such a jerk," she muttered,

directing a glare into the rearview mirror. "Now what are you going to do? Huh?"

Lacking an answer, she stared at the front door of the house. She wasn't sure if it was her imagination or not, but the door appeared to be open wider. In order to get a better view, she opened her window a few inches, sat up straighter, and squinted.

It *was* open farther than she'd left it earlier. She was absolutely certain. And even as she watched, the door appeared to open even farther. Beth's heart catapulted into her throat.

Okay. Maybe she should call Blanche back. Maybe she wouldn't mind so much right now if Constable Sam came to her rescue.

Help!

She was turning the key in the ignition, intending to back out of the driveway at about seventy miles per hour, when she saw a female backside emerge from the doorway. Above that rounded, jeans-clad backside hung a long, fat, honey-colored braid. The person's identity registered in an instant. It wasn't some strange intruder. It was her old friend, Kimmy Mortenson.

Beth breathed a long, shaky sigh of relief while she turned off the engine, then once again got out of her car, happy to be home.

Kimmy waved as she came down the front porch steps. "Beth," she called. "Hey. I didn't expect you until tomorrow. Your mother had me come in to get the house dusted and spiffed up for you."

"You're looking great, Kimmy."

"I'm feeling pretty good. A whole lot better than the last time I saw you."

As Beth well knew, that had been last year at Shelbyville's

annual Halloween bash, when Kimmy had been poisoned by a cup of punch intended for Shelby. Poor Kimmy had nearly died that hellish night. Thank God they'd gotten her to the hospital in time to keep her alive.

Reaching out, Beth gently touched the woman's arm. "I'm so glad you're better."

"Me, too. My hands still shake a little. I get headaches once in a while, and my memory's not as good as it should be, but — hey! — I'm alive. No complaints. It sure beats the alternative." Kimmy gave a little laugh, accompanied by a shrug. "Anyway, your mother's been paying me to come in and clean twice a week, and just generally to keep an eye on the place."

"I know. She told me." Beth now told herself that she should've remembered that fact earlier when the door creaked. She wasn't usually spooked so easily.

"So, you're back to stay, Beth?"

She looked up the lawn to the house. It seemed she loved it more with every glance if that was possible. How could she even consider leaving? she wondered. The truth was — she couldn't consider it.

"I'm back to stay," she said firmly.

No sooner were the words out of her mouth than the roar of a car engine could be heard not too far away, and mere seconds later, Sam's rusty jeep came clattering and careening into the driveway. The vehicle had barely come to a halt before he sprang out of it.

Beth flicked a quick glance toward Kimmy. Oh, Lord. Only a person blind from birth couldn't have recognized that the sudden flush on the woman's cheeks and the smile on her face betrayed more than friendly feelings for the man who was just then walking toward them.

As for Sam, his feelings were inscrutable, and Beth was

disgusted with herself for even trying to discern them.
What did she care how Sam felt about Kimmy, or vice
versa? It didn't matter a bit to her.

"What's going on?" he asked.

"Nothing, Sam," Kimmy said, looking surprised by his
question. "Why?"

Sam shifted his gaze to Beth. "Blanche said you called
about an intruder."

She nodded, feeling really foolish now. "I did," she
said, "but it turned out to be Kimmy. I guess I should've
called Blanche back."

His expression, inscrutable as it was, seemed to relax
considerably. "Okay. Well, that's good."

Kimmy's eyes widened as she stared at Beth. "You
thought I was somebody breaking into the house? A bur-
glar?"

*"Well . . ."*

It was one thing to feel stupid, Beth thought, and quite
another thing to feel both stupid and skittish, like an em-
barrassing combination of the Scarecrow and the
Cowardly Lion in *The Wizard of Oz*. She quickly changed
the subject.

"So," she said as gaily as she could, "what's new since
I've been gone?"

"Not all that much," Kimmy replied. "Sam's our new
constable, but I guess you already know that."

Beth nodded and finally made eye contact with Sam.
"Congratulations."

"Thanks."

That one softly spoken word, uttered without sarcasm
or embarrassment, suddenly made Beth realize how much
the two of them had changed in the past decade and a half.
The Sam she remembered — the nineteen-year-old boy —

would've rolled his eyes and made some sort of silly, self-deprecating remark comparable to *Aw, shucks*. But this Sam was a man, one full of quiet confidence, obvious humility, and something that Beth could only describe as an aura of bone-deep pride. It nearly took her breath away, and she could barely speak.

"Well . . ." *Well what, idiot? Get a grip, will you?* "I guess I better start getting settled in."

She walked to the back of the car and opened the trunk, where most of her worldly possessions were crammed.

"Here. Let me help," Kimmy said.

"That's okay," Beth answered. "You don't . . ."

Sam didn't bother volunteering. He simply grabbed two heavy suitcases from the trunk and started walking up the hill.

And so it went for the next twenty minutes, with Kimmy babbling about how good it was that Beth was home and Sam doggedly emptying the Miata of everything that wasn't nailed down.

When they were finished, he offered to drive the blushing Kimmy home, and it was only when Beth stood on the front porch and watched Sam's jeep back out of the driveway that she realized she was feeling a weird blend of disappointment and relief, and that somewhere lurking beneath those emotions was pure green jealousy. How many times had she backed out of that driveway with Sam during their years together? Hundreds of times? Thousands?

She told herself that what she was feeling was simply a knee-jerk reaction to seeing her old flame with somebody else. It was perfectly normal to experience a certain twinge of envy, wasn't it? Well, wasn't it?

Briefly, she fingered the cell phone in her pocket, sorely

tempted to call her sister, Shelby, for some much-needed advice. But then she decided that was a terrible idea. Just the worst. After all, if it weren't for the wisdom of Ms. Shelby Simon, Beth and Sam would be celebrating their sixteenth wedding anniversary this year.

☆

Sam was negotiating the narrow, winding road that led from the Simon place to the blacktop, and his passenger was being far too quiet. He'd known Kimmy Mortenson since kindergarten, so he knew her uncharacteristic silence could only mean one thing. The woman was busting to talk. She was sitting there, bubbling inside like a little cauldron. Sooner than later, she'd boil over.

If he drove fast enough to her trailer on the west side of Heart Lake, if he really floored the jeep's bare metal accelerator, maybe he'd be able to avoid the inevitable commentary and speculation.

But when they emerged from the woods to turn right on Eighteen Mile Road, Kimmy could no longer contain herself.

"So!" she chirped. "Beth's back!"

Sam sighed. How could so few words carry so much drama and baggage? *Beth's back. It was the best of times. It was the worst of times.*

"It looks that way," he said, feeling Kimmy's eyes boring two hot, smoking holes into the right side of his skull.

"Sam, maybe this time . . ."

He cut her off right there, lifting one hand from the steering wheel in a halting gesture. "Let it go, kiddo. Okay?"

Kimmy wasn't about to do that. "It's just that the two of

you had something so special, Sam. Even all these years later, I can't picture either one of you with anybody else. And now you're back, and Beth's back. You're both single. It just seems like destiny."

He kept his eyes on the road and his mouth shut, relieved to see the turnoff to West Heart Lake Drive directly ahead, while Kimmy went on. And on.

"I really always thought of you and Beth as true soul mates, you know. The way you guys used to be able to read each other's minds. Remember that? And the way you'd finish each other's sentences. And do you know what I remember most of all?"

Sam didn't bother to respond, certain he was about to find out whether he wanted to or not. He felt as if he were about to receive forty lashes.

"I remember that night we played Truth or Dare in the Simons' sunroom," Kimmy said. "I guess Beth and I were fourteen, maybe fifteen, which would've made you sixteen or seventeen. Somewhere around there. It was Beth and you and me, Richie Melton, and a couple other kids. I don't remember Shelby being there. Anyway, when it was Beth's turn, she asked you 'Truth or Dare?' and you said . . ."

"Dare," Sam said now. He remembered. Jesus. That night could've been yesterday for all its clarity.

Kimmy spoke faster, more excitedly as she continued. "Yes! You said 'Dare,' so Beth crossed her arms, looked you straight in the eye, and said, 'I dare you to tell me you love me.'"

How could he forget?

"You never even flinched, Sam Mendenhall. You didn't even blink. You stared right back at her and, clear as a bell, you said, 'I love you, Beth.'"

It was the very first time he'd said those words to her, and Sam clearly recalled the fear in the pit of his stomach as he spoke. Apparently, according to Kimmy at least, he'd maintained an exterior aura of cool and an air of calm. That was good to know. For what it was worth at this point in his life.

His attention caught up with Kimmy again a few babbles later, then he swung a hard right, forcing his chatty passenger to squeal and grip the dashboard, then he hit the brakes in front of her green trailer with its white picket fence border.

"Jeez, Sam." Kimmy wrenched open the door, then glared back at him. "I've got enough problems without adding whiplash to the list. Thanks for the ride."

"Kimmy, I'm sorry."

"Yeah, yeah." She jumped out of the jeep and slammed the door.

"Kimmy, wait," he called.

She didn't, but yelled at him over the long braid flopping against her back. "I just hope you don't screw it up this time, Bozo, the way you did before."

# CHAPTER FOUR

By the time Beth had all her luggage and boxes distributed to their proper places around the house, she'd managed to eyeball almost every room pretty thoroughly and was relieved to see that her parents' year-long residence hadn't disturbed the place all that much. In fact, it was a revelation to see how her mother had rearranged the occasional piece of furniture in order to make "real life" more comfortable.

For her own comfort, Beth had decided to appropriate the master suite on the lake-side of the second floor for herself. This was the room her parents had used, and the only space intruded upon by twentieth-century décor, with its spacious closets and huge windows.

Here, at the far west of the house, she'd be well away from any guests. Well, if she ever had any, she thought as she began unpacking. There was still a huge amount of promotional work to be done, pictures to be taken, copy to be written, ads to be purchased in travel magazines and on Web sites, not to mention good old word of mouth to be circulated around the area. She toyed with the notion of

using her mother's former office on the third floor while
she unpacked.

Then, as she was folding her favorite flowered silk
nightgown and tucking it into the middle drawer of the
dresser, she remembered that there was something else to
be done. And soon. Sam was coming for dinner tonight,
dammit, and there probably wasn't a speck of food in the
kitchen.

She trotted down the back stairs, muttering to herself,
then went into the Victorian modern kitchen she'd
designed — no easy feat, that — and checked the contents
of the refrigerator. It was pretty bare, but there, nestled between a half-empty bottle of ketchup and a small squeeze
jar of mustard, was a bottle of champagne with a note
attached.

*Beth — To toast your success — Mom and Dad.*

A lump gathered in her throat as she pulled the bottle
from its shelf, read the note again, studied the label a moment, then held the chilly green glass between her breasts
while she fought back tears.

Success! What was that? Something that seemed to
come so very easily to everyone in the Simon family but
little Beth. Something that eluded her again and again, year
after year, no matter what she did and no matter how hard
she tried.

Her father — Harry Harry Quite Contrary — had risen
through the ranks of the criminal defense fraternity in
Chicago without breaking a sweat. Her mother — the
stunning Linda of Linda Purl Designs — had turned her
hobby of knitting sweaters and shawls into a multimillion-
dollar fashion business. Her sister, Shelby, had walked

into the offices of the *Chicago Daily Mirror* her first day out of college, and landed a column of her own, one that would eventually make her rich as well as famous.

And Beth?

Beth was always tagging along behind them, running as fast as she could, as hard as she could just to keep the family pack in sight. It wasn't that she felt sorry for herself. It seemed that there was only just so much success granted per household, and she was always at the back of the line, clinging to her weird, unconventional, nineteenth-century interests and uncanny ability to choose men who always let her down.

It was probably the latter that bothered her most deeply — the fact that she longed to share her life with somebody and start a family of her own. It struck her as such a simple wish, yet it forever confounded and eluded her. First there'd been Sam, who'd shattered her heart when he married somebody else. After that she hadn't been willing to risk her heart again until a few years ago when Danny came to work for her as a painting contractor here at the lake.

It wasn't love at first sight with Danny, but very gradually he won her over. Best of all, they shared the same passion for bringing back old Victorian wrecks. He was a wizard with wallpaper as well as a prince of paint. There was nobody who could construct a perfect scaffold so quickly or labor on it tirelessly for twelve hours at a stretch. He was her Michelangelo.

She'd moved to San Francisco with him two years ago to start a restoration business with him, hoping their partnership would be for life, both personal and professional. But her Michelangelo had turned out to be crazier than Van Gogh. He was jealous to the point of obsession. He never cut off an ear, but he did ram his fist through several lengths of drywall and one plate-glass window. It wasn't until he rammed that fist into her face that Beth finally moved out a year ago.

Her hope was to continue being his partner in their rapidly growing business, but it was an impossible proposition, given his feelings for her. A month or so ago, when he wouldn't take no for an answer to his perpetual "Marry me," when he wouldn't let go of her, it was Beth who shocked herself by ramming her fist into his face, leaving Danny pretty much unscathed while garnering herself a fractured bone.

It took six weeks for her hand to mend while she closed out her end of the business. And then, instead of hitting Danny again, she hit the road.

At the age of thirty-three, she'd just about given up hope that true love — like her parents', like Shelby and Mick's — would happen for her.

But maybe that was good. She clasped the champagne bottle a bit more tightly to her chest. Maybe her success was destined to be professional rather than personal. After all, that was the conclusion she'd come to on the long drive from California, and she'd felt good about it. She'd felt strong and independent and full of optimism.

Go, Beth! You go, girl!

Thinking back, that moment of intense independence was probably when she'd stomped her foot on the accelerator on her way through Shelbyville.

Then Sam had appeared, and her newly adopted sense of going-it-alone had faltered. But only for a moment.

"Well, screw you, Sam Mendenhall," Beth said as she twisted the wires atop the champagne bottle and prepared to pop the cork and celebrate her new self.

Go, Beth! And this time don't stop. For anybody.

☆

Sometime later, Beth was awakened by the insistent, skull-piercing buzz of the doorbell. She opened one eye and realized she had a slight buzz of her own going on thanks to her celebratory champagne. Opening her other eye, it became apparent that the master bedroom was no longer flooded with afternoon sunlight as it had been earlier. The room was damn near dark now.

Since she hadn't set the bedside clock yet, she had no idea what time it was, but she had a sinking feeling that it was eight o'clock and it was Sam leaning on the damn doorbell.

Shit.

At least the floor didn't pitch and roll beneath the soles of her feet when she hauled herself out of bed. The walls didn't waver or blur as she made her way out of the bedroom. After that, she was able to negotiate the long second-floor hallway well enough, but the staircase felt a little bit like one on a cruise ship. No. Not a cruise ship. Make that a rusty ladder on a shrimp trawler in rough seas.

Ay yi yi.

By the time she reached the front hallway, the buzzing of the doorbell felt like a dentist's drill on her molars. What happened to the lovely chimes she'd installed two years ago? She had to answer the damn door if only to bring that horrible noise to a brutal end, so she grabbed the knob, muttered a curse, and opened the door.

Sam.

Dear God. Why did he have to grow up so incredibly good-looking? Why hadn't he turned out to be a ninety-pound weakling with crossed eyes and a major overbite?

His perfect bod was wonderfully clad in faded jeans and a pale blue oxford cloth shirt whose sleeves were rolled up to expose a pair of tan and ropy forearms. A few wisps of damp hair fell so casually across his forehead that they looked as if they'd been styled by a pro. His eyes weren't crossed at all, but deep set and direct and a heavenly hazel. He looked like he'd just showered and shaved, and he smelled better than Key lime pie.

Beth swallowed hard for fear of drooling.

A quick grin worked its way across his lips. At least she thought it was a grin. It could have been a twitch. It could have been indigestion. She really wasn't in any condition to tell.

"You're blitzed," he said.

"I beg your pardon?" she answered, drawing herself up with the righteous indignation of an inveterate tippler.

"You're snockered, Bethie." Now Sam, damn him, laughed out loud as he held up a bottle of red wine that Beth hadn't noticed before. "I guess that would make this redundant," he said.

She blinked at the bottle, then sighed a damp little gesture of surrender as she swayed and had to reach for the doorframe to steady herself. "Okay. Okay. You caught me, Sheriff. I was celebrating my homecoming with some champagne my parents left for me. I may have overdone it a bit."

"I'd say so."

He stood there just gazing at her, and Beth couldn't tell if the look on his face was amusement or disapproval. Sam used to be so easy to read in the old days, but then she'd never tried to read his mind when she was drunk out of hers. For a moment she couldn't even remember why he was here, looming in her doorway.

"Dinner," she muttered almost to herself. "Oh, damn."

"Let's have coffee," he said. "Come on."

He stepped over the threshold, and the next thing Beth knew he was steering her toward the kitchen, where he plopped her in a chair at the table, then deftly set about filling up the Mr. Coffee from the faucet at the sink. Without missing a beat, he reached into a cabinet and came up with a can of Maxwell House. He popped off the lid and poured what looked like the perfect amount of grounds into the receptacle, then closed the lid and switched on the machine.

Just like that. In charge. The host with the most. Beth suddenly felt like a guest in her very own home.

"How do you . . . ?"

Sam was searching through other cabinets, talking over his shoulder. "Know where stuff is? I stayed here for a couple days last winter after a pipe burst at my cabin. Your parents left me a key so I could keep an eye on the place."

"Oh. I knew that," she said. She didn't, but she said it anyway, not wanting to sound more out of it than she felt.

He had turned the tap on again and was filling a big six-quart pot. "Do you still like spaghetti?" he asked.

Beth's stomach flinched, but she mounted a little smile and said she was crazy about it. Under normal circumstances she loved any kind of pasta. Right now, though, she thought she'd be hard-pressed to keep down even a saltine.

"Good," Sam said, "because it's the only thing I know how to cook." He put the big pot on the stove and fired up the burner beneath it before he moved along to another culinary task.

He was humming, for God's sake! Beth was doing her utmost to remain upright and not toss her cookies while Sam was flitting around the kitchen humming.

"There's no ground beef," he announced, "but I could open a can of anchovies. What do you think?"

Oy. "I think I'm going to be sick."

☆

Sam leaned against the wall outside the little powder room off the kitchen, sipping a cup of coffee. Beth had been in there about fifteen minutes, but she'd turned the faucets on full force so he couldn't hear a thing, which was probably good. He'd had his fill of listening to puking on an operatic scale while he was living in Army barracks.

He shouldn't have come tonight. He'd argued with himself half the afternoon, practically talking out loud like some demented guy in the back room of an asylum.

*Go. See her, goddammit. Get it over with.*

*Don't go. Just let it all die on the vine right now.*

*Go.*

*No.*

*You chicken shit.*

Yeah, well . . .

So he'd showered and shaved and grabbed his only bottle of wine, then climbed the front steps of the Simons' house like a guy on his way to the guillotine, only to find Beth stewed to her little green gills. That was when his take-charge mode automatically kicked in, and he became Staff Sergeant Sam Mendenhall, for whom no task was too difficult and no challenge too small to be ignored.

He'd pranced around her kitchen like some sort of hyperactive chef on cable TV. Coffee — Bam! Spaghetti —

Bam! As if he knew anything more than how to open pickle jars and cans of soup or how to boil a pot of water. For the past year or so since he'd returned to Heart Lake, he'd been eating a big lunch in town in order to avoid having to fix a meal at home.

Well, in all honesty, his lunchtime routine did a bit more than merely satisfy the hunger in his stomach. It also served as a means to fill his social calendar. There were several women in town who were just as lonely as he was, and they seemed to have designated him Shelbyville's Most Eligible Bachelor for some reason. Sam didn't know how eligible he was, but he admitted to taking advantage of that reputation from time to time.

He took another sip of his coffee, then tipped his head back against the wall and closed his eyes. Technically, he supposed, he wasn't a bachelor at all. For over fifteen years the box he'd checked for marital status on any form had been a W for widower. That always made him sad despite the fact that he couldn't even picture his young wife's face anymore.

Hell, they'd hardly been married at all before he was buying her a headstone bearing the surname that had been hers for a few brief months. Sam always wondered if it bothered her to go through eternity as Susan Mendenhall instead of Susie Flynt, the name she'd been known by before some asshole on the rebound ruined her life.

Sam was almost glad when his cell phone beeped in his back pocket, putting an end to his mournful thoughts. He reached for the phone, hit the answer button with his thumb, and said, "This is Sam."

"Oh, Sam. God, am I glad I reached you."

He recognized Kimmy Mortenson's voice and identified a note of panic in it. "What's up?"

"I think there's a prowler out behind my trailer. I heard a funny noise and, when I looked out, I think I saw a man's shadow. I know it wasn't any stray dog or possum or anything. Could you come over, Sam, and take a look around? I'd really appreciate it."

Knowing Kimmy wasn't the Nervous Nellie type, Sam took her concern quite seriously. "Sure. I'll be there in a couple minutes."

She sighed gratefully on the other end of the phone. "Thank you so much."

Sam rapped on the closed bathroom door, but all the running water probably made it impossible for Beth to hear him. Either that or she was ignoring him, maybe hoping he'd go away. Happy to have an excuse to do just that, he found a pen and a pad of paper in the kitchen, left Beth a brief note, and got the hell out of Dodge.

☆

Beth slunk out of the bathroom, fully prepared for whatever remark Sam might make at her appearance. She'd looked like death warmed over in the mirror over the sink, and there was no improving upon it.

If Sam was sweet, she'd be sarcastic. If he was disapproving, she'd be indignant. If he was still behaving like the frigging Galloping Gourmet, she'd run right back to the bathroom and throw up again.

What she wasn't prepared for, however, was Sam's absence. She spied the white memo pad on the table immediately but decided to pour herself a cup of his freshly brewed coffee before sitting down and reading his note.

*Duty called. See you later. The Sheriff.*

Seven little words. Thirty-one letters. Three deep and precise punctuation marks.

Beth probably read the note seventeen times while she pondered the handwriting that was still frighteningly familiar after so many years. They'd been in love back in the dark ages before e-mail, so naturally during the months when Beth was home in Chicago, the two of them had kept the post office busy with letters flying back and forth nearly every day.

She knew Sam's handwriting even better than her own, those handsome block letters that appeared almost engraved on a page, written with such force that she could run a finger over the reverse side of the paper and feel his words like braille. She flipped the top sheets of the memo pad, seeing how far down the imprint of his writing went, and counting five pages at least on which she could see an impression.

If she were a spy, she'd be able to rub a pencil lightly over a blank page, making his words suddenly appear like magic.

Beth scowled. She didn't believe in magic. Not anymore.

She tore the top six pages from the pad, ripped them into two pieces, then four, then eight, and finally sixteen, before dropping the confetti into the trash can. No way was she going to start collecting Sam souvenirs again at this point in her life.

Sixteen years ago, in a fit of rage, she'd burned all his letters, only she'd immediately regretted her act, so she gathered the ashes and kept them in a vase sealed tightly with duct tape and stashed at the back of her closet. It took her at least five more years to gather the courage to finally pitch those stupid *cremains*.

Somewhere in the distance Beth heard a phone ringing, and realized it was the cell phone she'd left in the master bedroom. She turned off the coffeemaker, turned out the lights in the kitchen, and headed off to the west side of the house. Ringing phone or not, it was time to go to bed. A good night's sleep might help the headache she'd be certain to have tomorrow.

The phone kept ringing and ringing, like a transponder on a downed aircraft, guiding her to the proper location. Beth finally found the little black shrieking device under the covers she'd thrown back earlier when the doorbell woke her. She squinted at the caller ID with its San Francisco area code.

Danny.

Great. Terrific. Just what she needed right now. A half hour of mental abuse across two thousand miles.

She turned off the phone without a twinge of guilt and nary a recrimination. That's why she'd spent most of the past week putting all that mileage between herself and the Man Who Wouldn't Take No For An Answer.

It was nice, being able to silence him with a mere pressing of a button, Beth thought as she sagged onto the bed, sighed, and hoped like hell she'd fall asleep before the room started spinning.

# CHAPTER FIVE

For the next few days Beth was a model of sobriety and efficiency, waking early to make lists and spending her days checking off the various tasks she'd set out for herself. She had no actual deadlines to meet; the bed-and-breakfast would be up and running when it was up and running. Period.

Her parents had no plans for taking up permanent residency at Heart Lake again, whether or not Beth's business took off or failed. This would always be the family home where they'd vacation several times a year, and they would never sell it out from under their daughter. There weren't any mortgage payments to be made. There was no payroll to be met. Any pressures Beth felt were completely self-imposed, based on her deep desire and her overwhelming need to succeed. At something.

Using the computer her mother had left behind in her former office on the third floor, in what used to be the ballroom, Beth got to work. At the top of her To Do list was the choice of a name for her resort. When she'd attempted this three years ago, she'd chosen the name Heart Lake

Lodge. Now, though, that struck her as far too casual and way too woodsy. This was not, after all, a place with great stone fireplaces and moose heads mounted on knotty pine walls.

The name she finally settled upon was Heart Lake Manor because it had a certain air of elegance and maybe just a whiff of Elizabeth Barrett Browning. Then, once she'd pinned down the name, it was on to other tasks.

She contacted the Web design group in San Francisco who'd done such a great job for her when she and Danny were setting up their renovation business in California. It didn't take long — just a quick exchange of e-mails — to let Georgia Kane, designer extraordinaire, know exactly what Beth wanted the bed-and-breakfast site to look like and to accomplish for her. Beth outlined the basics and promised Georgia to get back to her with copy and pictures within the next week.

Those pictures, she decided, would have to be professionally done in order to present Heart Lake Manor properly in all its Victorian splendor, but a tour of the local Yellow Pages yielded not a single photographer who claimed to do anything more than weddings and portraits of families or precious pets.

As luck would have it, Beth just happened to mention her photographer problem to Thelma Watt when she went into town to pick up her mail. The postmistress had immediately pointed to a wonderful framed color print on the wall behind her and said, "Nobody's as good at taking pictures as my nephew, Steve."

Leaning across the counter, Beth studied the photograph. It was a shot of Shelbyville's Main Street, looking west, taken at sunset. Granted, it wasn't Manhattan with the Brooklyn Bridge lit up in the foreground or a crimson sun about to dip gloriously into the Pacific, but it was a very competent, well-composed, and well-thought-out picture, certainly as good as she'd seen in most brochures for small bed-and-breakfast establishments.

"Here." Thelma shoved a business card toward Beth. "Give him a call. He sells insurance, too, if you're interested."

"Thanks." She stuck the card in the back pocket of her khaki cargo shorts. "I'll do that."

While Beth gathered up her mail, Thelma just stood there staring at her, and Beth couldn't help but remember all the years this woman, in her official uniform and sturdy shoes and steady gaze, had terrified her. As a child, Beth had always thought of Thelma Watt as Oz, the All-Knowing. For a year or two, she was even convinced the old lady had eyes in the back of her head, perhaps one eyeball on each side of the prim gray bun she used to wear.

If there was a Mr. Watt somewhere in the woman's past, Beth had no idea. She couldn't imagine Thelma as a wife or a mother. As a child, Beth had always assumed that the postmistress lived right there in the post office, probably sleeping in one of the canvas bins in the storeroom with a sack of mail as her pillow.

"So, you're back," Thelma finally said, her words seeming to carry far more significance than a mere observation.

"Yep. I'm back," Beth responded, eager to leave the premises now before the Great Oz went on to other subjects. One in particular.

"Guess you've seen Sam," the postmistress murmured.

That was the one.

"Briefly," she replied, trying to sound casual and unconcerned, as if the name and the man to whom it belonged meant absolutely nothing to her. Sam? Sam who?

Beth wished she were more like her outspoken sister, Shelby, who — in a similar situation — would've probably aimed a withering glare across the post office counter and loudly proclaimed "None of your beeswax" to the snoopy woman.

"Guess he told you all about our crime wave," Thelma said.

"A crime wave?"

"Some criminal is making off with things. Curtains. Coffee cups. A trophy from school. My brand-new flag, which, in my opinion, is a federal offense. I need to look up the statute on that so I can tell Sam." Her pale lips thinned indignantly.

It didn't sound too serious to Beth, but she gave a small, sympathetic cluck of her tongue anyway just to appease the elderly woman. "Well, I need to get going. I've got a list of errands a mile long. It was nice seeing you, Thelma."

"I'd keep an eye out, if I were you, Beth Simon, with all those antiques you've got out at the lake. Make sure Sam swings by there at least a couple times a day."

*Oh, right. That was just what she needed. The distraction of Sam every hour on the hour.*

"Thanks for the warning," Beth said. "I'll batten down the hatches. Bye, Thelma."

Clutching her bundle of mail, she stepped out onto the sidewalk, breathed a little sigh of relief at having once again escaped Shelbyville's primo busybody, and got blasted right between the eyes with a shot of ice-cold water. By the time she could see again, she spotted a little boy with a bright green squirt gun the size of a cannon as he stepped out from the side of the post office, once more taking aim. Beth yelled at him, and he let her have it again.

"Bam!" he shouted, while he sprayed her from head to toe. "Bam! Bam! Gotcha!"

She didn't know how to defend herself. No way was she going to hold out the mail as a shield. And since she was wearing flip-flops, if she tried to run, she'd probably wind up breaking her neck.

"Bam!" He shot her again. "Bam! I gotcha good that time, lady!"

Beth was about to curse the little creep up one side and down the other when she heard a deep voice say, "I'll take that."

Suddenly the boy was no longer standing on the pavement, but was several feet in the air, and there stood Sam, like a cartoon Colossus, squirt in one hand and squirt gun in the other.

"Lemme go!" the kid wailed.

"Not till you apologize to the lady."

"I was just having fun. Lemme go."

"Tell her you're sorry, and you won't do it again. Ever."

The sound of Sam's voice was so strict and his expression so severe that Beth found herself almost beginning to apologize for being in the wrong place at the wrong time. It wouldn't have surprised her if the rotten little squirt gunner wet his little pants out of sheer terror.

"I'm sorry, lady," he blubbered, tears running down his face. "I won't do it again. I promise."

Feeling sorry for the poor kid now, Beth responded, "Oh, that's okay. What's a little water?"

Her quick forgiveness earned her a wet and grateful sniff from the boy and a stern glare from his captor.

"Just don't do it again," she added, shaking a finger at him for emphasis.

"No. I won't. Cross my heart."

Sam lowered him to the sidewalk, and as soon as the boy's red canvas high-tops made contact with the pavement, he raced away.

"You can pick up your weapon in my office next week, Mr. Dolan," Sam called after him.

"Dolan!" Beth exclaimed. "Is that Joe Dolan's kid?"

Sam nodded.

"Well, that explains it." She laughed. "I should have connected the freckles. I think his dad did the same thing to me about twenty years ago."

Oh, damn. No sooner were those words out of her mouth than she realized that Sam had rescued her from that dousing, too. She wondered if he remembered, then decided he probably did because he was looking at her a bit oddly. Then, when Beth realized the exact direction of his gaze, she looked down and suddenly discovered that she was standing there looking like the winner of a wet T-shirt contest, or if not the winner, then definitely the first runner-up.

If only Thelma's flag were flying, she could use that as an excuse for her nipples' outstanding salute.

In an effort to cover herself, Beth clutched her bundle of mail to her chest. MasterCard be damned. She didn't care if the bill got soaked all the way through.

Sam cleared his throat, but the wolfish gleam didn't leave his eyes. "He got you pretty good," he said. "I've got a towel in my car if you want to dry off."

"No, thanks. I'm headed back to the lake anyway." That was a lie. She'd intended to proceed from the post office to the Gas Mart to buy a replacement tire, but in this condition there was no way she was going to visit that bastion of loitering, leering masculinity.

Predictably, Sam was eyeing the Miata parked just a few feet away at the curb and that stern, almost military look he'd used on the Dolan boy was creeping back into his expression. "Did you get that tire changed?" he asked her brusquely.

*What's it to you, Sam Mendenhall?* Beth wanted to scream. You're not the boss of me. Just because they'd been the hot couple of Heart Lake a million years ago didn't give him the right to be her overseer now. She whipped a damp piece of mail from her bundle, waved it at him, and said, "It's on my list."

"Good."

They just stood there then, facing off on the sidewalk like a cat and a dog in front of the post office. Beth felt a kind of internal pressure, the result of her "nice" upbringing, to apologize for getting hammered on champagne and ruining their former dinner plans. She felt horribly compelled to reissue an invitation, but instead she dredged up every molecule, every single atom of antisocial behavior in her body to fight that ingrained urge to be polite.

Finally, it was Sam who broke the silence between them when he said, "Well, I've got rounds to make. Take care, Beth." Then he turned and disappeared behind the post office, presumably returning to wherever he'd come from.

Probably some damned phone booth, Beth thought. Like Superman. Which meant that Beth was that ninny, Lois Lane, forever getting into hot water. Or cold squirt gun water, as was the case right now.

She drove back to the lake, sodden and shivering, with the car's heater turned up full blast even though it was June.

☆

Continuing on his rounds, Sam stopped by Kimmy's place to see if daylight yielded any clues about the prowler she thought she had seen the other night. He hadn't seen any evidence then, but he'd only been using a flashlight to walk around her trailer.

He'd meant to get back sooner because he worried about Kimmy. She seemed a lot more jumpy and distracted since the poisoning incident last year. Still, who could blame her? One minute she was drinking orange punch at the annual Halloween party, and the next minute she was on the floor having a seizure, barely minutes from death's door.

From what he'd been told about that night last October, it could just as easily have been Beth or Shelby or Shelby's bodyguard, Mick Callahan, who was poisoned because their punch cups were tampered with, too. Poor ol' Kimmy. It was her bad luck that she'd been thirstier than her companions.

He parked, got out of the jeep, and walked around the green-and-white trailer again, not seeing anything more interesting than a ladybug on a piece of birch bark or more suspicious than a crushed diet soda can.

"Sam!" Kimmy came out the front door of the trailer, carrying a plastic milk crate crammed full of spray bottles and cleaning products and colorful rags. She pulled the door closed behind her, testing it to make sure it was locked.

"Any more visits from your prowler?" he asked.

"No. I think it was probably a dog or a raccoon. Or maybe it was just my imagination. I don't know. I'm really sorry I made such a big deal of it."

"No big deal," Sam said. "That's my job. You should call me when you think something's wrong."

"Well, everything's fine now. I'm on my way over to the Simon house to do a little dusting. I was planning to walk, but since you're here . . ." She smiled and batted her eyelashes at him.

"Hop in," he said, gesturing toward his car, glad to be able to help her with transportation if he couldn't solve her prowler problem.

During the short drive, Kimmy seemed like her usual chatty self. Sam was relieved that she steered clear of the topic of Sam and Beth and the Great Romance. He'd spent most of the morning trying to steer clear of the subject himself, especially after seeing Bethie looking like a little drowned rat in front of the post office. A sexy drowned rat, though. Damn.

When he pulled into the Simon driveway, he saw her again, out on the front lawn, stomping around with her cell phone clamped to her ear. She was wearing a dry T-shirt now, much to his disappointment.

"Thanks for the ride, Sam." Kimmy hopped out.

"Sure thing."

Hugging her milk crate, she tilted her head and gave him a challenging little grin. "I guess you don't want to stick around, huh?"

"You got that right, kid." He rammed the gearshift into reverse.

"Scared?" she asked, her grin sliding into a definite taunt.

"Smart."

He shot backward out of the driveway, all the while trying to ignore Kimmy's cackling laughter and fighting the powerful urge to cast one more glance toward T-shirt Woman on the lawn.

☆

"Stop calling me, Danny!" Beth shrieked into the phone.

Her face was burning with anger and frustration as she stomped around the yard. Her free hand was curled into a fist that every so often she would jab toward the heavens. Once she even flipped the bird in a westerly direction, vaguely aimed at San Francisco.

She couldn't keep her cell phone turned off indefinitely because too many people used that number exclusively. But every time she activated the damn thing, there was Danny, calling from San Francisco, apologizing for the past, making promises about the future, begging her to come back. She was beginning to wonder if there was such a thing as a phone restraining order.

"I can't make it without you, Beth." He sounded on the verge of tears.

She couldn't even respond to that. His desperation might have tugged at her heartstrings if he'd never hit her. But he had hit her. All it took was once. She knew he'd do it again if he ever had the chance, so Beth had locked him out of her heart for good.

It didn't seemed to matter to him whether she replied or not. Danny just kept rambling on. With his voice droning in her ear, begging her to come back, telling her how glorious the weather was out there today, she watched Kimmy get out of Sam's jeep and stand beside it, smiling and laughing, further confirming Beth's suspicion that the woman was head over heels in love with him.

And Sam? Beth was too far away to see his expression, but he was with her, wasn't he, driving her around like an obedient chauffeur.

"I have to go, Danny. Don't call me again. Just don't. It's over." She disconnected, then held her breath, expecting him to call her back in the next few seconds. When he didn't, Beth closed her eyes and let out a long, grateful sigh.

"Trouble?" Kimmy asked, setting her cleaning stuff down on the grass. "You looked pretty stressed out, Beth."

"No. It's nothing," she said, not wanting to discuss Danny at the moment, much less talk to him. "Just a few loose ends with my business in California. You look pretty cheerful, pal."

Even as she spoke the words, Beth realized how very true they were. Kimmy looked so happy. Her eyes were bright, and her mouth didn't seem to be able to keep from smiling. Her long braid swung back and forth like the tail wagging on a happy puppy. Suddenly Beth felt a little woozy, which she attributed to Danny making her blood pressure soar. Rather than fall down, she folded her legs and lowered herself casually to the ground.

Kimmy followed suit. Her smile turned into a look of concern as she leaned forward. "Hey. Are you feeling okay?"

"Just a little shaky," Beth said, putting her cell phone on the ground between them. "That was Danny on the phone. Remember him?"

"The guy who worked with you fixing up the house a couple years ago? Didn't you move out to California with him?"

"Yep. That's the guy." Beth sighed. "It didn't work out, but I just can't get him to accept that it's over between us. He calls me constantly. He's driving me crazy."

"Get a different number."

"Easier said than done, I'm afraid. I'd have to contact about a zillion people with my new number. I dunno. It just doesn't seem fair to have to change my life because Danny's such an asshole."

"Tell me about it." Kimmy clucked her tongue. "I've known more than my share of those. Remember Jimmy Mayhew?"

"The Elvis guy?"

"Yep."

"Oh, God." Beth couldn't help but laugh remembering Jimmy with his greasy pompadour, humongous sideburns, and pleated pants with skinny belts. He'd strutted around the lake for a whole summer saying little else but *Thank you Thank you very much* in a voice that always cracked between *very* and *much*. "I do remember him. What's he up to these days?"

"I have no idea," Kimmy said. "He left town about ten years ago, or maybe I should say he left the building."

They sat there laughing on the sunlit lawn while Kimmy dredged up more disastrous romances from her past. There was Sneaky Pete, Handy Andy, and last but not least, Farty Arty Kostlich, whom Beth remembered all too well. Finally, with a disgusted shake of her head, Kimmy muttered, "Assholes, every one. I think I'm a jerk magnet. At least that's what my mother always said. She was, too, I guess."

Beth remembered now that Kimmy's late mother, Sally Mortenson, had been a single mom, raising her daughter without a husband or companion. She'd never asked Kimmy about it, but once Beth was old enough to know about such things, she'd simply assumed that her friend had been born out of wedlock.

"Jerk magnets," Kimmy grumbled again.

"Well, but that's all changed now," Beth said.

"Excuse me?"

Beth angled her head toward the driveway. "You know. You and Sam."

Kimmy started to blink, obviously confused. "Me and Sam what?"

"Together," Beth said, already regretting that she'd brought up the subject. The last thing she wanted to do was sit there on the grass — just us girls — and listen to her old friend pour out her heart about her new love, Sam. She didn't think she could bear it.

"You think there's something going on between Sam and me?" She tossed her braid over her shoulder, then sat back laughing. "Are you crazy, Beth? Are you completely nuts?"

Now it was Beth's turn to be confused. "Well, no . . . I . . . You and Sam aren't together, then? I thought . . ."

"Together? Are you kidding me?" No longer laughing, Kimmy looked truly astonished. "Where in the world did you get that idea?"

"Well, I've only been back at the lake for a couple days, and I've already seen the two of you together twice now."

"Big whoop. We're not *together* together. Sam's just nice enough to drive me sometimes. I'm not supposed to drive myself for a while because I could have a seizure. From the poisoning. At least that's what the doctors tell me."

"Oh, Kimmy. I'm so sorry. I didn't know that."

"Obviously." She laughed again. "I guess there's a lot you don't know, Beth. But as far as Sam is concerned . . ."

Her expression changed all of a sudden as she fell silent. Beth was scared to death that her friend was about to have a seizure.

"What's wrong?" she asked Kimmy.

"Is that smoke I see coming from the back of your house?"

"What?" Beth turned and looked. "Oh, my God!"

# CHAPTER SIX

Beth pitched her cell phone into Kimmy's lap, screaming "Call the fire department!" then took off, running up the lawn and around the lake side of the house. By the time she came around the back, flames were shooting at least six feet high up the clapboard siding near the small back porch off the sunroom.

For a second she stood there, frozen in horror, her hand to her mouth, trying to think of something, anything she could do while trying not to think how fast a 120-year-old house — wood, most of it — could be eaten alive by fire.

No. Not *her* house, by God.

She raced to within a few feet of the flames, prepared to smother them with her hands if she had to, but suddenly she spied a beach towel hanging over the railing of the back porch. Grabbing it, she began slapping at the fire, which was already turning a good portion of gray-painted clapboard into charred black wood. As she aimed the towel again and again at the flames, sparks flew up, and bits of burning wood popped out at her. Beth could feel their hot sting on her skin, but she didn't care. Her efforts seemed to be keeping the fire localized, rather than spreading wider or higher.

She beat at the flames faster and faster, wishing she could race down to the lake for water, but there just wasn't time. There wasn't time to get the fire extinguisher she kept faithfully in the kitchen. If she stopped her frantic activity for even a second, the fire would get away from her and lick upward, where she wouldn't be able to reach it anymore. And if it started traveling along the second-story trim, there'd be no stopping it. Her beloved house would be engulfed in minutes.

Over the fierce crackling of the flames and the blistering of paint and the igniting wood, Beth listened for the wail of a siren. Shelbyville had a single, practically antique fire truck, a gift from her grandfather, Orvis Shelby III, in the mid or late 1940s. The volunteers kept the vehicle in wonderful condition and were amazingly quick getting to any emergency.

Until now.

What if Kimmy hadn't called? What if her current condition left her too befuddled to punch little cell phone buttons in proper sequence? Beth shouted out for her, screaming until her throat ached; but there was no answer.

Well, if she was on her own, then she'd just have to try harder, wouldn't she? She slapped the towel harder and faster against the rear wall of the house until it, too, caught on fire, and she had to drop it before the flames raced up her arms. She stomped on the burning terry cloth, picked it up again, and resumed her frantic efforts.

She was just about to pass out from the heat and the smoke when she heard voices nearby. A moment later Sam came charging around the side of the house, carrying a fire extinguisher.

"Get out of the way, Beth," he yelled. "Move."

Then, when she didn't move fast enough, he rammed his shoulder between her and the flaming clapboards, and Beth went stumbling backward, winding up on her ass in the grass. All the energy seemed to go out of her then. She tried to stand up once, but when her shaky legs wouldn't support her, all she could do was sit there watching Sam with the big red extinguisher clamped under his arm, aiming a spray of white foam at the orange flames.

☆

Ten minutes later, it was all over but the macho conferencing — the shrugging and soft cursing and pats on the back — in front of the charred, wet clapboards that Sam, with the assistance of the volunteers from Shelbyville, had saved from a worse conflagration.

At first Beth couldn't stand because of fear, but now it was total relief that seemed to be sapping her strength. When Jerry Hoffman, the fire chief, motioned for her to come look at something, Beth could barely keep her balance.

"Look right here, Beth." Jerry pointed to something on the ground right below where the fire had apparently begun. "See that?"

Beth shook her head. "I see something. It looks like burned paper. What is it?"

"Some kind of fireworks," he said. "Roman candle, if I had to guess."

"You think that's what started the fire?"

"Probably. We're just a couple weeks away from the Fourth of July. Kids are getting an early start this year, it looks like." He looked over his shoulder at Sam. "You've already rousted a few of them for illegal fireworks, haven't you, Sam?"

"Just one," Sam said.

The fire chief continued. "I think it was just a fluke, Beth. Damned thing probably got away from some kids, and they took off. What I'm saying is I don't think anybody set this on purpose. You needn't worry about that."

"Well, that's good to know," Beth told him while she remained as worried as before. Arson. Roman candles. A freaking book of matches. What difference did it make? Her house had almost burned to the ground.

"Don't worry," Jerry said. "If you want, I'll stop by Dave Early's office on the way back into town and tell him to come out here to give you an estimate on replacing this siding."

"That'd be great," Beth said. "Thanks, Jerry."

"No problem. We'll clean up as much as we can back here. Come on, fellas."

Beth stepped out of the way, so the volunteers could get to work, and in doing so she collided with Sam's shoulder.

"Sorry," she said.

"Hold still."

"What?"

"I said hold still," Sam told her with that now-familiar note of sternness in his voice. "You've got some ashes and stuff in your hair."

"Oh."

He seemed to tower over her, standing so close she could feel the heat emanating from his body and the warmth of his breath on her neck as his fingers combed gently through her hair. Beth stood, staring into the front of his black polo shirt, unwilling to lift her gaze for fear she might meet his.

"There you go," he said, moving back a step. "I think I got it all."

"Thanks, Sam. And thanks for putting out the fire. I don't know what I would have done without . . ."

"That's okay. No thanks necessary."

"No, honestly. I mean it," Beth insisted. After all, she knew when she was grateful and when she wasn't. "And thanks *are* necessary. Listen. Why don't you let me fix you a really great dinner to show my gratitude?"

*Or why don't I just start walking west toward the lake and keep going until I drown myself? Even better, why not just keep on truckin' toward California and seek a watery grave in the Pacific? What about a rope around my neck?*

She'd just done it again, hadn't she? Dammit. It was all Beth could do not to smack herself upside the head with the palm of her hand. After narrowly escaping one dinner with Sam, she'd just invited him for a second. She cursed herself for her spontaneous invitations, but even as she cursed herself she had a brilliant idea.

"Hey, Jerry," she called out to the fire chief. "I'd really like to thank you and your crew. Why don't you all come back for dinner tonight?"

*Take that, Sam Mendenhall. You're not so special after all.*

There was some mumbling and shrugging among the volunteers, then their leader called back. "Thanks anyway, Beth. Maybe we could take a rain check on your offer?"

"Oh, sure," she answered. "Anytime."

*Well, nuts.*

"Look, Beth," Sam said. "You don't have to . . ."

"I invited you, didn't I?" she asked irritably, her gaze snapping up to his. "How's eight o'clock?"

"Works for me." A small grin played at the edges of his mouth. "Don't get a head start on the libations this time, okay?"

"Very funny. Just for that I'll be cooking liver and onions."

She gave a little farewell snort — a really juvenile thing to do — and walked away before Sam could see how completely he unsettled her.

☆

Sam stood there, trying not to notice or react to the smug little twitch of Beth's shapely butt as she disappeared around the side of the house. Or the way her curly blond hair swung softly at her shoulders the same way it had when they were kids. Or the fine shape of her smooth calves and the delicacy of her ankles.

He wished he'd never gotten the call from Blanche about the fire. When it clicked through on call waiting, he'd been parked by the side of the road, talking with Lt. Col. Roy Shearing, who called at least once a week, sometimes twice, to entice Sam back to Fort Bragg and the Delta Force training program there. Roy had the personality of Attila the Hun, a voice like John Wayne, and a swagger that somehow managed to transmit itself over a phone connection. Sam had known him and deployed with him for a dozen years, and there was no one he respected more.

This time Roy was trying a new tactic by appealing to Sam's sense of patriotism. Ordinarily the guy relied on nostalgia for the good old days with fellow warriors. He'd offered reenlistment bonuses, superior housing, a Hummer, and just about every enticement shy of his three daughters' affections.

Sam was in the midst of telling the persistent officer that he wasn't interested in *training* patriots if he couldn't participate in actions as one of them, when Blanche's call interrupted their conversation, and Sam found himself going eighty miles per hour toward Heart Lake.

Thank God he had the fire extinguisher in the back of the jeep because when he'd arrived the flames were just about to get away from Beth and her brave but ultimately futile efforts. He looked at the charred boards in front of him, trying to picture what Heart Lake would be like without this old monster of a house that had been there since the 1880s. He couldn't even imagine its absence and didn't want to think of what might have happened if he'd arrived a few minutes late. Certainly Bethie's heart would break if anything happened to this place she'd always loved so much.

He wasn't sure he agreed with Jerry Hoffman's appraisal of the fire and its origin, though. It was started with fireworks, sure, but Sam wasn't so certain it was an accident. Not that there were any outstanding clues. Not that he was qualified as an arson investigator. It was just a feeling he had. He'd learned to trust his instincts over the years because they rarely led him astray.

Just what he needed — more intrigue to go along with the mysterious disappearing junk around town. Could it be the same culprit? Would a crackpot thief start fires just to get a bigger rise out of an already skittish local population? And if so, what was next on the guy's warped agenda? Sam wondered.

And last but not least, why in hell had he said yes to Beth when she asked him to dinner again? And why the hell had she even asked when it seemed pretty obvious to him that she wasn't the least bit interested in his company?

Not when she'd gone on to invite the entire volunteer fire department for a bit of home cooking.

Worst of all, why was he going to show up at her front door at eight o'clock, just as he had before?

Because, in spite of his reluctance, and no matter how much he argued with himself and debated the pros and cons of her second invitation, Sam already knew he'd go.

☆

It was probably a blessing that the rest of Beth's day was full of frantic activity; otherwise, she would've obsessed about the fire. In between picking up a new tire for the Miata and shopping for groceries in the busy burg of Mecklin, she managed to avoid all but one of Danny's calls on her cell phone.

She didn't mention the fire when he asked her what was new. For heaven's sake, she'd already talked to him once that day, and anyway, she only wanted to relay good news to her former partner in California. There was no way she was going to give him any kind of ammunition to use against her decision to come back to Michigan when he'd already said, "It'll never work out. You'll be back. You'll see."

Over her dead body.

He called two more times while she was putting together her tried-and-true *boeuf bourguignon*. While that simmered on the stove, her cell phone rang another two times when she was in the big claw-footed bathtub upstairs. Such harassment didn't do a lot for her mood, but the good news was that she was stone-cold sober when she opened the front door to Sam at precisely eight o'clock.

After one look at his handsome face and amazingly

great, all-grown-up physique, she wished she'd fortified herself with a glass or two of something.

Almost as if he'd read her mind, Sam held up another bottle of wine. "Shelbyville's finest," he said, pointing to the label. "It was the best I could do. You're probably used to great Napa Valley wines."

It seemed amazing to Beth to be standing there discussing wines with Sam when the last time they'd truly been together neither one of them was of drinking age and the most they'd ever done was share an illegal beer or two.

"Thanks, Sam." She took the bottle from him. "You didn't have to do this. I still have the burgundy you brought the other night." Beth laughed. "That probably surprises you, considering the condition I was in then."

He smiled. "It's hard to picture you drinking."

"Funny," she said. "I was just thinking the same thing."

Beth felt herself relax a notch or two and sensed that Sam relaxed a little bit, as well. The situation seemed less awkward all of a sudden. The tension in the air lightened considerably. They were adults, after all. They could behave amicably in spite of their romantic history. Maybe this wouldn't be so horrible.

"I'll open this and get some glasses," she said, stepping back to allow him in. "Have a seat in the living room, Sam. I'll be right back."

☆

Sam settled on the couch and stared at the portrait of the old lumber baron, Orvis Shelby, over the fireplace, remembering how the old guy's hard glare from behind his spectacles and his humorless nineteenth-century demeanor used to completely unnerve Sam when he and Beth were dating. Making out here, with her geezer great-great-grandfather leering down at them, was never an option.

"You're not as big as you used to be, Orvis," Sam muttered to the man in the painting.

Well, hell. Who was? At the age of nineteen, Sam had been a giant of optimism and expectations. He'd been like that kid on the prow of the *Titanic*, sailing headlong into life and feeling like the king of the world. Then, by the time he was twenty, all that had changed. He'd been cut down to size and slapped around, chewed up and spit back out by life and by the consequences of his own foolish behavior.

He didn't blame Beth even though it was her rejection that led to his stupid mistakes. If the Army had taught him nothing else, it was how to be a man and take responsibility for his own actions. Besides, sixteen years was a long time ago. As far as he could tell, the woman wasn't carrying any torches for him.

Beth had lived a whole life without him. He looked around the room, admiring what she'd done with it. It wasn't really a surprise that she'd come home to the place she'd always loved so much.

Somewhere in the big house a cell phone began to ring. Sam listened, expecting Beth to answer it, counting seven rings, before he rose from the couch and followed the tones to the main staircase where the little phone perched on the banister. Obviously Beth couldn't hear it in the kitchen, so he eyeballed the caller ID window, identified the California area code, and finally answered it.

"Simon residence," he said, only to be greeted with a few seconds of silence before the caller disconnected.

"Who was that?" Beth asked, suddenly just a few feet

away with the wine bottle in one hand and two stemmed glasses in the other.

"Dunno. He hung up."

"He?"

"He. She. Whoever." Sam shrugged. "The call was from California."

Her expression darkened. "Damn. That was . . ." Her voice trailed off in a kind of growl, then she forced a smile. "Never mind. Let's go sit and enjoy the wine. Dinner will be ready in about half an hour."

Sam followed her back into the living room, then realized he was standing in order to choose his seat after Beth chose hers. When she landed on the couch, he lowered himself into an adjacent chair. He felt like a nervous teenager, not wanting to be too close for comfort. Once again, Orvis glowered down at him.

Beth poured the wine, handing him a glass and raising hers.

"It's been a long time, Sam," she said. "Here's to you."

He lifted his glass, and without even thinking said, "*Salaam*," the greeting and toast that came so naturally to him during his long months in Afghanistan.

Not surprisingly, Beth blinked. Perfectly accented Arabic, especially the Pashto dialect, wasn't often heard in this part of Michigan, if ever.

Hoping to distract her from asking him any questions about it, he tilted his wineglass toward her, and said, "Here's to you, Beth. Or maybe I should say *Here's look-ing at you, kid*."

That earned him a laugh and the hoped-for detour in conversation. "I'd forgotten that you could do such a good Bogart impression," she said. "You used to keep me in stitches, Sam. Remember?"

He nodded, taking a sip of the deep red wine, glad that Beth had opened the good bottle he'd brought the other night instead of the swill he'd picked up in town this afternoon. He didn't want her to think he was nothing more than a local yokel after all these years. Beth was a city girl at heart, despite spending all her summers at a rural lake.

"So, tell me what your life's been like these past sixteen years, Sam." Beth tucked her feet beneath her on the couch. "Good, I hope."

"Tolerable," he answered, anticipating further questions he wouldn't be able to answer other than in the most cursory fashion. He was used to that, though. It was standard policy not to discuss the Delta Force, its operators, or any of their activities outside the group itself.

"I'm sorry about your dad," Beth said. "I would've come up for the funeral, but I didn't find out about his death until a week or two later."

"That's okay. I didn't get back for the funeral either."

"You look like him, Sam," she said, her gaze roaming slowly over his face. "Especially now that you're older."

"That's what people say."

"How's your mom? Didn't she move down to Florida? My mother said . . ."

Sam stood up so abruptly it even shocked him. He was on his feet before he knew it and speaking even before he knew what he was going to say. "I can't do this, Beth. I can't sit here and chitchat like this, like two people at a high school reunion."

He set his wineglass on the table, feeling like a real jerk, like a socially inept kid who couldn't sit through an adult conversation, like a victim of Tourette's Syndrome who was going to say something really inappropriate unless he got away this instant. And Beth was looking at him as if that were exactly the case.

"Sorry," he told her, already moving across the living room under the steely gaze of old Orvis, heading toward the front door and the cool dark and anyplace he didn't have to look at her lovely face or hear her sweet voice or remember how they'd once loved each other and fucked it up beyond all recognition.

"Good night, Beth."

# CHAPTER SEVEN

By the time Beth stomped into the kitchen for something to eat it was after ten o'clock, and her wonderful *boeuf bourguignon* had simmered on the back burner of the stove so long that it tasted little better than crummy beef stew out of a can. She ate it anyway as the punishment she deserved for being such a wimp a couple of hours ago with Sam.

Worse than a wimp. She'd been a doormat, almost literally.

Sam had really thrown her for a loop, walking out on her the way he had. The ironic thing was that all the while Beth had been sitting there in the living room with him, she'd been groaning on the inside, clenching her teeth behind a sweet smile, detesting the polite formality of their small talk, but determined to get through the evening as best she could and finally to put the inevitable reunion with Sam far, far behind her.

Actually he'd done more than unsettle her with his abrupt exit. He'd pissed her off. Royally.

Instead of behaving like a good little hostess, she wished now that she'd been the one to jump up, and scream, "This is ridiculous. It's bogus. I hate this bullshit. Either we talk about what really happened with us sixteen years ago, Sam Mendenhall, or we shouldn't talk at all. Ever."

But she hadn't said that, had she?

Nooo.

She'd sat there and smiled like a good little girl, a prim and proper welcome mat, politely initiating, then sweetly enduring, their perfunctory exchange. Instead it was Sam — who seemed to be as short on good manners as he was long on good looks — who had seized the moment and gone storming off into the dark of night.

Bully for him.

Score one for the sheriff.

Yay, Sam.

With her elbows propped on the kitchen table while she force-fed herself the horrible stew, Beth wondered how she could possibly live happily ever after, not to mention temporarily, in the same small town as Sam. Shelbyville wasn't exactly a major metropolitan area where a person could sink into anonymity. How could she endure the continual stress and just plain aggravation of encountering Sam on what would certainly turn out to be a weekly if not a daily basis?

So, he couldn't sit and chitchat like two people at a high school reunion, huh? Well, neither could she. Dammit. Was that what was in store for the two of them in the coming years? Passing on Main Street or meeting by accident at the post office, then irritating the hell out of each other just by saying "It looks like rain" or "How's your mom?" or "Have a nice day."

At least she and Danny were capable of intelligent and often fascinating conversation. At least they could talk to each other for more than five minutes without one of them throwing a fit and stomping out of the room. Now that she thought about it, she sort of missed those wonderful, rambling conversations that had made Danny so attractive to her in the first place.

Her phone rang then, as if on cue, and for a brief moment Beth was tempted to answer it. She knew it was Danny. This would make his tenth or eleventh call today, not nearly a record for him. Besides, who else could it be, calling at this hour?

She pictured him as she'd first seen him three years ago when he'd answered her inquiry about a painting contractor for the house. He'd looked intriguing — sexy as hell, actually — with his long blond hair pulled back in a rough ponytail and a blue-and-white bandana wrapped pirate-style around his head. Okay. So she'd hired him based primarily on his looks; but he'd turned out to be the best painter, plasterer, and wallpaper hanger that she'd ever worked with.

Beth glanced at the clock on the stove, noting that it would be a little after eight o'clock on the West Coast. Danny would be standing at the window of the apartment they'd shared, looking at the sunset over San Francisco Bay while he held the phone to his ear and listened to ring after ring, obviously undaunted, undiscouraged, and utterly persistent in his attempt to get her to come back. It struck Beth as a flattering contrast to the man who'd walked out on her earlier in the evening.

At least somebody wanted her. At least somebody prized her conversation.

Maybe she should talk to Danny, or at the very least listen to him. Maybe she should give him one more chance to prove he could really love her up close and personal without abusing her. Maybe, considering her bone-deep tendency to be polite, she hadn't stood up to him the way she should have. Maybe she'd enabled the bursts of anger and physical abuse. Maybe . . .

Nah.

She'd stood up to him in grand fashion. She'd slugged him, hadn't she? And hard enough to break her hand. So much for all that inborn, bone-deep politeness. Beth had given him more than enough chances to change, and he'd blown them all with his temper and his misplaced jealousies.

She let the damned phone keep ringing while she rinsed her plate and put it in the dishwasher. It was still ringing downstairs when she finally flopped into bed. She was growing accustomed to the sound in a weird sort of way. It didn't even keep her awake.

☆

At three o'clock in the morning Sam finally gave up any attempt to sleep and rolled out of bed with a curse. What else was new? Hell. He'd had trouble sleeping ever since returning from Afghanistan.

Initially it was the relentless pain from his broken leg and hip that kept him awake. Then, when surgeries and metal screws and medications gave him some relief, it was nightmares that had him sitting up wide-eyed and soaked with sweat two and three times a night.

The Afghan landscape seemed all too real in his dreams, almost more vivid than his actual memories of it. The skies were nearly sapphire in his dreams. Naked aspen trees reached up against those dark blue skies like bleached bones. The peaks of the Hindu Kush were wild beneath their blankets of brilliant white snow. The women who populated his dreams all had emerald eyes and graceful hands with golden rings and bracelets, beckoning him, always beckoning, while they swayed suggestively behind their veils.

Invariably one of the women would have startlingly familiar blue eyes, and he'd follow her, wondering how his Bethie came to be in Bamayan or Khandahar or Kabul. In those dreams he'd pursue her through crowded marketplaces and bazaars, down dark and narrow alleys, into homes with dirt floors, across multicolored carpets, into mosques and caves and along frozen riverbanks. For the most part, the dreams were about the pursuit alone. But sometimes he'd catch up with her.

"Bethie?" he'd ask, searching those beautiful, veiled blue eyes.

More often than not the woman would throw off her veil or step out of her *burqa*, revealing herself as someone else. A crone with no teeth. A blind woman whose eyes turned out to be a pale and hazy hue. Once, God help him, the object of his pursuit turned out to be his very own mother. Little wonder he dreaded falling asleep.

Despite the wee small hour of the morning, Sam fired up the stove, filled his battered coffeepot with water, and poured the grounds directly into the pot without measuring. The stronger the better in his opinion. Plus, he'd gotten used to and even fond of infinite varieties of bad coffee in the Army. Later, if he was home, he'd switch from coffee to Afghan *chai*, the strong tea he'd come to appreciate after consuming untold gallons of it.

If he hadn't accepted the responsibilities of constable, chances were good he'd be pouring himself a couple fingers of Jack Daniel's Black right then to ease himself back to bed. But his phone might ring at any minute, and he'd have to go check out some teens parked in a cul-de-sac, a drunk who refused to leave a tavern, or a missing pair of burlap curtains. God forbid that he wasn't sharp enough to handle such emergencies. And God forbid that anything really important came up.

Like the fire at the Simon house.

He thought about that as he sat on his little screened porch, sipped his coffee, and stared out at the dark waters of the lake.

It was hard to imagine anybody having an ax to grind with the Simons. Harry and Linda Simon had contributed so much to this area. Over the years Harry had probably donated at least a hundred thousand dollars in free legal advice to the township. Linda, with her wildly successful knitting business, paid plenty of taxes here and employed a dozen or more knitters, both full- and part-time. Nobody around here would want to tamper with that golden goose.

Their daughter, Shelby, was a different story, though, and Sam could easily believe that somebody had it in for the opinionated advice columnist. Somebody had actually tried to kill her last year, but wound up poisoning poor Kimmy instead. Hell, even he had an ax to grind with Shelby after she interfered with his relationship with Beth, scuttling them completely, and ultimately changing his life dramatically. Whether it was for better or worse, Sam had yet to decide.

Still, Shelby had never had much to do with the family house after her teens and even less to do with it now that she was married to a Chicago cop. The place mattered to her, Sam supposed, but she didn't love it the way her sister did.

Setting fire to that big old Victorian hulk was almost the same as setting fire to Beth herself. He could still picture her slapping at the flames with that burning beach towel. She would've done the same thing when she was a kid, the way she loved that place.

He remembered when a storm brought a poplar branch down on the roof one summer, and Bethie had cried over the damage as if it had happened to her instead. He hadn't known how to comfort her. Hell, he was just a kid, maybe fifteen at the time, and it was all he could do not to cry himself, seeing her hurt that way. Now that he was thirty-five, he'd do a better job at soothing her sorrows. He'd know how to hold her, how to kiss the tears from her eyes, how to . . .

Sam shook his head to clear it of those dangerous thoughts.

He'd had the good sense to walk away from her earlier. No sense letting that burst of courage go to waste with thoughts of the way they used to be.

That was the past, and even though it haunted his dreams, he wasn't going to breathe life into it again, no matter how many times he had to walk away from her.

☆

For the next few days Beth got down to business with a vengeance.

She contacted Thelma Watt's nephew, Steve, who was clearly thrilled to be chosen to photograph "the old *grande dame* of Heart Lake," as he referred to her house. Considering his outspoken fondness for the place, Beth was utterly confident in her choice.

Before the *grande dame* was ready for her pictures, though, there was a lot of primping to do to get her ready. Kimmy came over with her box of cleaning supplies and brought every surface to a glistening shine. It took her a full four hours to rub lemon oil into all the woodwork in the dining room alone.

While Kimmy did the basic cleaning and polishing, Beth concentrated on the spiffing up required for the photographs that would go into her brochure. In the two bedrooms she planned to feature, she collected all the items and knickknacks left over from her parents' residence the year before. Most of those were her mother's belongings. Her father had spent a good six months of their residence exiled in the carriage house while the two of them worked to keep their marriage from falling apart.

Now Beth carried a load of extraneous family items across the lawn to the carriage house, which she'd redone in pure twentieth-century comfort and convenience rather than the Victorian trappings of most of the property. Actually, her father had insisted on it.

"Why you think anybody wants to revert to those fussy old times is beyond me, Bethie," he'd told her. "But do whatever you want with the place. Have at it, honey. Just leave a few square feet of this century for me, all right?"

"Here you go, Pop," she said now, dropping an armful of her mother's beautifully knitted but decidedly contemporary throw pillows onto the long, curved sofa in the loftlike main room of the carriage house.

Actually, she had nothing against most contemporary design, with the exception of stark Danish Modern, and she was fond of this large room with its big, comfy sofa and big-screen TV and the sleek but small kitchen just beyond the curve of granite counter space. If Heart Lake Manor turned out to be as successful as she intended, Beth herself would be spending more and more time out here, allowing her guests their privacy inside the big house.

Once she'd rid the two bedrooms of personal effects, it was time to spiff up the front porch, so Beth hopped in her car and drove to Johnson's Tree Farm and Nursery a few miles away at Pretty Lake. There she found some wonderful Boston ferns potted in hanging baskets that would be perfect for the porch. They were so enormous that she couldn't fit all six in the Miata, so she had to make two trips.

It was on her second trip, driving south back to Heart Lake, that she passed Sam's northbound jeep with Sam at the wheel and a redhead — a very attractive one as far as Beth could tell — riding shotgun.

So?

So what?

It didn't bother her a bit, seeing him with another woman. Why should it?

And because it didn't bother her one little bit, Beth found herself readjusting the rearview mirror and glaring into it so long, watching the vehicle and its passengers recede in the distance, that she nearly ran off the road.

☆

The jeep's engine idled in the Cutlers' driveway while redheaded Julie Cutler thanked Sam for the hundredth time for his quick response to her call and his assistance in finding Gordo, her ancient and arthritic toy poodle, who, despite his aching joints, had shot out of the front door this morning at the sound of firecrackers in the backyard.

The dog was cradled under her arm at the moment, obviously happy to be back where he belonged.

"Why don't you come by for supper later, Sam? I've got some really nice steaks I can throw on the grill, and I know you love corn on the cob."

He'd taken the pretty divorcee up on similar offers during the past year, but an evening with Julie suddenly didn't
hold much appeal for him. He cursed himself silently when
he realized why.

Beth.

Dammit.

He told Julie he already had plans for that night and that
he'd call her soon, both lies meant to get him quickly off
the hook and spare her feelings. He despised the words
even as he was speaking them, and they left a bad taste in
his mouth as he drove back to town.

Less than a week after Beth's return, Sam had turned into
a lying, equivocating coward. In other words, a damned
weasel. For a man who had a fairly strong notion of truth and
duty and honor, as well as a reputation for living up to those
ideals, this transformation wasn't a good sign.

And for a man with his finely honed military skills,
tracking down runaway poodles didn't provide much challenge or satisfaction.

Considering all that, Sam decided it was probably time
to revisit his career options and redeploy.

He couldn't stay here.

Not now.

Beth's mere presence was making him miserable.

☆

When Beth pulled into the driveway with her second
load of potted ferns, she noticed immediately that one of
the three pots she'd unloaded earlier was missing. Rather
than schlep them all up the lawn before her return trip to
the nursery, she'd left all three of them beside the driveway. And now there were only two.

It struck her as odd, but then she decided that Kimmy had probably lugged one of them up to the porch, then gotten busy with something else and promptly forgotten about the remaining two. Beth proceeded to unload the car, and carried the huge ferns one by one up to the house.

The sixth pot wasn't on the porch, so she called out to Kimmy. When no answer came, Beth shrugged and set about hanging her purchases. Lucky for her there were already good, strong hooks screwed into the roof of the porch, so it didn't take long for all five to be hanging securely overhead.

Beth stood back to admire her handiwork. They looked great — all green and healthy and wonderfully Victorian. But they looked decidedly lopsided with three on one side of the front door and two on the other, so Beth went in search of the missing plant.

Kimmy, as it turned out, was gone, having left a shakily printed note on the kitchen counter, saying she'd forgotten about a doctor's appointment this afternoon. Jeez. Poor thing. She'd become so scatterbrained since the poisoning incident that she probably took the fern with her, never giving a second thought to what was in her hand.

Still, Beth didn't doubt her own tendency to be somewhat absentminded lately, what with all the crank calls from Danny and the repeated sightings of Sam. In light of that, after searching the house, the porch, and her car again, she called the nursery to see if she'd left a plant behind.

Mr. Johnson told her he remembered putting all six pots into her car — "that little red machine," he called it. "I charged you for six, and six is what you got."

"Boy, that's really weird," she said.

"Well, there's been a spate of missing stuff around here lately," the nursery owner said.

"Who'd take a fern?" she asked, sounding truly dismayed.

"Dunno. Same joker who took Thelma Watt's flag, I suppose. She's fit to be tied about that. Maybe you should give Sam Mendenhall a call, Miss Simon."

*Oh, sure. I'll get right on that, Mr. Johnson. Yessirree Bob.*

"Well, thanks anyway," she told him. "I'll just keep looking. I'm sure it'll turn up. And if not, I'll be back for a replacement."

"Only two left," he said. "You just about cleaned me out this afternoon. Want me to put one away for you just in case?"

"Thanks. I'd appreciate that. I'll come by for it sometime tomorrow."

"Anytime," the man said. "Best keep those other ones inside, so they don't take off, too."

Beth hung up, thinking maybe that wasn't such a bad idea.

# CHAPTER EIGHT

At least some things were going right, Beth thought the next morning when she picked up the replacement fern at the nursery. Mr. Johnson had done as he promised, putting one aside for her.

Despite her protests, the man insisted on showing Beth his copy of the sales receipt for *six* potted ferns.

"Just want you to know it wasn't my fault," he said as he ran her credit card through his machine. "I'll bet you anything it was that thief. Did you call Sam and alert him?"

"No, but I will," Beth told him, telling herself she'd call Sam about the same time that pigs flew over the frozen landscape of hell.

By the time she had all six ferns hung securely and symmetrically on the front porch, Steve Watt, the photographer, showed up at the appointed time.

He was far younger than Beth had anticipated. Knowing that the elderly postmistress was his aunt, she'd expected to greet a man in his forties or fifties, but Steve, with his blond crew cut, half dozen tattoos, and flip-flops, barely looked twenty. She commented on that while he was setting up his equipment in order to photograph the front of the house.

"Aunt Thelma's my great-aunt," he said. "Or great-great. I forget."

"Oh. Well, that explains it."

He laughed. "She must be 212 if she's a day, huh?"

"I just hope I'm in such great shape when I'm her age, whatever it is," Beth said.

"No kidding. You know, I feel sorry for the poor dumb bastard who made off with her flag. He'll be plenty sorry when she gets her hands on him."

Now Beth laughed as she angled a hip onto the porch railing. "Who do you think is taking all this stuff? Any idea?"

Steve shrugged as he continued to pull what looked like lens cases out of his big canvas bag. "Kids probably. Kids with nothing else better to do. I better not catch one of them trying to make off with any of my stuff, I can tell you."

"You could sic your Aunt Thelma on them."

"Damn straight," he said. "Hey, I really appreciate your giving me this opportunity, Miss Simon. I've been by here a lot in the past few years. You did an amazing job with this place. It's awesome."

"Thanks." Beth was liking this kid more and more. "I don't think anyone has ever called it awesome before."

"Oh, yeah." He gestured toward a window. "That trim's great. I really like the maroon against the dark blue. You've got a good eye for contrast."

Beth thanked him again, not bothering to mention that it had been Danny's good eye that was responsible for those particular touches on the windows.

"I can't wait to see the inside," Steve said as he set up a

black metal tripod. "So tell me more about the history of the house. This is great."

It was indeed, Beth thought. It wasn't often that she had such an eager audience for her favorite stories.

She didn't have to be asked twice.

"My great-great grandfather — you'll see his portrait in the living room — came to Michigan in the early 1840s and . . ."

Beth paused for a second just to make sure Steve was truly interested, that he hadn't asked about the house just to be polite. Unlike her sister, Shelby, who didn't care whether she was boring the pants off somebody or not, Beth had always been cautious when speaking. It was probably because so few people really shared her interests.

Either young Steve was a very good actor, or else he really was curious about the history of the house.

"Go on," he said to her. "So he came to Michigan in the 1840s, then what?"

Beth smiled. Bless his heart. If this kid weren't about twelve years old, she swore she'd be half in love with him.

"Well," she continued, "first he bought some virgin timberland in the Upper Peninsula, then . . ."

She was still happily yakking by the time Steve had lugged all of his equipment into the house, photographed the living room from every possible angle, and was ready to take on the two bedrooms upstairs that Beth had prepared. While he carried his equipment up the big staircase, Beth went to the kitchen to get them something to drink.

With a cold can of diet cola in each hand, she was just about to mount the staircase when Steve called out.

"You better come here, Miss Simon."

There was something in his tone that immediately set off a warning bell in Beth's head. It was the same thing whenever she used to hear her mother say "Uh-oh." She knew something must really be wrong.

She raced up the broad stairs and entered the bedroom that used to be hers for so many years when her family summered here. Beth knew every curve and nick in the massive antique furniture in the room and every imperfection in the floral wallpaper. It was brighter than usual now because Steve had pulled back the massive blue velvet drapes, allowing bright north light to penetrate what was usually a cool Victorian dimness.

"You must've really pissed somebody off," the photographer said to her over his shoulder as he stood in front of the casement.

Every single pane of the tall window had been shot out. A few were missing their square of glass entirely, but most looked like angry, hectic spider webs with distinct holes in their centers.

Beth gasped, and rushed forward.

"Careful," Steve told her, holding up his hand in a gesture of warning. "There's glass all over the floor here."

"Oh, my God. When did this happen?"

"Hard telling. Could've been anytime, I guess. The curtains were covering everything up." He shook his crew-cut head. "Good thing, though. Otherwise, the BBs could've done a lot of damage in the room itself."

"BBs?" Somehow that sounded less serious than bullets. Beth felt briefly and stupidly relieved. "How do you know they were BBs?"

He pointed down. "They're all over the floor."

She saw them, scattered among all the bits of glass. Little silver balls. There must've been dozens of them. Perhaps a hundred. Like beads from a necklace that had broken.

While she stared at them, Steve eased back the drapes on the adjacent window. The movement was accompanied by the tinkling of broken glass and the sound of metal BBs hitting the hardwood floor.

"Looks like the same deal here," he said. "What a mess."

The news of the second window and the sound of the falling glass seemed almost too much to bear. When her knees felt weak, Beth let herself down onto the bed. The soda cans were still in her hands. She noticed now that her thumbs had deeply dented the aluminum.

"Is there a phone nearby?" Steve asked her.

Beth blinked.

"A phone?" he repeated, holding his hand up to his ear.

"Oh. Yes. The phone. It's downstairs in the kitchen."

"Okay. Be right back." He paused beside the bed where she sat and asked in a voice full of concern, "Want me to take those off your hands?"

"Excuse me?"

"The cans?"

"Oh." She'd already forgotten they were there, lodged in her fists. Loosening her grip, she handed them to the young man. "Thank you."

"Sure. Be right back." He paused in the doorway. "Are you okay, Miss Simon?"

Actually, she wasn't okay at all, but Beth mumbled that she was fine. Then she sat there, perched on the side of the big bed, for what seemed like a very long time before Steve returned.

She felt oddly violated, almost physically attacked herself by whoever had attacked her house. It might have affected her differently if the damage had occurred elsewhere, say in the living room or in the sunroom or in any other bedroom but this one. This room, where she'd spent so many treasured hours over so many summers, seemed like a real part of her. If not an actual physical part, then surely it was a significant piece of her psyche and her soul.

The windowpanes with their waves and small imperfect bubbles in the glass probably weren't original from the 1870s, but they'd undoubtedly been here since the 1930s or 1940s. Beth didn't have any records for work done on the house prior to 1952, when her grandparents did a fairly extensive — and awful — renovation. Still, the window glass was old. And even if it wasn't ancient, her memories of these windows were so special.

As a little girl, she used to open the drapes and gaze through the tall windows when she was supposed to be taking a nap.

She could almost hear her sister back through the years, standing in the doorway.

*Mommy said to keep those curtains closed so you can sleep. I'm going to tell on you, Beth.*

Shelby always threatened, but she rarely carried through, so Beth always kept the curtains open.

The waves in the glass would so distort the images of treetops and clouds that it was like a different world from the one she was used to. In fact, Beth called it her Wavy World where there were no straight lines or sharp edges or even smooth shapes. Everything was disconnected and undulating.

Sometimes she pretended that the Wavy World outside her windows was situated high above the clouds, and it was easy to imagine herself flying. She was a bird. She was an angel. She was queen of the air.

Most of the time, she imagined her little world underwater and pretended she was a beautiful mermaid, trapped in a castle on the ocean floor. Her fantasies were vivid and almost as cartoony as *The Little Mermaid*.

"There's no such thing as a mermaid, Beth," an eight-year-old Shelby informed her. Beth already knew that, but it didn't matter.

As she grew older, her fantasies grew more real and often included being rescued from her underwater prison by an old fisherman's handsome son, who sometimes looked like John Travolta; but, more often than not, bore an amazing resemblance to a very young and very heroic Sammy Mendenhall.

Oh, God. She just wanted to cry. She wanted just to let go for a few minutes and weep. Why would somebody vandalize her house this way? Why destroy her precious view of that childhood Wavy World? If bored kids with BB guns wanted to shoot out windows, there were plenty of abandoned fishing cabins around here. Why didn't they vandalize those? Nobody cared about those ramshackle shanties. The kids probably wouldn't even have gotten into trouble.

Oh boy, were they in trouble. Beth decided she wasn't going to spend another minute being sad. She was mad as hell, and she was going to find out who was responsible and . . .

"Sam'll be here in a minute," Steve said, walking into the room.

"What?"

"I called Sam Mendenhall. He's the town constable." Steve stopped speaking abruptly, stared at Beth, and then, after a little gulping sound, said, "Aw, damn. You two have some sort of history, don't you? Aunt Thelma mentioned it. I'm sorry, Miss Simon. Listen. If you want, I can call Sam back and tell him . . ."

"Tell me what?"

Beth hadn't heard his footsteps on the stairs. Both she and Steve looked at the doorway in surprise when Sam appeared.

"Tell me what?" he asked again, looking from Beth on the bed to Steve at the window.

The young photographer's face reddened considerably. "Oh . . . well . . ." The poor guy stammered, shrugged helplessly, then glanced toward Beth as if to say *Help me out here, will you?*

Meanwhile Sam was walking toward the windows on the north side of the room. He stood in front of one, squinted at the damage, crossed his arms, then shook his head.

"Jesus Christ, Bethie," he said so softly that it was almost a whisper. "Look what they did to your Wavy World."

Despite all her best intentions to let anger replace her sadness, and despite her fierce desire not to wimp out, Beth dissolved in tears.

☆

Well, hell.

He hadn't meant to make her cry.

Sam dragged his fingers through his hair, then went to the bed, sat down next to Beth, and wrapped her in his arms. God. She felt so familiar — her soft-yet-supple flesh, the warmth of her hair, the faint fragrance of flowers and spices emanating from her smooth neck. Even her tears felt familiar as they moistened the front of his shirt.

Just as much as ever, she fit perfectly in his embrace.

This was what he'd dreaded all along. This was what

he'd feared from the moment he stopped her on the road. Bethie had been in his heart even when she wasn't in his life, and now that she was in his arms, his heart was pounding so hard he thought it might explode.

Even on the far side of the room, young Steve Watt probably heard it because the kid suddenly cleared his throat and announced, "Well, I think I'm through taking pictures for the day. I'll just get my stuff out of here and be back tomorrow, Miss Simon." He cleared his throat once more. "Is ten o'clock okay?"

Beth sniffed and nodded against Sam's chest.

"That's fine," Sam said by way of translation.

It didn't take long for Steve to gather up his equipment and make his exit. All the while, Sam kept holding Beth. At some point he realized that he was rocking her slightly and stroking her hair. Just the way he used to do when she cried when they were kids.

Not that she ever cried that much. In fact, now that he thought about it, he could only remember three occasions. The first was when her mother was rushed to the hospital for an appendectomy. Beth was maybe nine or ten at the time, and scared to death that everyone was lying to her and that her mother had actually died.

The second time was after an argument with her sister, Shelby. After all these years Sam couldn't recall what they'd argued about, but knowing Shelby and her big mouth, he was sure that she'd verbally ripped her little sister up one side and down the other.

The third and last time he'd seen Beth cry was the night before he'd left for basic training. It was also the last time he'd held her in his arms.

Ah, God. Sam sighed. He hadn't thought about her Wavy World in decades. It amazed him that he remembered it at all. But maybe it wasn't so surprising. How could he forget anything about Beth?

With a muted curse and a wet sniff, she pulled away from him now.

"What a wuss, huh?" she said, trying to ramp up a smile as she scrubbed the tears from her cheeks and her chin.

"Nah," Sam said. "Those windows meant a lot to you. Lots of good memories."

"You remember that?" She blinked those wet, red-rimmed, bluer-than-blue eyes.

"Sure. Does that surprise you?"

"No," she said, then shook her head in apparent dismay. "Well, yeah, I guess it does surprise me. That was a long time ago, Sam."

Just then it didn't seem that long ago to Sam. Being with Beth right now felt like a mere continuation of yesterday somehow.

She pushed up off the bed and went to the dresser to examine her face in the mirror. Sam sensed that their brief moment of intimacy, or whatever the hell it was, had ended. Beth obviously didn't want or need his comfort anymore. Still, in light of these episodes of vandalism — the fire and now the windows — he knew she definitely needed his help, whether she'd acknowledge it or not.

He stood up. "I'm going to go outside and have a look around. It'll be getting dark in a couple hours, so it's too late for the county cops from Mecklin to do much. I'll have them come over in the morning."

"Thanks," she said, still making repairs in front of the mirror.

"Keep these drapes closed, Beth," he told her. "Not that anybody's going to be firing BBs, but we've had some problems with Peeping Toms in the woods out back. So just be aware."

She strode to the closer window immediately and yanked the heavy curtains closed. "Vandals," she grumbled. "Peeping Toms. A bizarre mystery thief. My God, Sam. What's going on around here?"

Her tone struck him as more accusatory than quizzical. As if this were all his fault somehow. Hell, maybe it was. Maybe somebody with proper police training would've at least caught the mystery thief by now.

"I don't know, Beth," he answered, trying not to sound too defensive. "Things were fairly quiet until you came back."

She whirled around, planting her fists on her hips. "Just what is that supposed to mean? That this is my fault?"

"That's not what I meant." When did she become so hot tempered? he wondered. "Jesus," he muttered under his breath.

"Well, what are you saying, Sam?"

She was standing in front of the open drapes of the second window with her chin lifted defiantly, pointed right between his eyes, when what was left of the wavy glass behind her suddenly started to shatter and rain down upon her head.

Beth didn't even have time to scream before Sam had knocked her to the floor and covered her body with his.

# CHAPTER NINE

He didn't know he could still move that fast!

Sam lay stunned for a moment, as much by his abrupt encounter with the floor as by the knowledge that his reflexes weren't as impaired as he had come to believe in the past two years since he got banged up overseas. It took a second or two for him to realize that Beth was lying beneath him, and they were both covered with broken glass. Luckily, he'd protected her head with his hand when he tackled her. Using his forearms, he rose, wincing as shards of glass bit into his flesh.

"Are you okay?" he asked, looking down into her wide and frightened eyes.

When she didn't reply, he asked again, more urgently, afraid that his solid 190 pounds might have broken one of her delicate ribs or at least knocked the breath out of her.

"Bethie, honey, are you all right?"

This time she nodded awkwardly, no doubt as best she could with her head on the floor and his not-insignificant weight still pressing down on her. God help him, in spite of the danger they might be in, his body betrayed him completely just then, and it was all he could do not to close the distance between them and sample the softness of her mouth.

"I'm okay. At least I think so," she said. "But . . . Could you get up, Sam? I can't breathe."

"Sorry." He practically scrambled off her and to his feet, then reached down a hand to help her up.

Bits of glass tinkled onto the floor as they both brushed gingerly at their hair and clothes. Sam turned and pulled the curtains closed. The room darkened considerably, but wasn't dark enough to keep Beth from exclaiming, "Oh, God. You're bleeding."

He followed the direction of her gaze to discover that both his forearms were slick with blood. "Aw, shit." Sam immediately clasped his arms to his shirtfront, far more worried about dripping on Beth's carpet than he was about a few superficial cuts. "It's nothing. Get me a couple of towels, will you?"

"I don't think so."

She moved behind him and put a hand on his back, pushing hard when he didn't respond fast enough.

"You're coming into the bathroom and letting me take a look at those cuts. You've probably still got some pieces of glass stuck in there."

"Hey, it's okay, Beth. Really. You don't . . ."

This time she shoved him hard enough to make him move forward, so he compliantly kept going in the direction of the adjacent bathroom, a huge space with a black-and-white-tile floor and a white claw-footed tub right out in the middle of the room. And windows. Too many damned windows, all on the north side of the house, just like the ones in the bedroom.

"Stay out until I've closed the curtains in here," he told her.

He peered from the edge of one of the unbroken panes, trying to see if anybody was hanging around on the fringes of the woods in back of the house. He ought to have raced out there himself mere seconds after the shots were fired, but . . . Hell. It seemed he never did what he should when he was around Beth and being distracted by her blue eyes or her glossy pink lips or the swell of her hips or the oh-so-fine shape of her little butt.

"Are they closed yet?" she called impatiently from the other side of the door.

Seeing nothing suspicious outside, Sam pulled the black satin drapes closed and told Beth to come in.

☆

"Hold still, dammit."

Sam was worse than a four-year-old, squirming to get away while she tried to see if there were any more bits of glass in his arms. First he hadn't wanted to kneel by the tub so she could properly wash the blood off of him. Then as soon as she'd run warm water over his arms, he insisted he was fine and needed to get outside to take a look around. She practically had to sit on him to do a thorough inspection of his cuts.

How she'd escaped similar injuries to herself was a miracle. Well, maybe it was Sam who performed the miracle because no sooner had the glass started flying than he was knocking her out of its path. She'd never seen anybody move so fast.

"Are you about done there?" he asked, making no effort to disguise his impatience.

"Just hold still."

Beth was concentrating on a little sliver of glass on the inside of his arm, just a few inches above his wrist, hoping to extract the tiny shard from his skin and catch it with the tip of her fingernail. Despite her intense focus, though, as she tended to Sam, she became increasingly aware of the scent of him so close to her and the feel of him — how his tan flesh barely shielded her fingertips from sensing the powerful musculature beneath it. Sam had arms like a young blacksmith.

And just then, in an instant, she flashed back to another time when she was also tending to his wounds. They'd been horsing around with one of her mother's silk scarves in the woods behind the house. Beth was — what? — maybe ten or eleven, which would have made Sam twelve or thirteen.

She remembered it so perfectly, even including the abstract pattern of the pink-and-white scarf she'd "borrowed" from her mother's dresser drawer. She could even picture what they were wearing, both of them in cutoff jeans and ratty sneakers without socks. She wore the Hard Rock Café T-shirt her parents had brought her from Los Angeles, and Sam wore one of his favorite camouflage-colored shirts.

It was a glorious summer day, with a dazzling sapphire sky and puffy white clouds scudding along in a breeze. For want of a kite, she and Sam were holding up the scarf, letting it catch on the wind and watching it fly deeper and deeper into the woods. They were laughing like loons as they chased after it, then all of a sudden an unusually strong gust lofted the silken square high up into a pine tree, where it snagged on a branch. And stuck.

"Uh-oh," Beth said. "My mother's going to absolutely kill me if I don't get that back."

Almost before the words "No problem" were out of his mouth, Sam was already halfway up the tall tree.

"Be careful," Beth called up to him. "Maybe we should get a broom or a ladder, Sam."

"Nah."

His footing was so sure as he climbed higher and higher. His legs were so strong and tanned. Looking back on it, he reminded Beth of some sort of Greek god in training. And when he finally reached out to clutch the scarf, the look on his face was pure triumph as he grinned down at her.

"Your banner, my lady," he called to her.

And then he fell.

Branch after branch after branch.

Beth stood there frozen. It felt as if her heart had stopped, and she couldn't even breathe. When he finally hit the ground, which thankfully was cushioned with pine needles, the scarf was still clutched in his fist.

Then, as now, he tried to fend her off when she wanted desperately to help him.

"I'm okay."

"You're bleeding, Sam."

"It's no big deal." He grinned, offering her the flyaway scarf. "I got it."

Then, as now, she practically had to sit on him to wipe the blood from all the scrapes on his arms and legs and face.

"You'll probably have a scar from this. It's kinda deep," she told him, gently touching a gash just below his knee.

"Good," he said, laughing. "Then I'll always remember today. It'll be my souvenir."

"Sam, you jerk. What am I going to do with you?"

She used her mother's scarf to dab at all his scrapes and cuts, not caring what the punishment might be for ruining the expensive little square of designer silk. Sam meant more to her than anyone or anything in the entire world.

Oh, God. Beth remembered that feeling so vividly it was almost as if she were experiencing it again, two decades later. As if she, too, carried a permanent scar from that day. It threatened to overwhelm her.

"I should have gone with you," she whispered. "I wanted to, only . . ."

He pulled away from her as if her hands had suddenly turned as hot as branding irons.

"Thanks for the help," he said brusquely. "I'm going out back to have a look around."

"Sam, I shouldn't have said . . ."

"And keep those fucking curtains closed," he bellowed as he strode out of the room, leaving Beth with her mouth hanging open and no words coming forth.

Already she bitterly regretted the ones she'd just spoken.

☆

Sam slammed the front door and jogged around to the back of the house, not really expecting to find anything or anyone. Basically he wanted to put as much distance between himself and Beth as he could.

*I should have gone with you.*

What the hell was that? An apology after all these years? An expression of regret? A fond wish to wipe their shared slate clean and start all over again?

Not on your life, Elizabeth Eleanor Simon.

No freaking way.

Sam found that he was walking faster and faster as thoughts of Beth ricocheted through his head. In addition, he was trying his best to ignore the aroused condition of his body, which had sprung to life at about the same time that Beth was running warm water and her warm fingers along his arms. Since he couldn't really ignore it, he told himself it was no more than a visceral, automatic response to being touched by any female and that it had nothing to do with Beth personally, to say nothing of his wanting her physically.

Because he didn't.

Yeah. Right.

While berating himself, Sam walked along the edge of the woods where the rough, untended ground met the clipped lawn of the Simon property. There was nothing much of interest there. A few weathered gum wrappers. The carcass of a small bird. A baseball that had seen better days. Certainly there was nothing that alerted him to anyone's presence in the past hour.

He was about to walk farther into the woods when he saw the drapes open on the second floor of the house and Beth's blond head poked out the bathroom window.

"Sam Mendenhall," she yelled down at him. "I'm so angry at you."

"Well, go be angry somewhere else inside the house. That's a damn good way to get a BB or worse right between your blue eyes, Beth."

Even at this distance, he could see her blink those blue eyes, as if the thought of personal danger hadn't once occurred to her. And even at this distance the mere sight of her provoked his arousal again.

Maybe he should just shoot her himself and be done with it. Better yet, maybe he should just shoot himself.

She pitched him a withering look, then ducked her head back inside and closed the drapes.

Once again, Sam started toward the woods, but he'd only taken a step or two before someone else called out his name. He turned around to see Dave Weller in his civilian clothes. The Mecklin County sheriff was apparently off duty, and his beer belly was unrestrained by his police utility belt.

"Hey, Dave. What brings you out here?"

"Whoo-ee." The sheriff was staring at Sam's bloody shirt. "What happened to you? You look like you've been gut shot, Sam."

"I got hit with some broken glass." He pointed to the second-floor windows of the house. "I was going to call you about the incident tomorrow."

"Steve Watt already did," the man said. He studied the broken windows a moment, then looked back at Sam. "That's why I'm here. What's going on around here, Sam? All these weird things missing, and now the Simons' windows shot out. Didn't I hear something about a fire, too?"

"Yep."

Dave scratched his head. "Weird, as I said. Just plain weird. You think the same person is responsible for it all?"

Sam shrugged. "I don't have a clue."

"Know anybody who's got it in for the Simons? What's her name? Shelby, maybe? The columnist. She was a target last year."

"Shelby's in Chicago," Sam said. "It's just Beth, the younger sister, here now."

The sheriff squinted west, where the sun was getting close to the tree line on the opposite side of the lake. "I don't get over here to Heart Lake a lot. Seems like nothing untoward ever happens."

"Until now."

"Yeah. What is it with these Simon sisters, anyway? Seems like they just attract trouble."

Sam shrugged again. "Damned if I know."

"Yeah. Well, it's too late to do any snooping around today. I'll send some guys over tomorrow." He pointed up to the broken windows. "And, if you want, I'll send over the fella from town who does our board-up work. Don't want to leave those uncovered too long. S'posed to rain tomorrow."

"I'd appreciate that, Dave."

"Sure. He doesn't charge much. We'll just send the bill to Miss Simon."

"That'll work."

The man was staring at Sam's shirt again. "You sure you don't need medical attention?"

"Thanks. I'm fine. It looks worse than it is."

"Well, okay then. See you later, Sam."

After the sheriff left, Sam decided he was wasting his time trying to find anything in the woods. He'd let the pros investigate tomorrow. In the meantime, he needed to decide what he was going to do about Beth.

First, there was the matter of her safety alone in this monster of a house.

Second . . .

Don't even think about it, he told himself.

☆

Not long after Sam yelled at her from below her window, Beth did something she didn't think she'd ever do. Not in a million years. She called Shelby for advice.

Even Shelby was shocked.

"I can't believe you're asking for my opinion," she said almost breathlessly. "God, Beth. You're serious, aren't you?"

"Of course I'm serious," Beth shot back. She held the phone to her ear with her shoulder while she poured a glass of milk to go with the ham sandwich she'd fixed as an early dinner. "Just tell me what to do."

"I can't do that."

"Since when?" Beth rolled her eyes as she put the milk carton back in the fridge. "Shelby, I don't know that you've ever *not* told me what to do."

"Well, this is different," Shelby said, sounding flummoxed and, for the very first time in her life, unsure of herself.

"This is a mess," Beth said with a distinct moan, pushing her sandwich aside. She just wasn't hungry anymore. "What am I going to do, Shelby?"

"About Sam?" her sister asked.

"About Sam. About everything."

"Talk to him, Beth. Just tell him the truth. Tell him how you feel."

"Ha! I don't know how I feel. For a minute today, for one heart-stopping moment, I felt as if I'd never stopped loving him. And then five minutes later I was so angry with him I wanted to kill him."

As she was speaking, Beth heard her phone's call waiting click.

"Damn. I've got another call," she said.

"Go ahead and take it," Shelby told her. "I'll wait."

"No. I'm sure it's Danny."

"Danny!" Shelby might as well have exclaimed "Cockroach" from the tone of her voice. It was pure contempt. "Why is he still calling you? You're not talking to him, I hope."

"No more than I have to. There are still a few bits of business we need to wind up, which isn't easy when he's in San Francisco and I'm up here."

"Well, wind it up as fast as you can, then don't ever talk to the creep again, Bethie. If I've told you once, I've told you a thousand times . . ."

Now she sounded like the Shelby Simon that Beth was all too familiar with. She couldn't stifle a groan of aggravation. She didn't want her sister's advice about Danny, for God's sake. She needed Shelby's advice about Sam.

And just as she was about to inform Shelby of that, Sam tapped on the screen door of the kitchen. Beth's heart lurched.

"I have to go, Shelby."

"Well, not to talk to Danny, I hope."

"No. Thanks for listening. I'll talk to you later."

"Oh, I get it. Sam's there, isn't he? I can tell just from the sound of your voice, Beth. Now you listen to me . . ."

Beth not only clicked off, she turned the phone off completely before turning her attention to the man coming through the kitchen door.

☆

"The sheriff from Mecklin is going to send somebody over to board up your windows," he said.

"Oh, good. I wasn't sure what I was going to do about them, and it's supposed to rain tomorrow."

He remembered how innocent and unconcerned she looked a little while ago when she stuck her head out the window, and it irritated him that she wasn't taking this vandalism more seriously.

"You've got a lot more than rain to worry about," he said. He jabbed a finger toward the door he'd just walked through. "Keeping the doors locked might be a good place to begin."

"I'll do that," she snapped. "Thank you ever so much for the advice."

"And don't go sticking your head out of windows."

"Yes. You've already pointed that out." Her chin ratcheted up a notch, and she crossed her arms. "Anything else?"

Actually, there was something else, but Sam was loath to suggest it because he didn't trust his own motivations. This was all too damn personal, too fraught with ancient history and baggage.

"You really shouldn't stay here alone," he finally said.

"Well, I'm not leaving if that's what you're suggesting. I've waited too long to come back and get this business up and running." She did one of those irritating little clucks with her tongue. "I'm here. I'm staying. Period."

"Then call somebody to stay with you. Maybe your mother? Shelby? A girlfriend?"

"Mom and Shelby are too busy with their own lives to babysit me. Besides, they'd drive me crazy after a few hours. As far as girlfriends go, there's only Kimmy, and I doubt she'd be much help in a crisis."

Sam found himself nodding in agreement. He certainly didn't want Shelby around with her free-floating opinions and extreme reluctance to keep them to herself. As for Kimmy, she was having a tough time just making it from one day to another.

"What about you?" Beth asked.

"Excuse me?" he responded, not because he hadn't

heard her, or understood her, but because he needed to buy a little time. It had already occurred to him that his presence in the house was the logical way to keep Beth from harm. But he still wasn't sure if that was his sole reason for wanting to move in. Or indeed what difference it made whether his intentions were pure or not.

And just what were her intentions? he wondered. Then he *really* wondered about those intentions when he realized that the expression on her face was a direct challenge as she repeated her question.

"I said what about you, Sam?"

He swore he could feel the air nearly crackle between them. Judging from the spark in Beth's eyes and the hint of color on her cheeks, he thought she must've felt it, too. Sam narrowed his gaze and threw his own challenge back at her.

"Just what is it you want from me, Beth?"

She didn't even flinch, the brazen little wench. "Protection, of course. What else would I possibly want?"

Every atom in his body urged him to step toward her, to pull her into his arms, to kiss her until her knees buckled. He must've been insane even to be contemplating it.

"I'll pay you," she said.

Sam snorted. "You couldn't pay me enough."

That made her wince, and he took perverse pleasure in the reaction. But then he felt guilty. She really did need somebody to look out for her.

"I'll move into the carriage house for a while," he said. "How's that?"

"Fine," she replied crisply.

Sam couldn't tell if she was pleased, relieved, or completely pissed off at him. There was a time when he could translate every single emotion that made itself visible upon her face. Now he couldn't read her at all.

"I'll put fresh sheets on the bed out there," she said.

"No need. I'll get my sleeping bag. Be back in about an hour." He was already heading for the door, probably because he thought if he lingered she'd change her mind.

And God help him, he didn't want her to change her mind, whether he could read it or not.

# CHAPTER TEN

$S$hit.

Shit. Shit. Shit.

Beth slapped both hands on the kitchen counter hard enough for her milk glass to tremble.

What had she just done? What had she been thinking? Well, perhaps the more appropriate question at this point was why didn't she seem to be thinking at all lately. It was as if her brain wasn't even remotely connected to her mouth.

She'd practically dared Sam to sign on as her personal bodyguard. She didn't need a freaking bodyguard. She needed a mindguard to keep her from making stupid mistakes and coming up with stupid offers.

It was just that he'd stood there in the kitchen looking so damned hunky and at the same time so supremely arrogant, making her want to jump his bones and at the same time wanting to plant her knee in his groin. Instead, she'd asked him to move in.

"I must be losing my mind," she proclaimed to the empty room.

She didn't want Sam around on a permanent basis. My God, she had too much to do, and he'd be nothing if not a continual distraction, strutting around like some Lower Peninsula Greek god, some Mecklin County superhero inserting himself between her and danger, and reminding her every single minute of how much she'd loved him once upon a time.

Shit.

Talk to him, Shelby had advised her. Tell him how you feel.

And what had Beth done just moments after that little piece of sound advice. She'd freaking asked him to move in!

He'd probably expect her to cook and clean for him now that he'd be living in the carriage house.

Fat chance.

She glared at the ham sandwich she hadn't touched yet, resisting her inclination to make a second one for Sam just in case he hadn't eaten any dinner, fighting her natural instincts to feed people, to comfort and nurture them. That was why she was going to be such a success with the bed-and-breakfast if she ever got it off the ground.

At the moment, though, it looked like it might turn out to be her own private loony bin, where she and Sam could just drive each other bonkers twenty-four hours a day until the vandals were caught.

Just then she heard footsteps mounting the steps of the little porch outside the kitchen, and it dawned on her that not only hadn't she followed Shelby's advice, but she also hadn't followed Sam's either by locking the doors. With her heart beginning to feel like a drum, she gauged the distance from where she stood by the sink to the door, wondering if she could get there and bolt the screen door before the unknown person reached it.

Yes, she probably could, she decided, if only she could move. She next gauged the distance to the knife block on the counter, which was within her reach if necessary.

Through the screen she could see the person's silhouette. It was a man, rather tall and slim. It certainly wasn't Sam's muscular form. How long ago had he left, saying he'd be back in an hour?

Rather than reaching for a ten-inch chopping blade, Beth was considering flight into the interior of the big house where she knew of at least a dozen great hiding places, when the stranger knocked on the frame of the screen door.

"Miss Simon? My name is Roy Shearing. Sorry, I didn't mean to frighten you. The front doorbell doesn't seem to be working."

Her panic immediately decreased. An intruder wouldn't ring the doorbell or knock, would he? Someone bent on violence wouldn't introduce himself first, would he? If this person wanted to hurt her, he could already have done it by now.

"Oh. You must be the man they sent to board up the windows," she said, walking toward the door.

"Uh. No. They told me in town that I might be able to get a room here."

"A room?"

"Well, now I'm not sure if I'm at the right place. Are you Beth Simon? Is this Heart Lake?"

"Yes," she said, "on both counts."

"Well, the man at the gas station in Shelbyville said you were running a bed-and-breakfast out here, and that you'd probably have a vacancy for a night or two."

"Oh, no," she exclaimed. "I'm not ready for guests."

Hearing her own words, Beth wanted to slap herself.

There was a real, live, presumably paying guest on her doorstep, and she was sending him away. She was close enough to the door now so she could discern the obvious disappointment on his face. His rather handsome face, she noted.

"Well, sorry I disturbed you," he said. "Would you happen to know of another place?"

"There aren't too many places on the lake with vacancies this time of year. On second thought, I do have a room that's *almost* ready, if you'd like to take a look at it."

"That'd be great."

Beth pushed the screen door open for him. "Come in, Mr. Shearing. It was Shearing, wasn't it?"

"That's right, but it's Lieutenant Colonel Shearing, Miss Simon. Why don't you just call me Roy?"

"Okay, Roy." Beth reached out her hand. "Please call me Beth."

"Nice to meet you, Beth."

His grip on her hand was firm, not wimpy and tentative the way most men shook hands with females. She liked that. Without the screen between them, she could see him much more clearly. His face was lean and tan beneath close-trimmed graying hair. His eyes were nearly an identical gray. If she had to guess, she'd say he was forty, plus or minus a year or two. His white short-sleeved shirt was neatly tucked into a pair of khakis that had creases as sharp as razors. His bearing was military, enough to make Beth stand up a little straighter.

"The room is upstairs," she said. "If you'll just follow me . . ."

"Yes, ma'am."

Despite her cool outward demeanor, Beth was practically fizzing inside. A guest! Her first guest! Hot damn.

Heart Lake Manor had seemed like a fantasy for so long, it was hard to come to grips with its sudden reality.

Way to go, Beth!

Woo-hoo!

Then she decided she'd better stop fizzing and high-fiving herself and get on with being a good hostess.

"What brings you to Heart Lake?" she asked, while he followed her up the staircase.

"A former colleague of mine lives nearby. You might know him."

"Oh? Well, I know just about everybody in the area. What's his name?"

"Sam. Sam Mendenhall."

Beth tripped on the second-to-last stair, just lost her footing so completely that it seemed almost as if an invisible hand had pushed her, then she felt Roy Shearing's firm grip again, this time around her upper arm.

"Careful there," he said.

"Oops," she mumbled, embarrassed by her clumsiness. It wasn't as if she hadn't been bounding up and down this particular staircase her entire life. Jeez. She and Shelby had even named the steps for the first twenty-eight presidents of the United States to help them learn the proper sequence. Now she'd just been tripped up by Woodrow Wilson. Or maybe it was Sam Mendenhall.

Finally, at the top of the stairs, Beth recovered her balance and her voice sufficiently to say, "So, you've come to see Sam."

"In a manner of speaking. I've come all the way up here from North Carolina to convince him that the Army needs him a hell of a lot more than some one-horse town in Michigan." The lieutenant colonel grinned. "No disrespect intended, ma'am."

Beth forced a hostessy smile, and said, "None taken. But it's a nice little one-horse town, Roy."

"I'm sure it is."

She started down the hallway, feeling just a little woozy all of a sudden, blaming it on the fact that she hadn't eaten that ham sandwich. That was probably why she'd tripped, too. It had nothing to do with Sam. It really didn't. "The room is just down here."

☆

Back at his cabin, Sam stripped off his bloodstained clothes and stepped into the shower. As steam filled his glass shower stall and the hot water sluiced off his chest and shoulders, he sighed audibly and wished he could just stay there, alone, in a fog, for the next twenty-four hours.

His retirement from the Army had been bearable at first. There was his banged-up leg to tend to with surgeries and physical therapy. After that, he enjoyed the novelty of being constable. It hadn't taken long, though, for unadulterated boredom and frustration to set in. It was a half-assed job, and he was an ass for doing it when anybody with a flashlight and an authoritative voice could've taken his place.

But as long as he was constable, he didn't have to think about the direction his life was taking, and he didn't have to make any decisions about his future. It was limbo, but it felt safe somehow. At least it had before Beth showed up.

He rested his forehead against the warm, wet tiles. She was in trouble, he was sure, although he had no idea of the source. He wasn't an investigator, after all, trained to solve a crime. He was a warrior, his muscles trained to respond to an attack. Basically, his job was to react. In this case, he didn't know if that would be enough.

Finally, reluctantly, he got out of the shower, got dressed, then flung out his sleeping bag on his unmade bed, dropped his shaving gear, his toothbrush, wadded-up jeans, a fresh shirt, and some clean skivvies onto it, then rolled it up again. So much for packing.

He couldn't help but think about the rigors of packing when he and his team of operators were deployed, often on a few hours' notice, to various hot spots around the world. They went through detailed lists and checklists, going so far as to inspect one another's gear for any lapses or oversights. It didn't do much good to pack a sidearm if you didn't have the proper ammo for it or to pack a map without a compass.

Right now he didn't need a damn map or a compass to tell him he was getting in way over his head where Beth was concerned and that the chemistry between them was as volatile as it had ever been. The very thought of it made him cast a baleful glance at the nightstand beside his bed, where he kept a stash of condoms.

No way.

Nuh-uh.

Not on his life.

If he had to spend the next few days taking cold showers or diving into the lake before the sun had a chance to warm it and swimming a punishing distance, then that's what he'd do. He didn't care how blatantly she came on to him, like the way she'd done this evening. He was just too damn old at thirty-five to play those games anymore.

They'd run each other off the rails as kids. No need to do it again. His heart just couldn't take it. Not again. He'd keep her safe, but he'd keep her at arm's length while he did it.

The phone rang just as he was going out the door with his sleeping bag jammed beneath his arm. Now what? Had somebody's toothbrush gone missing? Or maybe the pickles disappeared from a hamburger? Maybe Lorna couldn't find the plus-size pair of panties that matched her stolen DD bra? His irritation was evident when he answered the phone.

"Don't you take that snippy tone with me, Sam Mendenhall."

It was Blanche Kroll, the town clerk and his officemate. Already he knew this wasn't going to be good news.

He softened his tone considerably when he asked, "What's up, Blanche?"

"Somebody's made off with every single flower in my garden out front. There's not a damn one left."

He almost laughed, but that would've earned him Blanche's silent treatment for at least three weeks. Anyway, he knew how hard she worked on the garden outside her office window, watering it every day and weeding once a week.

"When did this happen?" he asked.

"I guess it must've been sometime between five-thirty and six-fifteen because that was when I was having my supper at Doyle's. Dammit, Sam. You've just got to catch whoever's doing all this mischief."

He sighed. "Well, I'd like to, Blanche, but until I catch him or her or them in the act, there's not much I can do."

"You might start spending a bit more time in town, young man, instead of mooning around the Simon place. People are talking, you know."

"I'd be surprised if they weren't," he said. If he'd been standing next to a wall, he would've banged his head into it repeatedly. "I'll see you tomorrow, Blanche."

"Early," she snapped, just before she hung up.

By the time he'd driven around to the east side of the lake, Sam's mood had darkened from navy blue to a deep charcoal gray. And when he started up the lawn only to see Beth sitting with some guy on the front porch, his mood blackened completely.

☆

Her guest had already eaten dinner, so Beth had invited him out onto the porch where she opened a bottle of Chardonnay and attempted to engage him in conversation, which wasn't an easy feat.

Roy Shearing struck her as a man who simply wasn't comfortable in the company of a woman, in an unstructured situation, where there was no agenda. She thought he'd make a competent business associate, and he'd probably be a terrific date, but in the role of guest, he was a flop.

He crossed and recrossed his legs so many times that Beth began to wonder if he had a problem other than social discomfort. When she poured his second glass of wine and their fingers happened to brush, he jumped as if she'd held a lit match to his hand. The guy was clearly not comfortable with her, and that became even more evident when he practically moaned with relief at the sight of Sam walking up from the driveway.

Instead of approaching the house, though, Sam angled to his right for the carriage house.

"Sam," she called out. "There's somebody here to see you."

He turned to look just as Roy Shearing stood up, and shouted, "Staff Sergeant Mendenhall, I presume."

Even at a distance of fifty or sixty feet and in the deepening twilight, Beth could see the surprise on Sam's face. He shook his head, mouthed a curse, dropped the sleeping bag beneath his arm, and strode toward the porch.

"Good to see you, Lieutenant Colonel," he said, reaching out for the man's hand.

"You, too, Staff Sergeant. I told you if the mountain wouldn't come to Mohammed, Mohammed would come to the mountain, didn't I?"

Sam laughed. "Yeah, you did. Well, welcome to the mountain."

Beth stood there, thinking how right she'd been about the lieutenant colonel. He was a completely different person now that Sam was here. As for Sam, he looked truly happy for a change. She thought that ought to please her, but it bothered her instead. She used to make Sam so happy when they were kids.

Beth feigned a yawn. "Well, why don't I let the two of you have some privacy. Roy, if you'll just lock the front door when you come in, I'd appreciate it."

She turned to Sam. "The carriage house is open. Good night."

Both men bade her a cheerful good night, no doubt glad to see her go.

It would've been wonderful if she could've fallen asleep the minute her head hit the pillow, but she lay there for what seemed like hours, listening to the sound of their voices drifting up from the front porch to her open bedroom window. She couldn't distinguish any individual words. Occasionally they'd laugh or cough, but for the most part it was just the low, almost leathery tone of male camaraderie.

She didn't have to be a genius to know that Lieutenant

Colonel Mohammed had come to take the mountain back to the Army.

And if the mountain left Heart Lake?

It should be the best news Beth could imagine. The answer to her prayers.

But it wasn't.

Not anymore.

# CHAPTER ELEVEN

Beth awoke the next morning feeling as if she'd barely slept, which was pretty much the case. First it was the sound of the low-key banter and quiet laughter of the two soldiers on her front porch that kept her from drifting off to sleep, and then Bill the Board-up Guy arrived at almost midnight with his big slabs of paint-spattered, graffiti-laden plywood and his excruciatingly loud voice and hammer and nails.

Sam had offered to oversee Bill's endeavors so Beth could go back to bed, but she refused. It was her house, after all. These were her problems. She didn't feel right about foisting them off on somebody else in the middle of the night or at any time, no matter how gallant and sincere the offer.

"Suit yourself," Sam had finally said before returning to his old Army buddy on the porch.

It didn't take long, however, for Beth to regret her decision to play overseer when Bill the Board-up Guy took a full fifteen minutes to untangle the ropes that held his ladder to his truck, and another two long hours actually to cover the two windows. Granted, they were pretty tall windows, and they were on the second floor, and it was awfully dark out there. But still . . .

He took ten minutes to get his ladder properly steadied in back of the house. Up the ladder. Oops. Bill forgot his hammer. Down the ladder. Find the friggin' hammer in his beat-up toolbox. Up again. Oops. Wrong nails. Down the ladder. Now where were those durned nails? Back up the ladder. *Ad infinitum. Ad nauseam.*

"I'm not the regular guy," he told her.

"I'd never have guessed," Beth answered, her tongue planted firmly in her cheek while she stifled a yawn.

There was even a point when Beth suspected that Bill might've been the vandal who broke the windows in the first place just so he could try his hand at boarding them up.

Finally, at almost two-thirty in the morning, after Bill dragged his well-worn ladder back to his truck and lashed it back onto the roof, Beth and her headache dropped wearily into bed and didn't stir so much as a ligament or an eyelash until her alarm went off at seven.

With a guest in residence, she didn't have the luxury of sleeping in. She had to come up with a decent breakfast, so after she showered and threw on some clothes, Beth headed for the kitchen. Halfway down the hallway, though, she noticed that her guest's door was open, and when she got closer and peeked into the room, she could see that his bed hadn't been slept in.

It seemed odd, but then she decided that maybe Roy and Sam had taken their conversation into the carriage house to avoid all the hammering out back, and maybe Roy had simply fallen asleep out there. Or maybe they were still awake, knocking back beers and trading war stories.

She wished now that she'd informed Roy last night of a specific time for breakfast, lunch, and dinner.

Her To Do list included the printing of small cards, announcing time frames for meals. Breakfast would be in the vicinity of eight o'clock to nine-thirty. Lunch between one and two, maybe. Dinner would be fashionably late at seven-thirty perhaps, or even eight.

She hadn't quite decided on the times yet, but she knew she couldn't just be hanging around the kitchen all the time, waiting until her guests woke up or got hungry and wandered into the dining room. It occurred to her again that, beyond the décor and the advertising, there were still a number of bugs to work out before Heart Lake Manor was a smooth-running operation.

No big deal. She'd work them all out soon enough. It was just that she'd been distracted this first week. And right now, glancing out the kitchen window, she saw her primary distraction headed her way.

She had an instant and vivid flashback to all those summer mornings years ago, when Sam would appear just after breakfast, and the two of them would go off for hours of exploring, swimming, picnicking, chasing butterflies, climbing trees.

"I don't know what the two of you find to do for all those hours between breakfast and dinner," her mother used to say.

"Just everything," Beth had answered. "We just have fun."

"Jeez, Beth. You should play the field," Shelby would tell her. "You shouldn't put all your eggs in one basket named Sam. There are bigger and better fish, even here at Heart Lake."

"Put a sock in it, Shelby."

As she and Sam got older, of course, they added a few new activities to the exploring and chasing butterflies and climbing trees. Hand-holding, for one. Strolling arm in arm. Carving their initials inside hearts on trees and wooden benches and one time in wet concrete. Kissing entered their repertoire. Oh, yeah.

*Sam and Bethie sitting in a tree*
*K\*I\*S\*S\*I\*N\*G*

God, those were good times. Just the best. She almost wished she could go back and be thirteen again, with no obligations, no responsibilities, no plans other than having fun all damn day long. She wondered if Sam ever got nostalgic about those long-ago summers.

From the serious look on his face right now, she doubted it. The way his mouth turned down and his brow furrowed, he looked like he'd never had a moment's pleasure in his entire life. Mostly, he looked like he'd been up way too late the night before.

No. Mostly he looked sexy as hell.

No longer a gangly kid, Sam walked with such a masculine confidence and grace, as if completely unafraid of anyone or anything he might encounter along the way. It was easy to picture him in uniform, but she thought she preferred this casual civilian look of faded, snug jeans and dark polo shirt that clung to his broad shoulders and chest as if the garment had been made just for his physique.

She glanced down at her own attire, which consisted of a long, flowered, cotton skirt and a faded pink T-shirt and sandals, suddenly wishing she'd spent a bit more time with her clothes and makeup this morning. She looked like a northwoods frump.

Sam rapped on the screen door, then pulled it open before she could respond.

"Hey," he said.

"Hey yourself. Is the lieutenant colonel still sleeping?"

"Uh. No. Actually he's gone." As he spoke Sam reached into the back pocket of his jeans and produced several bills. "He left five twenties and said if that's not enough, just let him know and he'll make up the difference. I've got his address if you need it."

Beth stared at the cash in Sam's hand. "Gone? He's gone? I don't understand."

Roy Shearing was her first official guest. He was her Christopher Columbus. He was her friggin' Neil Armstrong. One small step for man, but one giant leap for Beth.

Gone? How could he be gone? He'd just arrived, for heaven's sake.

Sam shrugged as if the man's disappearance was of absolutely no consequence. "He got a call late last night to join up with his unit and pulled out of here around five o'clock."

"I don't know what that means," Beth said, totally frustrated yet determined to know exactly why she'd been cheated out of a famous first, why Heart Lake Manor, like the *Titanic*, had sunk in the middle of its maiden voyage.

"He had to go back to work, Beth."

"Well, I thought he was on vacation."

"It was canceled."

"Didn't he like his room?" she asked, ignoring Sam's response. "Was there a problem? I bet it was all that damned hammering last night."

"There was no problem, Beth. Roy had to go back on duty. That's all."

"What kind of duty?"

"I can't tell you that," he said. "Here. Take the money."

"Why can't you tell me?"

He grinned. "Because then I'd have to kill you."

"That's not funny, Sam."

Considering her state of mind, it wasn't funny at all, but Beth couldn't help but think that Sam hadn't meant it completely as a joke, and that there was a kernel of truth in his statement about the lieutenant colonel and his whereabouts.

She held out her hand and wiggled her fingers. "Okay. All right. Give me the money. I've earned it if for no other reason than pure aggravation."

"Here you go." He put the bills in her hand. "Is that enough?"

Beth fanned out the five twenties. "It's way too much for the little I provided. Next time you talk to Roy tell him he's got a free night coming."

"I'll tell him," Sam said, "but I doubt he'll be back this way anytime soon. His mission here wasn't a complete success."

"How so?" she asked, while folding the money and putting it under the sugar canister.

Sam shrugged again, clearly indicating he didn't want to discuss Roy's mission or its lack of success. "Got any toast, Bethie, or cereal? I'm ravenous. I could use a couple aspirin, too."

Now that she looked closely, Beth could tell he had a headache from the depth of the vertical line between his eyes. That had always been a dead giveaway when Sam was feeling tired or sick. Instinctively, she reached up to press her fingers to his unshaven cheek.

"Poor baby," she cooed.

Rather than pull back, Sam seemed to lean into her touch. His eyes closed, and for just a second the lines on his face appeared to smooth. He looked at least ten years younger. He looked like the young man she remembered so very well.

It was Beth who pulled back when she became aware of the sheen of moisture in her eyes. She moved quickly to the cabinet where her father used to keep his daily baby aspirins, hoping they were still there.

"Aha!" she said, taking them from the bottom shelf. "These should still be good. I guess three or four should cure what ails you."

"Four," he said.

"Four it is." Beth shook them out into the palm of her hand and avoided eye contact when Sam took them, for fear those damned tears would well up again.

While Sam filled a glass of water from the tap, she opened a fresh loaf of bread and dropped four pieces in the toaster, damned if she'd prepare the full-blown breakfast for him that she'd planned on fixing for the lieutenant colonel, her late, great guest. Sam had requested toast and aspirin, and that's exactly what she'd give him.

She had the sinking feeling that if he asked for her heart, she'd offer it once more, only to have it broken all over again.

☆

Sam took his headache and his toast and coffee to the front porch, making himself as comfortable as possible with his feet up on the porch railing, with all its spindles and fancy shapes.

It hadn't rained the night before as predicted, but he could smell it in the air this morning. The sky was overcast, and the wind was just starting to pick up as it blew east over Heart Lake. The water was choppy and gray instead of its usual smooth and sunlit blue.

God, he hoped Bethie made a success of this place. The disappointment on her face when she found out her guest had taken a powder was hard for Sam to bear, and he found himself wondering how she must've looked when she heard the news of his marriage to Susie Flynt when he was always supposed to marry Beth.

Hell, no wonder she'd sent all his letters back stamped "Return to Sender" and refused to talk to him on the phone.

He watched a group of teenagers walking along the beach, laughing and shoving one another. He thought he recognized the Tobin kid from the west side of Heart Lake, maybe one or two of the others. A few of them glanced furtively toward the porch where he sat, but he couldn't discern their expressions. Were they unusually worried, or was it just the typical apprehension of teens under the scrutiny of an adult? Were they the culprits who'd set the fire and shot out the windows? His gut told him no, but it was still too soon to rule anybody out.

It was also too soon to rule anybody in, he reminded himself. He was still clueless. Constable Clueless. He felt about as effective as Barney Fife.

"They look pretty carefree, don't they?" Beth asked, scaring the bejesus out of him because he hadn't heard her come out the front door.

"They're kids," Sam said, jerking his feet down from the railing, the same way he used to do when Beth's mother came out on the porch. "That's their job. Being carefree."

"I remember."

Her voice sounded not exactly sad, but nostalgic, as she lowered herself into the adjacent wicker chair. Once she and her coffee mug were settled, she plopped her own legs up where Sam's had just been. He couldn't help but notice that they were very nice legs.

"Your mother wouldn't like that, young lady," he said with mock sternness.

She laughed, a bright, spontaneous, almost crystalline sound, and turned her head toward him. "Oh, God, Sam. Remember that time when . . . ?"

As she'd done in the past, Beth stopped speaking with a little gulping exclamation, then muttered "Never mind. Just forget it," right before she lifted her coffee mug to her lips to preclude speech entirely.

At the sound of Beth's laughter, something snapped in Sam. He'd had his fill of uncomfortable silences, of avoiding the past, of walking on eggshells where the subject of their relationship was concerned, and of dreading such a conversation. This was really the last straw. He sat forward, his elbows on his knees, his own cup of coffee cradled in his hands.

"How long do you think we can avoid talking about the past, Beth?"

Her eyes flashed. "Indefinitely," she snapped, "when one of us keeps walking out on conversations."

Nodding in agreement, Sam closed his eyes. He had that coming. He'd been a boor that other night when he walked out on her. A boor and a coward, both. "I'm sorry about that. This isn't easy for me, Beth. It's damn hard."

"You think it's easy for me?"

"No. No, I don't."

"Because it's not," she said, cutting him off. "I didn't come back here from California to be swamped by the past. I came back for my future, only I've spent so much time thinking about the past that I'm not getting much else done."

"Yeah. Me, too." He took in a long breath and let it out slowly. "So, we need to talk."

"Yes, we do."

"Okay." He couldn't suppress a grin. "You go first."

Beth nearly choked on her coffee. "Me? You go first. This is your idea, after all. Sheesh."

"All right. Let's see. Do you want to hear the sweet and slightly sappy reminiscing part first, or should I cut to the bitter ending?"

Beth gave him a look that was half-wounded and half-belligerent. "There was nothing sappy about us, Sam. And the ending was a lot more bitter for me than it was for you."

It suddenly occurred to him that they were headed right for an argument of who hurt whom the most. That hadn't been his intention. At least not consciously. He had hoped to make things better between them and more open, but now he saw that they were just going to get worse. Shit.

With that realization, he wasn't at all disappointed to see a car come skidding into the driveway and Kimmy Mortenson jump out of the passenger seat with her cleaning equipment in one hand and a huge bouquet of flowers in the other.

Beside him Beth muttered, "Oh, damn. I totally forgot that I called Kimmy and asked her to come over and help out this morning. So much for our conversation."

It was probably for the best, Sam thought, without voicing his intense relief.

"Hey! Good morning," Kimmy called as she came up the lawn. "Look what I've brought!"

Sam was already looking. He was staring, in fact. Those flowers looked awfully familiar. If he wasn't mistaken, he'd seen just about each one of them bloom in the past few weeks outside Blanche's window.

Kimmy negotiated the front porch steps like someone who didn't take balance for granted.

"Where'd you get the gorgeous bouquet?" Beth asked her.

"Well, it was the weirdest thing." She set her cleaning stuff down, then straightened up and hugged the flowers to her chest as she buried her nose in the blossoms. "Oh, man, they smell so good. As I said, it was the weirdest thing. They just showed up on my doorstep last night. I haven't the vaguest idea who put them there."

"Maybe you've got a secret admirer," Sam suggested.

"Yeah. Right." Kimmy rolled her eyes. "I figured I'd bring them over here, Beth, instead of keeping them at my place, where I'm the only one who can enjoy them. There's a big cut-glass vase of your mom's around someplace. Maybe they'll impress your new guest." She glanced around. "Is he still sleeping?"

"Well, I hope not," Beth said, "considering that by now he's probably on an interstate in Indiana."

"He's gone?"

"Mm," Beth murmured. "I've probably made the *Guinness Book of World Records* for shortest stay by a guest at a bed-and-breakfast."

"What happened?"

"Ask Sam."

Kimmy looked at Sam, who said succinctly, "The man's vacation was canceled."

"Bummer," the young woman said. "So, do you still want me to work today, Beth?"

"Sure. Go on inside, Kimmy, and I'll follow you in just a minute."

The sight of the flowers had reminded Sam that he'd promised Blanche he'd be in the office early to *investigate* their strange disappearance. He thought briefly about taking them from Kimmy as evidence, but she was so damn happy that somebody had given her flowers that he just couldn't bring himself to deprive her of the flowers or her happiness.

"I need to go into town for a little while," he said to Beth after Kimmy was gone. "I want you to keep the doors locked and stay inside until I get back."

As he'd expected, Beth bristled. "Well, I . . ."

"Look, Beth. I can help you, or I can leave you on your own. It's entirely up to you."

"Oh, all right. But how soon will you be back because I can't hide away in the house the whole day."

"It shouldn't be more than an hour or two. A couple guys from the county police will probably show up sometime this morning to check out in back. Otherwise, don't open the door to anyone."

She saluted him. Badly. The way a movie pirate might salute his boss. "Aye, aye, captain."

"Yeah. Yeah," he growled as he stood up.

He was halfway down the porch steps when Beth said softly, "Come back soon, Sam."

He knew he would. It was getting hard to stay away.

# CHAPTER TWELVE

While Kimmy arranged her flowers in a huge cut-glass vase on the island in the kitchen, Beth did her best to hunker down at the nearby table to hammer out a meal schedule for Heart Lake Manor, but she kept finding herself looking out the window for Sam. Then, instead of seeing him, she'd see the sky growing darker each time she looked out and the wind picking up in the trees.

The imminent bad weather set her on edge. Storms always seemed worse here at Heart Lake, probably because there were so many trees. That was why she'd settled in the kitchen with Kimmy rather than working elsewhere. She didn't want to be alone.

"I'm surprised you don't have lead poisoning the way you chew on pencils," Kimmy said.

Beth immediately shoved the offending writing implement behind her ear. She'd been so lost in looking for Sam, worrying about the storm, and scheduling mealtimes that she hadn't paid any attention to the wondrous bouquet in progress. Now she stared in amazement at the blooms that seemed to explode in a profusion of color out of their sparkling cut-glass container.

"Kimmy, my God, that's absolutely gorgeous. It's incredible. When did you learn how to arrange flowers like that? And where?"

"TV," she answered, grinning as she stuck a long-stemmed daisy in just the perfect spot between two red zinnias. "I couldn't do much this winter after the accident, so I watched a lot of cooking and decorating and stuff like that on the tube."

"That looks professional."

"Does it?" The woman's face positively glowed, and her grin spread until it very nearly touched each earlobe. "Oh, I'm so glad. I really, really want to be good at something." She sighed. "I sure wish I knew who to thank for these, though."

"You don't have any idea?"

Kimmy shook her head hard enough for her blond braid to flop over her right shoulder. "Not a clue. I'm not seeing anybody. I haven't had a date since last Halloween. The guy I used to live with — You remember Joe Hutton, don't you? — moved to Detroit right after Christmas, so I know they weren't from him. I just can't figure it out."

"Weird," Beth said, gripping her pencil again and about to return to the breakfast, lunch, and dinner dilemma until Kimmy spoke again.

"You know what's really weird, Beth?"

"What's that?"

"My mother used to tell me how my dad picked these huge bouquets for her, then rang the doorbell and disappeared before she got there. She'd open the door, and there would be this humongous bunch of flowers on her doorstep."

It was the first time Beth's old friend had ever made reference to her father. Beth was sure of that, and the mention shocked her enough that she responded immediately, without thinking.

"I didn't know you even had a father."

Kimmy stared at her over the huge bouquet. "Everybody has a father, Beth. Jeez. What do you think — I was hatched?"

"No. That's not what I meant. I just never knew that you knew who your father was. When we were little I was curious, but I never knew how to ask." She tapped the pencil on the table, not completely comfortable with the turn in their conversation. Once in a while, Beth's curiosity went too far. She probably inherited the trait from blabby Shelby, who never met a question she didn't like.

But Kimmy didn't seem offended. On the contrary, she seemed quite willing to discuss the man who'd sired her thirty-some years ago.

"I didn't know him," she said. "My mother told me his name and a lot about him. He went to Vietnam not too long after I was born. They were going to get married when he came back, but he never did."

"Oh, Kimmy. I didn't know that. I'm so sorry he was killed."

"I didn't say he was killed," she said, deftly poking another daisy into her creation. "I said he never came back."

Beth blinked. "He didn't come back? I don't understand."

"My father was released from the Army in October, 1972, and he just disappeared. My mother never heard from him again."

"So he's alive? Or at least he was?"

"Yep."

"And did you or your mother ever try to find him?"

Beth tried to imagine her father simply disappearing but couldn't even wrap a part of her brain around the idea. Harry Simon often disappeared in his law office for ten or twelve hours a day, but he always came home, even if it was midnight.

"Nope."

"How come?"

Kimmy looked contemplative. She stood there, plucking the petals of a daisy as if she were mentally ticking off *He loves me, He loves me not*. Then she sighed, and said, "We thought about it. Mom and I talked about it a lot, especially when I was a little older, but then we decided that it was up to him to find us. And we were always here, you know, right where he'd left us. We were easy to find."

"I can understand that," Beth said. "I'd probably do the same thing. I wonder what happened to him. I wonder why he didn't come back."

Her friend shrugged. "Dunno. And after all these years, it's hard for me to care." She frowned as she looked down. "You know, I've got so many flowers here, I'm going to need another vase. Maybe I'll go get that pretty pale blue one in the sunroom. Would that be okay?"

"Oh, sure," Beth said, just as eager to drop the subject as Kimmy seemed to be. "The blue vase would be great, or you could use that other cut-glass one in the dining room."

"Okay. I'll go take a look."

When Kimmy left the kitchen, Beth gazed out the window again, hoping to see the sun breaking through some of the dark clouds.

No such luck.

It was looking really bad out there.

☆

The first thing Blanche said to Sam when he walked into the office was, "What'd you do? Get in a fight with a cat?"

He'd almost forgotten the cuts on his arms until then. When he told the town clerk about Beth's broken windows, she just shook her head.

"Whole town's going to hell in a handbasket this summer, Sam," she said. "I swear."

He felt a little guilty not telling her where her prized flowers had ended up, but the *where*, he decided, wasn't nearly as important as the *why* or the *who* in this case.

"You haven't made any fresh enemies, have you, Blanche?" he asked, only half in jest, of the woman who collected the local taxes with an iron fist and didn't hesitate to speak her mind anytime, anywhere. She'd once even told Thelma Watt that all the gum stuck under the counter at the post office was "a menace to society, not to mention a filthy health hazard." After that, Thelma hadn't spoken to Blanche for two whole years.

"None that I know of," she answered. "Sounds to me like Beth Simon has a few enemies, too."

He nodded even while he still hoped against hope that the vandalism at the big Victorian mansion wasn't personal, but merely directed at the biggest, most attractive bull's-eye around.

For another fifteen minutes or so he listened to Blanche's gloomy opinions about the state of affairs in Shelbyville and the world, then he went outside to snoop around town for a while. Who knew? With any luck, ol' Constable Sam might stumble into somebody in the act of snatching a pie from a windowsill or snagging an industrial-strength bra from a clothesline.

The weather had deteriorated in the quarter hour he'd been inside the office. There was a faint green cast in the western sky. The clouds were low and fast. The wind whipped Thelma's new flag in all directions. Out at Heart Lake, just two miles away, he suspected that the water was churning with whitecaps and the wind shrieking like a banshee through the white pines.

Beth.

All of a sudden he remembered that she used to be scared to death of storms. She hadn't been just naturally apprehensive as most people were in bad weather, but truly terrified.

He pulled his cell phone from his pocket and punched in the number of the Simon house without even searching his mental Rolodex. Hell, he'd probably called the number a million times between the ages of nine and nineteen.

While it rang, he thought about how Beth's mother always insisted on proper telephone etiquette. If he mumbled a quick, "Is Beth there?" Linda Simon wouldn't even deign to respond. The proper password was, "Hi, Mrs. Simon. This is Sam. May I please speak to Beth?"

Looking back, he was grateful the woman was such a stickler. The lessons she'd taught him over the years — annoying as they were at times — had served him well during his Army career, when he was up close and personal with the sticklers out of West Point.

Beth finally answered on the seventh ring.

"How's the weather out there?" he asked.

"Not so great."

There was a slight note of apprehension in her voice, but it wasn't anywhere near the hysteria he'd anticipated. He could picture her, the receiver to her ear, while she used her other hand to hold back some drapes in order to get a better view of the raging waters of the lake and the wild twisting of the trees.

"Is Kimmy still there?"

"Yes. She's arranging her flowers. They're just gorgeous."

"Can't wait to see them. I'll be back soon. Anything you need from town?"

"Oh, thanks, Sam. No, I . . . Well, as a matter of fact I do need some tea if you're anywhere near a store. Earl Grey or English Breakfast, preferably. Loose, if possible; otherwise, bags are fine."

"Okay. See you soon." As he disconnected, he was already walking toward Shelbyville's only grocery store, repeating to himself *Earl Grey, English Breakfast, Earl Grey, English Breakfast.* It was no surprise his Bethie wasn't a Lipton kind of woman.

☆

Beth was just hanging up the phone when Kimmy entered the kitchen, looking more flustered than usual.

"Mind if I use the phone, Beth? I want to call my cousin and have him pick me up. I need to get back to my trailer to close all the windows and bring my lawn furniture in before this storm comes through."

"Oh, sure. Go ahead."

*Oh, damn. Don't leave me here alone.*

"Thanks."

Beth watched her stabbing at the buttons on the phone and wondered if the aftereffects of the poisoning had affected her vision somehow. She seemed to keep getting the sequence wrong, then she'd swear softly, tug at her braid, disconnect, and begin again. Poor Kimmy.

As much as Beth didn't want her to leave, she couldn't stand her friend's obvious distress.

"Listen," she said, "I have a better idea. Why don't I just run you home?"

Kimmy's face brightened. "Oh, would you, Beth? That'd be great."

"Sure. I'll just grab my keys and we're outta here."

*Outta here and into the storm. Oh, joy.*

☆

Sam stepped on the gas. He should've figured that his choice of teas in Shelbyville would be limited to domestic bags. When he asked young Dory Brooks at the counter about loose tea, she'd looked at him as if he were crazy, and said, "What do you mean, loose tea? Like broken bags or something?"

So he'd sighed, jumped in the jeep, and was now heading for Mecklin, where his chances of finding what Beth wanted were only slightly better. He debated taking a right at Eighteen Mile Road and going straight to the lake without the tea, but since the storm had yet to produce anything but wind, he decided he had time enough to pick up the tea before all hell broke loose weather-wise.

A long jagged bolt of lightning split the dark sky to the west. From long experience on maneuvers in inclement weather, it was fairly easy to estimate where the strike had hit. Sam thought it was probably the tiny burg of Rodman, seven miles west of Mecklin.

With a bit of luck and a wind speed of fewer than twenty knots, he had a good chance of outrunning this monster.

☆

Beth was about to offer to stay and help drag furniture inside the trailer when Kimmy's big, strapping cousin showed up and volunteered to do it all himself.

"You two just go on inside," he told them, shouting over the wind, "before this thing really blows up."

Kimmy smiled. "Come on in, Beth."

It was all Beth could do not to scream "Are you nuts?"

A mobile home was the very last place she wanted to be in a storm. Well, no, under a tree would actually be the very last place. But jeez . . . Her own home had stood in place for more than a century, and she was *still* terrified it would blow away or get zapped by lightning.

"I think I'll just head on home," she told Kimmy, doing her best to mount a brave smile, or at least one that didn't wobble at the edges.

By the time she got back to the east side of the lake, the wind was blowing so hard that Beth had trouble keeping her hair out of her face long enough to insert her key in the front door, not to mention the fact that her skirt kept whipping up around her waist, revealing her hot pink thong for all the world to see.

God bless it.

She couldn't do three things at once — aim the key, tame her hair, and capture her skirt — so she decided the hell with everything but getting into the house, took the key in both hands, and focused exclusively on the lock.

☆

The wind picked up to a sustained thirty knots or so, and it was probably gusting around forty. Sam was still two miles from Mecklin when he looked in the rearview mirror, saw that the road was clear in both directions, and hit the brakes and turned the wheel to whip a quick U-turn in order to beat it back to Beth's.

The hell with the tea.

Dammit. He couldn't fight the powerful urge to protect her not only from vandals but also from the forces of nature. All things considered, it was a really stupid way to feel after a sixteen-year separation during which Beth had undoubtedly taken care of herself. On the phone a while ago she hadn't sounded frightened. Concerned, maybe. On edge. But not terrified, the way she'd get when she was a kid.

So what the hell was he doing rushing back to Heart Lake?

Damned if he knew.

The rain started just as he turned onto the twisting, forested road that led to the lake, and by the time he pulled into the Simon driveway it was pouring, with the wind driving the rain nearly sideways. Jogging up the lawn to the house, he could barely see until he was about ten feet from the porch when he saw something that nearly threw him into cardiac arrest.

A bright pink thong. Long sleek legs. A world-class ass.

He only got a brief glimpse before the wind tugged Beth's skirt back down, but that one glimpse was as effective as a lightning bolt for the shock it sent sizzling throughout his system. Sam nearly stumbled up the porch steps.

"I can't get this damn thing open," she muttered.

"Here," he said, taking the key from her hand and shoving it into the lock. "It's tricky. You have to sort of twist it upward."

He did, and the door blew open on the next strong gust of wind, with Beth right on its heels. Once inside the vestibule, Sam closed the door and locked it.

Both of them stood there, dripping like drowned rats on the marble floor, until a crash of thunder that shook the ancient timbers of the house sent Beth scurrying into his arms.

He decided then and there, for better or for worse, he'd never let her go.

# CHAPTER THIRTEEN

The storm had converged on the house with all its fury. Beth was sure of that. She could feel the thunder through the soles of her feet, reverberating up through her bones to the very top of her skull. Her skin prickled with each bolt of lightning, and those strikes were coming faster and closer together. God. It was like being in a horror movie that just wouldn't quit.

The wind rattled the windows as if it were trying to invade the place. It shrieked through crevices and crannies around the wooden frames, howling to get in.

If not for Sam's strong arms around her, Beth would be in her childhood hidey-hole under the staircase right now. It was one of the first places she'd checked when the storm began to blow up. She shined a flashlight into the dark, cramped space, sucked in her breath at the sight of the spiderwebs hanging like bunting, and decided the only thing that scared her worse than spiders was storms. Well, snakes, too.

Frightened as she was, there was something about being in Sam's arms that made her feel completely safe.

She didn't know if it was the sheer size of him or the warmth of his body against hers or the granite solidity of him. Or maybe it was just that he was Sam. She couldn't imagine that any other human being could infuse her with such a sense of safety while she stood in the raging eye of a storm.

Even so, once the lightning and thunder began to subside, Beth thought she'd better make a move, if only to assert that she wasn't a total yellow-bellied, lily-livered wimp. But as soon as she took a small step backward, Sam's arms tightened their embrace.

"Stay," he said softly, his lips against her hair.

Because his request was followed immediately by a deep, bone-rattling roll of thunder, Beth did exactly as she was told. If he didn't mind, she certainly didn't mind.

Only . . .

Now that she was able to focus on Sam rather than the storm, it slowly dawned on her that his arms weren't the only hard part of his anatomy. Just to make sure, she moved her hips against him, the thin fabric of her skirt encountering the solidity behind his denim fly. A muted growl sounded deep in his throat as he drew her even closer against him.

She knew if she tipped her head just so, if she lifted her chin a mere inch or two, Sam would kiss her, and the very thought sent a warm wave of desire curling through her abdomen. After all these years, she hadn't forgotten what a great kisser he was. He'd taught her an infinite variety of pleasures in combining four lips and two tongues. Or maybe they had learned together by lovely trial and error as they experimented hour after hour after hour.

But just then, as much as she wanted his mouth on hers,

she managed to maintain a shred or two of cool, enough to realize that she wasn't ready for all the complications that would be sure to follow.

The song might've said "a kiss is just a kiss," but Beth knew that wouldn't be true for her and Sam. A kiss would surely take them all the way. And where would they go after that? Where *could* they go?

It just wasn't smart.

She told herself to be smart.

*Don't be stupid*.

But then Sam's thumb ever so gently nudged up her chin, and stupidly, eagerly, hungrily, she complied. His mouth came down on hers, not with tiny, tentative, cool, getting-to-know-you kisses, but with the warm, wet passion of their final kiss sixteen years ago. Beth's stomach flipped over backward, and her knees nearly buckled. If Sam's arms hadn't been around her, she would've slid to the black-and-white-marble floor and melted into a passionate purple puddle.

The voice inside her head had suddenly changed its tune. Now, instead of warning "Don't do it, stupid," the vicious little traitor began urging her to "Go for it, girl."

Apparently Sam's inner voice was similarly prodding him because she felt his hand inching up the fabric of her skirt and fanning out warmly on her thigh.

Oh, Lord. She was going to do this, wasn't she? Well, she was a grown-up. She was on the pill. This wasn't some serial killer who'd picked her up at a bar. It was Sam.

And then he broke their kiss just long enough to whisper three little words.

"Tell me yes."

She did, but it came out as more of an affirmative moan than an actual word, and the next thing she knew Sam had swept her up in his arms and was carrying her, levitating her almost, up the staircase.

☆

They were in the room with the king-size bed formerly used by Linda and Harry Simon. The storm had abated, but not enough to lighten the interior of the house. Sam was grateful for that because somewhere between the front hall and here, he'd acquired a bad case of nerves. The specter of Beth's parents above the headboard wasn't helping any.

And it didn't help that Beth had stripped down to her hot pink thong the second her feet hit the floor, then promptly pulled the bedspread back and slithered between the sheets. At the moment all he could see was a bevy of blond curls on the pillow. Just below Linda's and Harry's ghosts.

As he remembered — and how could he forget? — every time he and Beth had made love in the past, he slowly, tenderly undressed her. It was almost a ritual. He always thought Beth was more comfortable somehow with his taking that initiative, as if she didn't want to lose the appearance of a certain feminine reluctance to screw her brains out or appear too hot to trot in taking off her own clothes.

Hey, it was fine with him. He loved doing it. Stripping her slowly, achingly slowly had always been a turn on for him. In fact, he missed the slow buildup of their ritual.

Oh, well. Sam shrugged out of his rain-soaked shirt and dropped it onto the pink pile of Beth's clothes on the floor. He unbuckled his belt. He was thinking too much. Way too much. Dammit.

Tugging the leather through the loops of his jeans, his thoughts shifted to all the scars on his body that Beth had never seen. Jesus. He was a mess. From his shoulders to his ankles, especially on his right leg, there was enough scar tissue to build a whole new human being. Was that going to turn her off? Or would she be turned off not by the scars themselves, but by his reluctance to discuss them?

"Sam?" The blond curls came up off the pillow a few inches. "Is something wrong? Are you having second thoughts?"

Second thoughts? Hell, he went through the second thoughts a couple minutes ago. It was a total miracle, probably one of the Wonders of the Modern World that his dick remained blissfully ignorant of his scrambled mental processes.

"I don't have any protection with me," he said, sounding as lame as a teenager about to lose his virginity.

Beth's response was immediate, although muffled somewhat by the sheets. "I'm on the pill."

Fresh out of excuses, Sam took off his shoes and socks, then his jeans, and finally his dorky white Fruit of the Loom briefs. If he'd known this was going to happen, he'd have at least worn his black Calvin Kleins.

His last cogent thought was that maybe he should write a quick, pathetic letter to big mouth Shelby and sign it "Reluctant and horny as hell at Heart Lake."

Then he slipped under the covers to encounter Beth's warmth and the dizzying, delicious, erotic fragrance of her.

☆

The mattress canted under Sam's solid weight, and Beth found herself rolling into his arms. If this was wrong and stupid, if it was far too soon for the two of them to make love, it was way too late to stop it.

And somewhere deep inside her, in some dark little corner, lurked the battered and bruised version of herself, the one who'd learned, slowly and painfully, not to provoke Danny. The mere thought of that experience sent a chill through her body despite the fact that she lay in Sam's warm embrace.

"Sam, what if . . . ?"

He leaned back slightly in order to see her face. "What if what?"

Beth shook her head against the pillow. "No. Never mind. It doesn't matter." She wished she didn't sound like a whimpering three-year-old all of a sudden. And, dammit, it did matter. It mattered a lot.

"Tell me."

"It's just that . . ." She dragged in a deep breath, then let it out with, "What if I changed my mind? Right now. What if I said no?"

He looked at her as if she'd gone a little mad. "Then we'd stop, Bethie. Is that what you want? To stop?"

"No, I . . ."

The truth was that she didn't know what she wanted just then. Maybe if Sam had whipped off his clothes faster, she wouldn't have had so much time to question what they were doing. Maybe . . . Damn. She'd never felt so torn between the red-hot needs of her body and the amber warning lights in her brain.

"Listen to me. We don't have to do this, Beth." He reached for her hand and pressed her fingers to his lips. "I'm not one of those assholes who doesn't know the meaning of the word *no*, you know."

Now he moved her hand over his heart, where she could feel the hard beat deep inside his chest.

"Whatever you want, sweetheart," he said. "Just tell me."

She wanted *him*. Oh how she wanted him! In sixteen years, she'd never stopped wanting him. The longing blazed through her now like a lit, sizzling fuse. It reduced all her misgivings to ashes.

"I want you, Sam," she whispered. "Love me. Love me now."

He didn't ask if she was sure. He took her at her word, and kissed her as if taking up where they'd left off sixteen years before. Only hotter. Deeper. More delicious and delirious than ever before. Than ever in her life.

It was as if kissing her and caressing her was his life's mission, and soon there was no unkissed or uncaressed patch of skin on her entire body.

At times she could've sworn that Sam had three or four hands. How else could he touch her in so many places simultaneously?

He was slow and thorough. He was gentle and undemanding and giving. It was as if he sought no pleasure at all for himself, but only wanted to pleasure her in every possible way.

It was a whole new world for Beth. When they were kids, there had always been a guilty, furtive aspect to their lovemaking. They were always afraid they'd get caught. The few other men she'd been with seemed far more interested in their own prowess than her pleasure. And then there was Danny, who used the act of love as an apology.

But this was a whole new universe, and Beth was its molten center.

Sam dipped his fingers inside her again, then returned to stroking her.

"There?" he asked.

"Oh, yes."

He shifted his touch a micron. "Or *there*?"

"Oh, God." She was a volcano now. Mount Beth. "Oh, God. Yes. There. Do that. Don't stop."

Sam's patience and persistence sent her over the edge, and while Mount Beth was still exploding, he entered her and fused with her completely.

They lay in each other's arms for the longest time then, getting their breath back, letting their heartbeats subside.

Whether this was right or wrong, Beth didn't know. She snuggled closer to Sam's warmth, refusing to let her brain compete with the climax that was still shimmering through her body.

☆

She must've drifted off.

Sam was gone, and the sun was making a valiant effort to shine through the windows on the west side of the bedroom. The leaves outside the window were glistening with raindrops.

Beth stretched languidly beneath the covers. She was glistening, too, until she suddenly remembered why.

Sam.

Sam and great sex.

Sam and great sex with no apparent future.

Her brain wasn't going to defer to her body much longer, she feared.

And with her afterglow thoroughly soured, Beth got dressed and went downstairs. Somewhere between the bedroom and the kitchen, she morphed from Sex Goddess to Chef, mentally inventorying the freezer and cupboards for a meal beyond compare. She owed Sam that, at the very least.

The clock in the kitchen said it was just five-forty-five. Beth would've sworn it was much later.

Sam had already installed himself at the table by the window with a beer from the fridge. He looked adorably rumpled.

"You're awake," he said by way of greeting.

Beth put a chirp in her voice. "Are you hungry?" she asked him.

"Famished."

"Well, okay, then."

This was her turf. This was what she was good at. Beth rubbed her hands together and got to work.

There were boneless chicken breasts in the freezer, which she popped into the microwave to defrost while she deftly sliced red and green peppers from the vegetable drawer. She chopped up an onion and several buds of garlic, and tossed them all into a pan of hot olive oil, letting them sauté until only someone without a sense of smell wouldn't react to the fabulous fragrance emanating from the stovetop.

"That smells good," Sam said, as if on cue.

"Mm."

Properly encouraged, Beth took the thawed chicken out of the microwave and replaced it with a mixture of boxed risotto. The chicken got dredged with seasoned bread crumbs, heavy on the oregano, and then plopped into the pan with the pepper slices, the onions, and garlic.

She could feel Sam watching her even though he didn't speak. His silence irritated her, although she didn't have a clue what she expected him to say under the circumstances.

*You were great!*

*Thanks for the hot jungle sex.*

*I'll be seeing you.*

All of the above.

"I think I'll open a bottle of wine," she said. "Red or white?"

"Either one."

*Aha! He speaks!* Even so, there wasn't a lot of enthusiasm in his voice. He sounded distinctly withdrawn. She might as well have asked him "How do you like your tap water? Cold or lukewarm?"

Grabbing a bottle of Chardonnay from the wine rack, she started to uncork it. It wasn't chilled, but what the hell. Sam obviously didn't seem to care. About anything. Or anyone.

She battled with the corkscrew until she thought she'd scream, but it wasn't until she began pouring the wine that she realized she was shaking. The bottle chattered against the rim of the glass.

All of a sudden Sam was beside her. He took the bottle from her trembling hands and proceeded to fill the goblets.

"Thanks." Beth turned toward him, pressing her forehead to his chest and muttering into his shirt. "I'm a postcoital mess. Sorry."

"It's okay," he whispered. "Do you want to talk about it?"

She nodded, her head still lodged against his breastbone. "You go first."

Sam chuckled. "Okay. How's this for starters. I never stopped loving you, Bethie."

For starters, that was a whopper.

"You didn't?" Beth sort of gulped the words. She looked up at him then, and his face was more serious than she'd ever seen it, with the possible exception of the day he left for basic training.

"I never stopped loving you," he repeated. "Angry as I was . . . Jilted as I felt when you wouldn't come with me . . . I never stopped loving you."

Beth swallowed audibly. This was what she'd always longed to hear, always, and yet Sam's words didn't match the facts as she knew them.

"You married somebody else," she said, trying to keep her tone calm rather than accusatory, but woefully unable to keep the ancient, awful hurt out of her voice.

Sam sighed with impatience and rolled his eyes. "I explained that to you in a ten-page letter that you wouldn't even read."

"What letter?"

"The one you sent back to me marked 'Return to Sender.'"

"I never did that."

"Well, somebody did," Sam growled.

"It wasn't me."

Both of them were silent for a moment, then at the same time both of them muttered, "Shelby."

"Goddammit." Beth pulled out of Sam's arms and stomped around the kitchen in search of something to break or kick. "That meddling, big mouth, know it all! I should've known. How could she do that to me? How could she do that to us?"

She wished her sister were there right now so she could plant her foot in the middle of Shelby's shapely ass. For years she'd blamed Shelby for talking her out of eloping with Sam, but she had no idea that the interference went further than that.

Then, to her absolute dismay, to her utter amazement, Sam started laughing.

"I'm glad one of us thinks it's funny," she grumbled. "I can't believe you're laughing."

"Well, it's a little late to cry about it," he said.

"I don't know about that."

"And anyway," he said, "who knows? Maybe Shelby, in her big-mouth, meddling way, actually did us a favor."

"A favor!" Beth snorted. "A favor! How can you say that?"

"We were really young, Bethie. If we had gotten married then, we might have really screwed it up."

"I doubt that," Beth shot back with a lot more force than conviction.

In all honesty, Sam was probably right. At seventeen, despite her love for him, she didn't have a clue about how to be a responsible and supportive mate. She would've been miserable, living on an Army base hundreds of miles from her family. Still, she was too pissed at Shelby right now to let go of this righteous indignation.

"Hey." Sam walked toward her with open arms. He gathered her against him and whispered, "Maybe it's not too late for us, Bethie. What do you think?"

She thought her heart was melting right along with all of her bones. She thought she was the luckiest woman alive. And she thought how scared she was that she and Sam might screw up their second chance.

# CHAPTER FOURTEEN

They talked nearly the whole night long, beginning in the kitchen over Beth's delicious chicken and risotto and the bottle of Chardonnay. It had been a long time since Sam had eaten anything more glamorous than the blue plate special at the local café.

After dinner Beth opened a second bottle of wine, and they adjourned to the living room, where Sam found himself once again under the painted eye of old Orvis Shelby, Sr. But the old coot's steady, steely blue gaze felt different this evening, as if the two of them — he and Sam — were somehow conspiring for the benefit of Orvis' great-great-granddaughter.

Sam lifted his glass toward the portrait above the big stone fireplace. "Here's to you, Gramps."

Beth laughed. "He used to make you nervous."

"Everything made me nervous where you were concerned," he confessed.

From her end of the couch, Beth gazed at him over the rim of her wineglass, and said, "I find that hard to believe. You were always so sure of yourself, Sam. So decisive and secure. I've never known anyone so self-assured."

"Well, I put on a pretty good act," he said, leaning back into the cushions of one of the few comfortable, contemporary pieces of furniture in the house. "Come on. Think about it, Beth. I was the local poor boy wooing the rich summer girl. My great-great-grandfather was a lowly lumberjack in Orvis's empire. Your dad was a hotshot lawyer. My dad pumped gas after he retired from the Army. I wasn't exactly on the social register, you know, even here in Shelbyville."

"I never thought about it," she said.

"I know you didn't. That was one of the reasons I loved you."

"Really?"

"Really. I don't think you had any notion that you existed on a playing field way above us regular folks."

Her eyes widened, expressing her sincere astonishment. "I didn't," she said. "I don't."

"Jesus, Bethie." He gestured around the spacious, expensively decorated room, just one of dozens of similar rooms in the huge old house. "What do you call all this?"

"It's just . . . Stuff! Things!" she exclaimed.

He realized once more, as he had so many years ago, how special this woman was, how very unique. Given all the advantages of her birth and upbringing, even now Beth still didn't consider herself special. He couldn't say it was genetic, remembering how Shelby used to lord it over some of the local residents on occasion. That was why the older sister was always referred to as "that little snip with the big mouth" while people tended to call Beth "that sweet young Simon girl."

"I'm glad that hasn't changed," he told her.

"Me, too."

"You did a great job getting this place spiffed up," he

said. "It's what you always wanted to do, even when you were little. So, tell me about your plans for the bed-and-breakfast."

"Well . . ." She grinned as she tucked her legs beneath her, took another sip of wine, and — obviously proud of her endeavor — began to wax poetic on her vision of the future of Heart Lake Manor.

Sam interrupted her occasionally with comments and questions, but all the while she spoke he was wondering how his own plans — or lack of them — fit in with Beth's agenda. They wanted him bad back at Fort Bragg as a Delta Force instructor. He hadn't exactly said no to Lieutenant Colonel Shearing, but he hadn't signed on the dotted line, either. And he also hadn't told Roy that the CIA had begun making overtures related to his language skills, in particular his fluency in Pashto. The spooks in Langley and Kabul wanted him bad, too.

It was nice to be wanted. It wasn't so nice when being wanted meant he would have to relocate to North Carolina or D.C., or, God help him, central Afghanistan.

His other option, of course, was to continue plodding along right there as the local Barney Fife. As he suddenly found himself contemplating a permanent life with Beth, he pictured himself in the capacity of host at Heart Lake Manor.

What a joke.

Sam wasn't sure which was worse. Barney Fife or Basil of *Fawlty Towers*.

"Sam?"

He blinked. "I'm sorry. My mind went off on a tangent for a minute."

Beth smiled a bit sadly. "Yeah. I don't blame you. All this Victorian bed-and-breakfast minutiae can get pretty boring." She reached for the wine bottle on the coffee table, and refilled their glasses. "Let's talk about something else."

Mostly, then, they talked about the past and all the adventures they'd had as kids. Heart Lake wasn't as populated then with summer people, so they'd had orchards and gravel pits and berry bogs and forests aplenty through which to roam.

"Remember the tree house we built?" she asked. "I wonder if it's still there."

Sam shook his head. "Dunno. I never had the courage to trek back in the woods to check it out. Too many memories."

She nodded, obviously remembering as clearly as he did that their tree house was where they'd lost their respective virginities one rainy afternoon a century or so ago.

They both steered clear of the topic of each other's romantic past — Sam because he had an alpha need to consider himself the only man who'd ever been with Beth, and Beth for reasons of her own.

Aside from the memory of the tree house, the closest they came to discussing sex was when Beth reminded him of the time he'd driven to Mecklin to pick up condoms at a drugstore where nobody would recognize him, and who should appear behind him in line at the checkout counter but Thelma Watt.

"What've you got there, young man?" she'd asked.

"Balloons, ma'am," Sam had replied.

Sam almost choked on his wine at the memory.

"It's good to see you laugh," Beth told him. "Are you happy, Sam?"

"Reasonably," he said. It wasn't a complete lie. He just didn't think about his happiness too often. At least he hadn't before Beth came on the scene. Now it seemed to be foremost in his thoughts.

"I'm glad," she said as she traced her index finger around the rim of her glass and stared thoughtfully into the pale liquid. "I almost turned around and went back to California that first day when you stopped me on the road. Or maybe I shouldn't tell you that."

"Why?"

"Why I shouldn't tell you? Or why I almost turned the car around and drove back to the coast?"

"Both."

"I didn't think we could ever be friends after all that happened," she said.

It stung him — the notion that she considered them to be just friends. Sam tried not to let his feelings show.

"Why did you feel you shouldn't tell me?" he asked.

"Oh, I don't know. Probably because I tend to be too candid sometimes. I say way more than I should." She laughed morosely. "It's probably genetic, just like Shelby. We both seem to get worse, the older we get."

"I want you to be honest with me," he said. "That's the only way this will ever work. You and me."

She nodded in agreement, and at the same time stifled a yawn.

"Tired?"

She nodded again. "A little."

And there it was. That awkward silence that told Sam their sexual encounter had exceeded the comfort level of their new relationship. He knew he should've waited, no matter how much he wanted to make love to her this afternoon. Dammit.

But then Beth reached out her hand to him, and said softly, "Don't go out to the carriage house tonight. Come sleep with me. We don't have to do anything. I'd just love for you to hold me, Sam."

"I'd love that, too," he said, enormously relieved as he stood and helped her up from the sofa.

Right now there was nothing he wanted to do more than hold this woman while holding everything else, all of the world, at bay.

He carried her up the big staircase again, just because he loved holding her that way and loved feeling her all sleepy and safe in his arms. Then, unlike the afternoon when she was in such a hurry, Sam took his time undressing her.

It wasn't quite as difficult as when they were kids. Beth used to wear the damndest bras, and it usually took him a while to even figure out whether they latched in the front or the back.

Tonight it was just a matter of whisking her T-shirt over her head. There was nothing underneath, which didn't come as a surprise since he'd been enjoying the lush form and texture of her unbound breasts all evening.

He thought he shouldn't be surprised that Beth's body had changed in the past sixteen years. She was a luscious and curvy thirty-three now rather than a skinny washboard seventeen. As he drew the hot pink thong slowly down her legs, he bent to kiss and to savor the sweet flesh of her belly.

"Mm," she murmured deep in her throat.

"You're not ticklish anymore," he said.

"No." She laughed softly as she reached for him. "And I'm not that sleepy anymore, either."

It was Beth who initiated their lovemaking, who took control, and it was Sam who was only too happy to comply in spite of his better judgment and his previous reservations.

She wasn't just good. She was great. And rather than allow his alpha self to begrudge her experience, he let go of all that and permitted himself to be grateful for it as she stroked him, touched and teased and tongued him, rode him, and pretty much wrung him out.

"Bethie, Bethie," he murmured when she collapsed on top of him.

"Was that good?" she whispered in the crook of his neck.

"Oh, yeah."

He would have praised her more, even thanked her, but just then the sound of a cell phone bleeped insistently from somewhere in the bedroom.

"I think that's yours," Beth said, levering up and edging to the foot of the bed where she reached down and began searching through discarded clothes. "Aha!" She pulled his cell phone from the pocket of his jeans and tossed it to him.

Sam sighed and looked at his watch before he answered. Four in the morning. This couldn't be good.

"This is Sam," he said into the mouthpiece.

"Sam, it's Kimmy." Her voice was high and tight with fear. "I'm so sorry to wake you like this, but there's somebody prowling around outside my trailer. Could you . . . ?"

"I'll be right there."

Drawing on all the reserves of energy he'd learned how to access while he was in the army, Sam got out of bed and into his clothes. "That was Kimmy," he said as he dressed. "Somebody's prowling around her place."

"Oh, no!"

"Bethie, I want you to get dressed and come with me, okay?" He tossed her clothes onto the bed. "I don't want to leave you here alone."

"I don't want to *be* alone," she said, whisking her T-shirt over her head.

They probably set some sort of world record for two naked lovers getting out of the sack and into their clothes, Sam thought. Beth would've made a good soldier.

He made sure the doors were locked before they left, kissed her just once more on the front porch before they loped down the lawn to the driveway, where his jeep sat in all its rusty splendor on four flat tires.

# CHAPTER FIFTEEN

They took Beth's car, and Sam cursed the entire way to Kimmy's place on the other side of the lake. In fact, he cursed in languages Beth had never even heard before. But she could hardly blame him. What a pitiful sight his old jeep was, with its tires looking like four black blobs of melted licorice on the driveway. She was selfishly grateful that the Miata had been locked in the garage, or else it would've probably suffered the same fate.

Kimmy was peeking out of a window in her trailer when they arrived.

"Go inside," Sam said. "Stay with Kimmy, and make sure the door is locked."

He had a flashlight in one hand and a scary-looking gun in the other. Beth assumed he'd retrieved both items from the jeep while she was unlocking the garage. The gun made her very, very nervous.

"Be careful, Sam."

"Always, sweetheart."

Then Kimmy opened the door and nearly pulled Beth inside.

"Did you see anybody out there?" she asked, her face pale and her eyes almost wild with fear.

"No. Nothing. But Sam's looking around."

As she spoke, Beth was also looking around the spacious yet cozy interior of her friend's place. She'd never been inside it before. To her right was what looked to be a fully equipped kitchen, which even had a center island. How cool was that? To her left was a living room paneled in a pale wood and decorated in warm shades of cream and beige. Both rooms were lit by overhead spots. Rather than appearing cramped, as Beth would've guessed, the interior of the trailer felt warm and comfortable and homey.

"I wish I knew what the hell was going on," Kimmy said. She flopped on a beige plaid couch and punched her fist into one of the cushions. "Jeez. And I can't even blame stupid Shelby now."

"What do you mean?" Beth was always more than a little defensive when it came to other people criticizing her big sister. It was one thing for Beth herself to do it. She was entitled, after all. But she bristled sometimes when others jumped on Shelby, whether she deserved it or not.

"Oh, I'm not ragging on Shelby, Beth. I know this has nothing to do with her. I guess I'm just rattled by all the stuff that's been happening around here lately. I just don't get it."

"Yeah. I don't understand it, either," Beth said, moving toward the window by the trailer's front door and pushing aside the curtain to peek out in an effort to see Sam.

It was dark in the little yard. Beyond it, she could barely make out the narrow strip of beach or the water of the lake. She squinted, but hard as she tried, she couldn't even see a flashlight beam. Oh, please let him be okay, she prayed.

She'd meant it with all her heart when she told him to

be careful. When they'd made love the second time, in the flickering light of the candle she'd lit beside the bed, Beth had seen all the terrible scars on his body, including the fresh cuts on his arms from the broken glass. Not that she'd said anything about them at the time, but a good deal of her amorousness was born from kissing each place he'd been wounded in the past and wishing away all the pain he must've experienced.

My God. What had he been doing for the past sixteen years? The man looked as if he'd hired himself out for target practice.

"Beth?"

She looked over her shoulder at Kimmy's anxious face. "I don't see anything out there," she told her, letting the curtain fall closed. "That's probably good news."

"Could I come stay at your house, Beth?" Kimmy was twisting her braid in both hands. "Just for a little while? Just till I get my nerves back in working order? I'm such a mess."

"Oh, sweetie. Of course, you can. Absolutely." Beth sat beside her on the couch and looped an arm around her shoulders. "I wish I'd thought to offer first. There's plenty of room, and it'd make me feel a lot safer just to have you there."

"Thanks." Kimmy sighed forlornly. "Don't you sometimes wish we could go back and be kids again? God. We never had to worry about a thing back then. Not one thing."

"I know," Beth murmured sympathetically even though she didn't completely agree. She remembered worrying plenty, especially around age sixteen and seventeen, when her periods were late.

Just as she was considering knocking on wood for continued good luck, there was a knock at the trailer's door. Both she and Kimmy flinched until they heard Sam's voice through the door.

"It's me," he said.

Kimmy rushed to the door. "Did you see anybody out there?"

He turned off his flashlight and shook his head. "Nobody. Not a sign that anyone was even around."

"Well, I'm sorry," Kimmy said, her voice heating up a bit, "but there was definitely somebody lurking out there when I called you. I'm not crazy, Sam Mendenhall. I know I was poisoned, and things are wrong with me now. I'm not too steady on my feet, but my mind still works reasonably well. There really was somebody prowling around out there."

Sam put his arms around her. "Honey, I'm not questioning you or what you saw. I believe you. But whoever it was isn't out there now."

As he spoke, he was looking over Kimmy's shoulder toward Beth on the couch, and all she could think was *Thank God Sam's all right. Who cares about anybody or anything else?*

Watching her friend in his embrace didn't inspire even a flicker of jealousy now. That was just Sam. There was something of the big, lovable, huggy bear in him. And if anybody needed a hug right now, it was poor Kimmy.

Beth stood up and smoothed out her skirt. "Kimmy's coming back to my place, Sam, for a couple days."

"Sounds good to me," he replied as he drew back his head and looked at Kimmy's face. "You'll be fine, honey. I promise."

Beth put her arms around the two of them. "I promise, too," she said. "I promise we're all going to be fine."

Of course, what "fine" meant, Beth couldn't have said just then.

☆

Back at the Simon place, Sam made a few calls, then staggered upstairs to catch an hour or two of much-needed sleep.

Beth was already breathing deeply when his head hit the pillow next to hers. She stirred.

"Sorry," he whispered. "I didn't mean to wake you."

"That's okay," she answered sleepily. "Where were you?"

"I had to make some calls. Where's Kimmy?"

"In the bedroom across from my old room. She wanted to stay in the carriage house, but I thought she'd feel safer here inside the house."

"Good idea."

Sam closed his eyes. Beside him, Beth turned on her side, jutting her warm buns against his hip. He remembered how easily sleep always came to her. The minute she curled up on her side, that was it. She was in dreamland.

God, he envied that. It had been years since he'd had a good night's sleep. His insomnia had grown worse after his accident in Afghanistan. Or maybe it was just that his dreams were worse.

Usually he relived the whole deal . . .

He'd be on horseback again, high in the mountains west of Bamayan, and bundled in so many layers of clothes — *jakat* and *jampar* and *kot*— to stave off the sleet and the bone-rattling cold. His horse, poor bastard, would be draped in whatever moth-eaten blankets Sam had been able to scrounge up each morning.

The high winds and the cold and the altitude played havoc with his transmitter that last afternoon, and to this day, even after the investigation, he still wasn't sure if he'd screwed up the coordinates or if it was a simple misunderstanding by the guys in the helo.

They came in too low and fired too early. In his dreams Sam could feel the icy downdraft of the Apache, hear the roar of its rotor just feet above his head, and worst of all hear the terrified screams of his horse just before the two of them fell man over beast, heads over heels and hooves, down the side of the mountain.

He could hear their bones snapping as they bounced off boulders and escarpments. It was hard to believe they were both alive by the time they hit bottom.

It was even harder to believe that his pistol was still in its holster.

He'd joked about it later with his Delta buddies. He said he'd handed the pistol to the horse; but the son of a bitch refused to put him out of his pain, so Sam shot him instead.

He only wished it were half that funny in his dreams.

"Sam! What's wrong?"

It was light now, and Beth was sitting up in bed, staring down at him.

"Nothing," he mumbled, blinking his eyes, surprised that he'd actually been asleep.

"You were thrashing around something awful," she said.

"It's just bad dreams," he told her. "I have them sometimes. I hope I didn't keep you awake." Then, fully awake, he grinned up at her. "Is that what they call 'bed head'?"

"Argh. It's horrible, I know. Don't look."

"It's perfect. Come here, Beauty." He pulled her down and settled her rumpled head in the crook of his neck.

"That's what my dad calls my mother," she said.

"I know. Like mother, like daughter."

He could feel her smile against his skin. In a family of beauties, his Bethie had always considered herself the second runner-up, and he vowed right now to tell her at least once a day how beautiful she was, no matter how long they were together, whether it was a few weeks or the next fifty years.

"Listen, Beth. I want you and Kimmy to stay here today with the doors locked. Okay?"

She nodded. "What are you going to do?"

"I'm going to do what I should've started doing long before this. Kicking ass and taking names."

☆

It was almost ten o'clock by the time Beth made it down to the kitchen. She cursed herself for falling back to sleep right after Sam got out of bed. She'd meant to get up, but . . .

Kimmy was in the kitchen breaking eggs into a bowl. "I thought I heard you in the shower," she said. "Want some breakfast?"

"Oh, I'd love it. Let me help."

"Nope. Sit. I want to earn my keep around here."

Beth sat at the table. It was nice to see Kimmy smiling again. Even her braid seemed to be bouncing happily between her shoulders. "Well, I'll let you pamper me just this once."

"Where's Sam? Should I fix some eggs for him, too?"

"To quote him, he's out somewhere 'kicking ass and taking names.'"

"Ooh." Kimmy feigned a shudder as she set a glass of

orange juice in front of Beth. "I wouldn't want to be on the receiving end of that."

"Me, either. I hope he gets some answers."

Beth sipped her juice and watched while Kimmy poured the beaten eggs into a skillet.

"Speaking of answers," she said, "how much do you know about Sam during all those years after we broke up?"

"A lot." The impish grin on her face was invitation enough, but then Kimmy tilted her head, smiled almost conspiratorially, and asked, "What do you want to know?"

"Everything," Beth said.

By the time they had finished their scrambled eggs, broiled tomatoes, and whole wheat toast, and were well into their second cups of coffee, Beth knew everything Kimmy knew about Sam. It wasn't everything, but it was a lot more than she'd known before.

"I can't tell you all the details of his career in the Army," Kimmy said. "His mother didn't even know everything, and what she did know I gather she wasn't supposed to tell. But she was proud of him, and people around here — Thelma, for instance — have a way of wheedling things out of people."

According to Kimmy, Sam wasn't regular army, but some sort of special operations group . . .

"Green Beret?" Beth asked.

"Dunno."

"Rangers?"

"Dunno."

"Delta Force?" She surprised herself with the names she was able to come up with in her curiosity. Except Kimmy wasn't able to be specific.

"Dunno," she said again. "I just know that he was on call, like all the time, and that he was sent all over the map.

Colombia. Haiti. The Philippines. A couple places in the Middle East. Mrs. Mendenhall said something about a kidnapping in South America, but she didn't know much else, or, if she did, she wouldn't say."

Kimmy filled their coffee cups a third time.

"The deal with his leg, the injury that forced him out of the Army, happened in Afghanistan, I think."

"He broke his leg?"

"Oh, yeah. In about a million places. Other bones, too. But his leg was the worst. His mom was scared he'd never walk again."

Beth winced. It hurt to know that Sam was hurt, and she had been nowhere around to help or comfort him. She wondered suddenly where his ex-wife had been during all this. She didn't know a thing about the woman. All she knew was that Shelby had called her last fall to say that Sam was back at Heart Lake and he wasn't married anymore. Beth assumed that meant divorced.

"What about his wife?" she asked, almost choking on the word. "Where was she while all this was going on?"

"His wife?"

"Yeah, Kimmy. The guy got married two or three months after we broke up." Duh, Beth thought, but didn't say it. "Remember?"

"Well, yeah, he got married, but I just assumed you knew all about that."

"What do you mean?"

"Everybody knows about that, Beth."

"Everybody but me, I guess. Tell me."

"He wasn't married all that long," Kimmy said, sipping her coffee. Because her hands weren't too steady, she held the cup between her palms. "His wife and baby both died after they'd been married only a couple months."

"Whoa." Beth held up a hand. "Hold the phone. His wife and *baby?*"

"Yeah." Now it was Kimmy who seemed to be thinking Duh and refraining from saying it as she stared at Beth across the table.

"What baby?" Beth asked.

"The baby that was the reason he had to get married in the first place, Beth. You never knew that?"

She shook her head. "No. I never knew."

But it explained a hell of a lot. It explained why Sam never made a concerted effort to contact her during those months when he was in basic training. Sure, he'd sent a few letters she never received, and he'd been pissed when they were returned unread, but he could've done more. Now Beth realized why he didn't. It was too late.

She'd been so hurt when she found out he was married, only a few months after their breakup. Now she understood the reason for the quickie nuptials, but she had yet to understand Sam's carelessness with another woman. That still hurt. It was years after their breakup — four years, in fact, when she was a senior in college — that Beth would even entertain the notion of sex with somebody else.

"I'm sure he didn't get in trouble on purpose," Kimmy said, as if she were reading Beth's mind. "That stuff just happens. Hey. Look at my mom, for heaven's sake. And my father didn't even have the decency to marry her. To tell you the truth, I've always thought what Sam did was pretty noble."

It didn't strike Beth as noble just then. She'd always assumed he'd married for love. Sam's shotgun marriage to the pregnant girl struck her as utterly sad and useless.

On the other hand, how could she fault him for doing the right thing?

Oh, man. When she'd asked Kimmy to tell her everything, she hadn't expected this. It was almost too much to wrap her mind around, not to mention her heart.

Just then the phone rang. Kimmy was sitting closer to it. "Want me to get it?" she asked.

"Sure. Go ahead."

After a minute of *okays* and *uh-huhs*, she passed the receiver to Beth. "Speak of the devil," she said under her breath.

Beth's heart lurched as soon as she heard his voice. "Is everything okay there?" Sam asked. "Kimmy sounds pretty calm."

"Yes. We're just finishing a late breakfast and catching up on old gossip," she said, then she changed the subject from old gossip to new mysteries. "Did you find out anything?"

"No. I've rousted just about every kid on the lake between the ages of ten and twenty. Male and female. Every single one of them looked me straight in the eye and said they had no idea who was responsible for all this shit. I've gotta believe them."

"I suppose you do. What now?"

"I'm heading into town, where I'll be obnoxious to some more kids. Thanks for letting me use your car, Beth. I should be back at the lake around two, maybe three."

"Oh, good. You know what I'd love to do this afternoon, Sam?"

There was a distinct chuckle in his voice when he asked, "Does it have anything to do with a mattress?"

"No." Beth glanced at Kimmy, hoping his voice hadn't carried past her own ear. She really didn't want to advertise the fact that she and Sam were sleeping together. There would be too much explaining if things didn't work out.

"If you get back early enough, I'd love to take a walk in the woods and see our old tree house." The idea had occurred to her the night before, but she never had a chance to mention it.

"Sure," he said. "I'll make it a point to get back early enough. See you later."

"What old tree house?" Kimmy asked, taking the receiver and hanging it up.

"It's a place that Sam and I built when we were kids, in the woods north of here. Way up near Little Glory Lake. Neither one of us has seen it since that last summer."

Kimmy laughed. "So that's what Shelby was snooping around for that one summer."

"Really?"

"She never found it, either. You guys must've really hiked way the hell into the woods."

"We did," Beth said. "We probably won't even be able to find it ourselves after all these years."

Oh, but she hoped they could. There were so many memories there. Good memories. Wonderful memories. And maybe once they were there, she'd be able to work up the courage to ask Sam about the bad ones.

☆

Sam was dead tired and disgusted with himself because his investigative attempts had failed to uncover a snitch or yield even a crumb of information.

Nobody saw anything.

Nobody knew anything.

Well, that wasn't quite true. Mrs. Belding, on the south side of the lake, knew for a fact that her battery-powered fan had been in her screened porch the night before, and now it wasn't there. She also swore up and down that several chocolate-covered cherries were missing from the box that also happened to be on the porch. Sam mentally added them to his growing list, which was in the glove compartment of his disabled jeep, now resting in the Gas Mart's parking lot.

He wasn't in the best of moods when he swung the little red Miata into Beth's driveway and hauled himself up the lawn to the house, where Beth was curled in a big wicker chair on the front porch. He bit down on his impulse to yell at her for not remaining behind locked doors. No sense putting her in a crappy mood, too.

"Oh, Sam. You look just exhausted," she said, jumping out of her chair and meeting him at the top of the steps. "Why don't we postpone this tree house thing?"

He looped his arms over her shoulders and kissed the top of her head. "No way. I've been looking forward to it," he said, when what he meant was that he knew how much *she* was looking forward to it, and he'd be damned if he'd disappoint her.

Kimmy declined their invitation to accompany them, so an hour later it was just Beth and Sam trekking through the tangled underbrush. It was hard to walk side by side, and when Beth forged ahead, she had a tendency to let branches snap back and whip Sam across his face and chest. He hardly felt them, though, because he had long since plugged himself into that automatic, military reservoir that kept one foot going in front of the other without much help from his body or his brain.

He used the compass on his watch to keep them on a north-northwest bead. Any path they'd worn through these woods was long gone, but he thought he recognized a few landmarks — a three-pronged birch tree, a rotting wooden blind long abandoned by hunters, a boulder thick with lichen.

But there were other things that caught his attention, too. Freshly broken branches. An occasional whiff of excrement. And finally, disturbingly, a few little brown pleated candy holders. The kind that might've held chocolate-covered cherries.

"Hold up, Bethie." He caught her arm and held tight.

"What's wrong?"

"I'm pretty sure I just saw a bear." It was the first thing that came into his head.

"A bear? You're kidding."

"No. About twenty yards ahead and just to the right."

She grinned. "This isn't a joke about what bears do in the woods, is it? Besides, I didn't know there were any bears around here anymore. Are you sure?"

"I'm positive. We better go back. No sense taking any chances."

Her grin faded, and disappointment vied with fear in her voice. "Oh, Sam, we've come so far."

"We'll come back, honey. I'll just bring a gun next time to be on the safe side."

"Well, damn."

He maneuvered her ahead of him and started her walking south while he kept an eye out behind them.

"If there is a bear, aren't we supposed to make a lot of noise so we don't surprise him?" she asked.

Sam looked down at another pleated brown candy wrapper. He didn't want to surprise anything or anybody, not with Beth by his side. "Uh . . . No. No noise. That's only . . . That's just with grizzly bears."

"Are you sure?"

"Absolutely. Walk faster, okay?"

# CHAPTER SIXTEEN

By the time he and Beth got back to the house — with the invisible bear breathing down their necks — Sam knew it was too late for him to go back alone and snoop around the tree house.

He went to bed early that night after one of Beth's great meals and much speculation among the three of them about bears and whether they did or did not (a.) live or (b.) shit in the woods. Beth and Kimmy thought it was hysterical. It might've been funny to Sam, too, if he hadn't been so apprehensive about just what or whom he was going to find in those same woods when he returned early the next morning.

He programmed himself to wake before dawn, then tossed and turned the whole night, falling down the mountain again, but this time tangled with a horse *and* a bear. At the bottom, the furry brown son of a bitch was unscathed. He lumbered away, glancing back indifferently over his humped shoulder at the broken man and the dying horse.

Just before dawn, Sam slipped out of Beth's warm bed and jogged to his cabin, where he shrugged into his old camouflage jacket, squeezed about half a bottle of Visine in each eye, loaded his .22, and attached the sniper scope.

He scribbled a note, saying where he was headed, and left it in plain sight, just in case. You always wanted to file a flight plan.

Then he followed the same path he and Beth had taken through the woods. Except he moved faster and far more quietly than they had the day before.

☆

Beth had fallen asleep looking forward to nudging Sam in the morning, then making love instead of making breakfast. But at seven-thirty, when she inched her foot toward the other side of the bed, there was only a cool void where Sam's warm body should've been.

She could almost taste her disappointment as she dragged her foot back, then drew the covers over her head and let out a muffled sigh.

Damn.

It wasn't easy to admit that she'd already grown accustomed to Sam's presence in her life as well as her bed. It was even harder to admit that she'd probably made a mistake letting things go so far so soon. They had started something, she and Sam, without the least notion of where it was going or how it might end. Not too smart, she told herself. In fact, it was pretty stupid.

What if they broke each other's hearts again? This time, without Shelby's advice and interference, they'd have no one to blame but themselves.

☆

Sam lay in the brush, his cheek pressed against the butt of his .22-caliber rifle. Through the 10x sniper scope he could see just about every wart and mole on the man who was climbing down the wooden ladder from the tree house.

Ironically, the man actually reminded Sam of a bear. He was a burly guy, probably carrying 220 pounds on his six-foot frame. His dishwater blond hair was streaked with silver, and he wore it long and shaggy, not for a fashion statement, but most likely because he couldn't afford the price of a cut. From the depth of the lines on his face, Sam guessed him to be in his fifties. Oddly enough, the guy was wearing an Army-issue camo jacket just as Sam was; but this particular jacket, judging from its clotted patterns of green and brown and black, had to be at least thirty years old, its colors meant to blend in with the jungles of Vietnam rather than desert sands.

What the hell was this guy doing out here in the woods?

Sam watched him walk to the edge of the little clearing, where he took a leak in some sumac bushes, then zipped up and shambled back to the ramshackle hut. He mounted the ladder once more, then descended with a scrap of red, white, and blue tucked under his arm.

And then the damndest thing . . .

The man clamped the fabric to a rope jury-rigged to a birch tree, and then with all due solemnity he raised the United States flag until it waved freely in the soft little breeze over his head.

If that wasn't Thelma Watt's flag, Sam would eat the thing, every last star and stripe of it.

He shifted the scope a fraction to the left in order to scrutinize the tree house itself.

*I'll be damned.*

Carol Dunlap's faded curtains almost covered one window, but not enough to disguise the bronze pigskin lifted from the trophy case at school.

Ol' Constable Sam had just found the phantom perp.

☆

The soft but insistent rapping on the bedroom door was accompanied by Kimmy's voice.

"Beth? Are you awake?"

Wasn't she? Beth whipped the covers from her face and turned her head to look at the clock beside the bed. Oh, god. She must've fallen back asleep. How could it be twenty after nine?

She cleared the sleepiness from her throat to call out, "I'm up. I'll be downstairs in a jiffy."

"Good," Kimmy answered brightly. "Your mom and dad are here."

Beth jackknifed up. She hadn't heard that right, had she? She was tempted to slap her hand to her ear to clear any obstruction that might be there.

"My what?" she called out, hoping Kimmy was still close by.

"I said your parents are here. They just drove up from Chicago."

"Why?" It was all she could think to say.

"Well, to see you, I suppose, silly. Get up and come downstairs."

"Yeah. Okay. Tell them I'll be right down."

But instead of getting up, Beth flopped back down on the pillows and stared at the ceiling. Her parents? Why were they here? Not that they didn't still own the house and have every right to appear whenever they chose, but . . . Why now?

Suddenly she felt like a teenager again, caught not with her hand in the cookie jar but with her boyfriend in her bed. She had this sudden, horrible, gut-wrenching urge to call Shelby and scream, "What am I supposed to do now?"

Thank God the urge passed almost as quickly as it occurred. With a beleaguered sigh, she hauled herself out of bed and got dressed.

Harry Harry Quite Contrary and Lovely Linda were in the kitchen, sipping coffee, chatting with Kimmy, when Beth came downstairs.

"There's my little girl," her father said, springing up from the table and opening his arms to her. As always, he hugged her hard and blew a wet raspberry into her neck.

As always, Beth exclaimed "Daddy!" and giggled as she hugged him back with equal force. For a minute she felt ten years old again and safe from everyone and everything in her father's dependable embrace.

Then she stepped back to look at him. God, his hair seemed to recede another quarter of an inch every time she saw him lately. But his eyes were warm and bright. He looked happier than ever.

And there was her mother, beautiful as always, wearing one of her own gorgeous sweater designs along with her signature black velvet headband to hold back her blond pageboy. Some things never changed.

"Hello, sweetheart," her mother said. "You look wonderful."

"Hi, Mom." Beth kissed her, then settled into the chair next to hers. "What a surprise!" she said, hoping to convey that she was pleasantly surprised instead of thoroughly flummoxed, even a bit annoyed, by their unannounced arrival.

Kimmy, obviously keying in to Beth's distress, got up from the table and carried her coffee cup to the sink, where she rinsed it quickly. "I'm going to get busy with some dusting," she said, then practically ran out of the kitchen before anyone could stop her.

"We thought it would be a nice surprise, and, well, we just missed you, sweetie," her mother said, her voice dripping with maternal good cheer. That alone was a pretty good clue for Beth that these two had an ulterior motive, which became evident when her father spoke.

He suddenly put on his dour courtroom face to match the solemnity of his tone. "Sam called us yesterday, honey. He's worried about you."

Oh, well. Beth was worried about herself, too, but not for the same reasons.

"Why don't you come back to Chicago with us for a little while?" her mother said. "You could stay with Shelby and Mick. They've got loads of room in their new house, and I know they'd love to have you there for a while. And . . ."

Beth held up her hand. "Mom, I'm not leaving, so just don't ask. I've got way too much to do here to get this place ready for the massive influx of guests I'm expecting in a few weeks."

She was exaggerating to be funny, but her parents didn't laugh. Neither one of them even cracked a smile. Oh, man. Beth wanted to throttle Sam within an inch of his life for siccing them on her like this. It was such a . . . such a Shelby thing to do.

"Who'd like more coffee?" she asked, seeking a few moments of distraction in order to pull her thoughts together and mount a solid defense against one of Chicago's best criminal lawyers.

But it turned out to be unnecessary when Harry Harry Quite Contrary rubbed his hands together, and announced,

"We'll talk about this later. I hear a couple dozen bluegills and perch calling me from the lake. Do you hear them, Beauty?"

Linda laughed. "I believe I do."

"Then you wouldn't mind if I . . . ?"

"Go, Harry," she said, then looked at Beth. "Bethie and I are long overdue for some girl talk, anyway. Right, sweetie?"

"Right, Mom."

Girl talk.

Oh, brother.

Beth needed a girl to talk to, that was for sure, but that girl wasn't her mother.

The next time she laid eyes on Sam, just as soon as her heart stopped bouncing for joy, Beth was going to kill him.

☆

Sam knew quite a lot just from watching the big blond bear of a man go through his morning rituals. For one thing, the guy was an excellent woodsman. He built a beautiful, compact fire in almost no time, over which he proceeded to boil a pan of water for his morning coffee — a handful of instant crystals tossed into the pot.

He had the appetite of a bear, too, and used a plastic knife to slather half a jar of peanut butter on half a box of saltines, all of them no doubt among the missing items at the market in Shelbyville. Sam didn't even wonder what had become of the stolen apple pie, but the missing bra remained a mystery.

As for Blanche's flowers . . . There was a pretty little bouquet stuck in an empty peanut butter jar on the tree house's tiny front porch.

So, he figured he wasn't dealing with a monster, but a man with fairly regular habits, competent skills, and not a total disregard for esthetics.

What he didn't know, however, was whether or not the guy had a weapon, so he had to proceed on the assumption that there was a hunting knife stashed beneath the camo jacket, or a gun within easy reach. Which is why Sam shouted out, "Get down on the ground and spread 'em. Now," just before he stood up.

"Down," he yelled again when the man didn't instantly respond.

"Yeah. Yeah. Okay, buddy." The bear went rather awkwardly to his knees.

"All the way down," Sam said.

"Aw, gimme a break here, pal. I've got arthritis in these old joints."

"Down." Sam started toward him, his rifle aimed at the man's midsection.

"Okay. Okay."

Sam reached him just as the guy's chest met the ground. He knelt, his knee pressing into the phantom perp's back, and patted him down for any hidden weapons.

The bear looked over his shoulder. "If you find anything more lethal than a plastic serrated knife, you let me know, okay?"

He smelled like a bear now that Sam was up close and personal, but there were no weapons on him other than his powerful scent. Sam stood up and stepped back a couple of feet.

"You can get up now," he told him.

"I could use a little help, son."

Sam held out his hand. The bear grabbed hold. Sam

lofted him onto his feet. As soon as he established his balance, the bear tilted his head toward the campfire and asked, "Want some coffee?"

"Sure," Sam said. "That'd be great."

☆

Linda Simon stood in the center of the carriage house with her hands on her hips. "I hate this place," she said.

Beth blinked. "What?"

"I said I hate this place. The carriage house. I hate every square inch of it. It reminds me of those horrible months when your father was camped out here last year."

"But everything's fine now, right?" Oh, don't answer that, Beth thought, especially if everything's not fine. She'd tried on the role of conciliator early in her parents' separation, and she hated it because trying to be fair to both of them nearly tore her in half.

She wasn't like Shelby. She didn't like to give people advice because it would be her fault if things didn't go right. This had been particularly true with her parents.

"Well, of course, everything's fine. What made you think it wasn't, sweetie?" As she spoke, her mother was walking around touching things. The back of the curved sofa. The pillows thereon. The granite-topped counter that separated the kitchen from the rest of the loftlike space. Finally, the overnight bag she'd tossed into a chair.

"Oh, nothing," Beth said. "I'm glad everything's going well for you guys. Listen, if you don't want to stay out here, if it bothers you, Mother, then stay in the house. There's lots of room."

The Lovely Linda flapped a hand in the direction of her younger daughter. "We'll stay out here, honey. Your father and I wouldn't want to make it uncomfortable for you and Sam."

Beth felt the hinges of her jaw loosen. It was a second or two or three before she could reposition her mouth adequately enough to say, "Um . . . Excuse me?"

"Beth." Her mother put her hands on her hips again, then skewered Beth with her gaze. "If you and Sam Mendenhall aren't sharing a bed by now, after all these years apart, I'd be very surprised. And I guess I'd be a little disappointed, too. There. I've said it. Does that shock you?"

Yes, it did. With the exception of a very uncomfortable discussion about the birds and the bees when Beth was ten or eleven, she and her mother had never talked about sex, not in the abstract, and certainly not in specifics. Namely Sam.

"No, I'm not shocked," she lied, following her remark with the truth. "I just don't want to talk about it."

Her mother was looking in the refrigerator now. She closed the door, then began going through cabinets.

"What are you looking for, Mom?"

"I thought your father might've left a bottle of wine out here. I know he had some Pinot Grigio last year. I could certainly use a glass of it right now."

"At eleven in the morning?"

Her mother turned, giving her daughter one of her legendary let-me-explain-this-so-you-understand looks. "Beth, I've been up since four, which makes it about, oh, midnight as far as I'm concerned."

"I see what you mean. I've got some wine in the kitchen. Let me go grab a bottle."

☆

"More coffee?" The bear, whose name turned out to be Kyle Ferrin, reached for the saucepan simmering on the campfire.

"No, thanks," Sam said. The stuff was worse than his, which made it nearly undrinkable. He crushed the empty paper cup in his hand and tossed it into the fire.

The cups, along with the king-size jar of instant coffee, had been pilfered from the Gas Mart. Sam guessed nobody there even noticed since they didn't report it. He wondered what else Kyle Ferrin had gotten away with.

"How was that apple pie?" Sam asked him.

"Damn thing was *hot*," the man said. "I burned my hand when I touched it on the windowsill."

A light went on in Sam's brain. He laughed. "So that explains the missing bra."

"Yep. I needed a pair of potholders. I can give it back to you, if you want."

"Nah. That's okay. Listen, Kyle, I don't mind your camping out here in the woods as long as you don't bother anybody." Sam narrowed his gaze. "And as long as you don't keep taking things. Why don't you make out a list of the stuff you need, and I'll get it for you?"

"That's a generous offer, son, but I don't know how I'd pay you back."

"Well . . ." Sam sighed. "Let's just say I'm making a long-overdue contribution to the Vietnam vets. Does that make it any easier for you?"

Like many of his fellow Vietnam vets, Kyle Ferrin had found it hard, if not impossible, to readjust when he came home from the war. He'd been living on the streets for the past three decades, unable to hold a job, unwilling to ask for help, uncomfortable in the company of his fellowman. And unapologetic about it all.

As Sam had listened to the man's story, he couldn't help but compare his own situation to Kyle's. Not that Sam's current plight was that extreme, but he understood the disconnect between military and civilian life and the difficulty of a good soldier finding his proper niche as a good civilian.

"Why here?" Sam asked him. It was one thing to live on the streets of Los Angeles, as Kyle said he'd done for years. But a shack in the woods in Mecklin County? "How'd you end up here?"

"I'm from here."

"No kidding? I thought I knew just about everybody in Shelbyville township."

"Well, I've been gone a long time," Kyle said. "Probably even before you were born. I came back to see my kid."

"Oh, yeah? Who's that?" Even as he asked the questio. Sam had an inkling that he knew the answer.

Across the campfire, he watched the man's expression darken. Sam thought he could read a bevy of emotions there. Shame. Regret. Apprehension.

"Sally Mortenson's girl. She lives in a trailer on the west side of Heart Lake. You know her?"

"Yeah. I know her."

So that's who was prowling around Kimmy's place and left the flowers on her doorstep.

"Well, don't say anything to her," Kyle said. "I've seen her. That's all I came back for. I just wanted to see her. I don't know if I'm ready to do any more than that. You swear to me you won't say anything to the girl."

"Yeah. Okay," Sam said. "It's your business. I won't say anything to her if you'll stop stealing and setting fires and breaking windows." He threw those last ones in just to see how Kyle would react.

The man reacted instantly and indignantly. "Fires! I didn't set any fires. Just this." He stabbed a finger at the campfire. "And I didn't break any windows, either."

Sam believed him. "Okay," he said. "Well, just stop stealing stuff, goddammit. Write me a list, okay?"

While Kyle shuffled to the tree house to get a pencil and paper, Sam poked at the white coals with a stick. The good news was that he'd solved one mystery. The bad news was that somebody was definitely out to hurt Beth. And if it wasn't Kyle, who was it?

He didn't have a clue.

# CHAPTER SEVENTEEN

Sam stopped by his place to lock up his rifle and tear up the note he'd written earlier. Before he showered, he called Beth to make sure everything was okay at the house, and when Kimmy answered the phone, he almost wished he'd never found her long-lost father.

"What's going on?" he asked her.

"Not much. Harry and Linda Simon got here a while ago. Harry's out fishing, and Beth and her mother are working their way through a bottle of wine in the carriage house."

Sam looked at his watch. It was barely noon. Those two were getting started a little early, he thought.

"Where've you been all morning?" Kimmy asked.

"Oh, just out and about. Doing my job. Keeping the township safe from vampires and werewolves."

She laughed. "And you're obviously doing a great job. I haven't seen any vampires or werewolves in months."

He felt lousy when they hung up. Lying, even if it was by omission, left an acrid, foul taste in his mouth. Plus, he wasn't sure he was doing the right thing by honoring

Kyle's wish to keep this knowledge from Kimmy. But if the man ultimately decided he didn't want to make contact with his daughter, Sam didn't want to give her any false hopes.

On the other hand, Kimmy might not want to have anything to do with the father who ran out on her so long ago. Sam just didn't know. Maybe he ought to talk it over with Beth, get her perspective on the situation.

Hopefully she and Linda would still be sober by the time he got to the house.

Even more hopefully, Beth would agree to go back to Chicago with her parents, if only for a while.

☆

Beth offered her mother a second glass of wine, but Linda covered her glass with her hand.

"No more for me," she said. "I don't want to wobble down to the dock when your father gets back."

Deciding she didn't care all that much about wobbling at the moment, Beth refilled her own glass from the bottle. She tucked her legs beneath her and saluted her mother on the opposite end of the big curved sofa.

So far, she'd been able to deflect most of her mother's questions about her relationship with Sam by changing the subject to her plans for the bed-and-breakfast. But the woman was getting that terrier look on her face, and Beth didn't think she'd be able to redirect their conversation much longer.

She watched her mother whisk off her black velvet headband, run her manicured fingers through her hair, then put the headband back on, only to have her blond pageboy fall perfectly into place once more. How did she do that?

"I don't know why you're so uncomfortable talking about Sam, Bethie."

"I just don't want to, Mother. Only . . ." There *was* something she wanted to discuss, she realized. "Let me ask you something."

"Anything," her mother replied, settling back against the cushions of the sofa.

"Did you know about the circumstances of Sam's marriage all those years ago?"

Bingo! The lovely Linda had never been good at disguising her emotions. What registered on her face right now seemed to be a blatant *Oh, shit*. Beth had definitely hit a nerve if not a veritable gold mine of secrets.

"You knew!" Beth said. "Oh, my God. I can't believe this. I'll bet Shelby knew, too."

"No, she didn't," Linda said forcefully. "But, yes, I did know. Sam's mother told me. She was so upset. But I didn't tell you because there was nothing you could've done about it, Beth. I thought knowing the truth would just hurt you more than you already were."

Beth could only sigh. It was true, of course. Knowing that Sam had gotten another girl pregnant would've broken her heart in a billion pieces instead of just a million.

"Honey, if it was the wrong thing to do, then I apologize. Truly. But it seemed right at the time. You were so young. Barely seventeen."

"Maybe it was the right thing to do." Beth took another sip of her wine. "I don't know."

"Did Sam tell you?"

Beth shook her head. "No. Kimmy finally spilled the beans. Sam still doesn't know that I know."

"Well, it was a long time ago, honey. By now it's just water . . ."

". . . under the bridge," Beth said. "I suppose so." She hoped so, anyway.

"Speaking of bridges, do you miss the Golden Gate?" her mother asked. "You never told me how things ended up with Danny. Did the two of you manage to part amicably or not?"

"Not," Beth said.

"Oh, dear."

She wanted to talk about Danny even less than she wanted to talk about Sam. Thank goodness a horn honked in the driveway just then.

Peering out one of the carriage house windows, Beth saw Sam's jeep with four brand-new tires. Gus from the Gas Mart was just climbing out from behind the wheel to shake hands with Sam, who seemed to have appeared out of nowhere.

"Is that Sam's voice I hear out there?" her mother asked.

"Yep."

"Well, go on, honey. I think I'm going to take a little wine-induced nap before your father gets back and insists on showing me his fish-cleaning skills for the zillionth time."

"Okay. See you later, Mom."

Beth was already on her way to the door, hardly wobbling at all, she was happy to note. Well, maybe just a little.

☆

Sam saw her coming down the lawn, and for a second he forgot how to breathe. He'd been giving Gus his credit card number to pay for the new tires, and he lost his place in the sequence, as well. He had to start from the beginning, while Gus chortled.

"Are you writing these down?" Sam snapped at the Gas Mart mechanic.

"I sure am, Sam," he said, stifling his grin.

"Hi, Gus," Beth said, arriving on a little gust of perfume and a brief whiff of wine. "Hey, Sam."

She leaned into him just a little, and Sam lost his place on the plastic card once more. He shoved the damn thing back in his wallet.

"I'll call it in later, Gus. That all right with you?"

The guy knew better than to laugh now. In fact, he practically saluted as he said, "Sure, Sam. Whenever you get around to it. No problem."

"You need a ride back to town?"

"Naw." Gus jerked a thumb toward the road just as the Gas Mart's tow truck appeared. "There's Tiny now. Well, I'll be seeing you."

"Gus! Wait!" Kimmy came flying down the porch stairs, waving her arms. "Can you give me a ride back to my place?"

Beth whipped around. "You're not leaving, are you, Kimmy?"

"Yeah." She tossed her bouncing blond braid back over her shoulder. "Your folks are here, Beth, and I just don't want to be a fifth wheel."

"Oh, you're not," Beth said.

"Well, anyway, I'm going back to my place. I just want to get back to my own bed and my TV shows."

"But . . ."

Sam cut off Beth's protest. "I'm sure you'll be fine there, kiddo. And I'm just a phone call away if you need me."

"That's what I figured," Kimmy said, trotting toward the tow truck. "Thanks, Beth. I'll talk to you later. Tell your mom and dad I said bye."

"Okay."

His Bethie sounded a little befuddled, and Sam didn't know if it was the afternoon wine, her friend's abrupt exit, or both.

"Harry and Linda are here, huh?" he said.

She gave him a look somewhere between Man 1 and Man 2. "Yes, they are. Thank you *so* much."

Sam draped his arms over her shoulders and pressed his forehead to hers. "I had to call them, baby. I want you to go back to Chicago with them. For a couple days, at least. Will you do that? Just to be safe?"

Her head snapped back. "Wait a minute. It's perfectly all right for Kimmy to go back to her trailer alone, with some prowler stalking her, and I can't stay here with you?"

"I want you to be safe."

"So, keep me safe!"

"Beth, for God's sake . . ."

"I'm not leaving, Sam."

"Beth . . ."

"No. Absolutely not. No way. I've waited too many years for this chance to make something really, really special out of this house. This is my dream, goddammit, and I'm not leaving. Not even for a few days. Period. The end."

Jesus Christ. How could anybody listen to a woman defying all good sense and be so frigging distracted by the blue fire in her eyes and the wild flush on her cheeks and the rise and fall of her beautiful breasts? What the hell was wrong with him? He used to be a serious, sensible kind of guy.

Right this minute he felt like a Neanderthal, wanting to club his woman over the head, fling her over his shoulder, and carry her back to his cave.

He raised his hands, not to club her, but to surrender. "I give up."

"You what?"

"I give up."

"You do?"

"Yes. I'll call off your parents if you'll promise to do everything I tell you to. If you want me to keep you safe, you're going to have do that. Is that clear, Beth?"

"Well . . ."

He wasn't about to take a dithering and noncommittal "well" for an answer. "No. I'm not kidding. It's either that, or I take you back to Chicago myself. Wrapped in duct tape in the trunk of a car, if necessary. I mean it."

"Okay. Okay. I promise."

"Promise what? Say it."

She groaned softly. "I promise to do whatever you tell me to do."

"Without arguing."

"Without arguing," she echoed.

"You swear."

"I swear."

"And if I say jump?"

"I'll jump," she answered. "I'll even ask how high."

Sam didn't trust her completely, but at least he figured he'd gotten his point across. It was time to loosen up.

"Where's your dad?" he asked.

"Where else? Fishing."

"And your mom?"

"She's taking a nap in the carriage house. Why?"

God help him, if he'd had a mustache, he'd have twirled it. Instead, he waggled his eyebrows suggestively, probably for the first time in his entire life. He wasn't a man given to silly gestures. Well . . . until now.

Beth laughed and clasped her hand over her heart. "Sam!"

"You swore you'd do anything I told you to," he reminded her.

"Well, I know, but . . ."

"Love me, Bethie." Damn. He sounded a lot more needy than he'd meant to. He'd sounded pretty pitiful, actually. Still, Beth didn't seem offended. Just the opposite, in fact.

Her blue eyes twinkled.

"Walk this way," she said, grabbing his hand and pulling him up the lawn toward the house, then up the big staircase toward heaven.

☆

This time Sam made love to her so slowly, so deliciously, so sensually that Beth felt like the lucky paramour of some reincarnated Greek god who'd invented all these techniques in the first place. She'd never had a lover as generous as Sam. Not even Sam himself when they were kids.

She loved the weight of his warm body on hers. She loved the way his eyes sank closed just before he kissed her. She loved the depth of his kisses, as if their breath truly became the same breath.

She loved the way the cords in his neck stood out on the verge of his climax, and the sound of the groans of pleasure in his throat that he couldn't suppress. The way his face tightened when he came. The way his body arched.

Maybe most of all she loved the way he turned her body inside out and made her feel every cliché ever associated with lovemaking. Fireworks. Crashing waves. Rockets blasting off and deep red roses blooming. All of the above.

Once again, he left her breathless, basking in the afterglow of their loving.

She'd opened the windows in the bedroom earlier, and outside she could hear the buzz of boat motors as they towed skiers around Heart Lake. There was the sound of children playing on the beach and the gentle repetition of water slapping at the pilings of the dock. The breeze was riffling the leaves. They sounded like the petticoats of women gathering on the lawn for afternoon tea. She thought she could almost hear the sun shine.

Best of all was Sam's even breathing and its warm flutter on her neck.

Everything felt perfect in her world at that moment. Her tiny little world, no bigger than a king-size mattress in a not-so-big room in a Victorian house on the shores of Heart Lake. This was her place in the universe. To share it with Sam . . . Well, that felt like the cherry on the whipped cream on top of perfection.

But she cautioned herself to slow down. Great sex between bygone lovers did not a future make. She knew better than to let herself get carried away by a sizzling climax and its afterglow. What would be, would be.

It was a frustrating philosophy, but Beth couldn't come up with anything better at the moment.

Hard as it was to shunt Sam to the back of her brain, even as she was lying in his arms, she tried. If she kept letting herself be distracted, she'd never get this place up and running.

She needed to call Steve Watt and set up another photo session. And there was the price for the printed brochures to be nailed down. She needed to check back about the Web site. Oh, and she had to call somebody about putting in new windows in her old bedroom. She should have done that yesterday. She should've done a lot of things yesterday, dammit.

Outside the window she heard the distinctive sound of the motor on her father's fishing boat. No fancy schmancy fiberglass for Harry. He used the old wooden rowboat that had belonged to Beth's grandfather, along with its ancient three-horsepower motor that had to be coaxed to life with curses and prayers. The sound grew louder. Soon, she heard him latch the boat to the dock, then whistle as he walked up toward the house.

"He probably caught the limit," Sam said softly, his hand moving over her flank.

Beth laughed. "I didn't know you were awake."

"Just barely. You wiped me out."

"Sorry," she said.

"Don't be. I love it."

"Mm. Me, too." Beth nuzzled her backside closer to his warmth.

It occurred to her that this might be the perfect moment to broach the subject of "us." She was framing her first question when her father shouted from the vicinity of the driveway.

"Linda! Linda, come out here. Hurry."

Beth knew immediately that it wasn't his "Come watch me clean fish" tone. He sounded really upset.

Even Sam seemed to sense that something was amiss. "What's wrong?" he said, levering up on an elbow.

Harry yelled again. "Linda! Beth!" He hurled a few expletives into the air for good measure. That wasn't like him at all.

"I better go see what's wrong." Beth threw the covers back and reached for her clothes, scattered on the floor beside the bed.

Sam tugged on his briefs and jeans, then whipped his shirt over his head.

They raced down the staircase side by side. Beth was out the front door first.

Her father, in his ratty fishing overalls, was pacing back and forth beside his big black Mercedes in the driveway. All four doors were open. All four tires were flat.

"Oh, my God, Daddy."

Harry held up a hand in warning. "Don't come any closer, Bethie. I don't want you to see this."

"What?" she asked.

"Just stay where you are," he told her, then said, "Sam, come here and take a look, will you? There's some kind of dead animal in the backseat."

In spite of her father's warning, Beth rushed forward on Sam's heels.

She stared through the open door of the car. She couldn't tell what kind of animal it was. There was too much blood.

# CHAPTER EIGHTEEN

Beth was only too happy to leave the grisly sight. She met her mother halfway up the lawn.

"You really don't want to see this, Mom," she said, linking her arms through Linda's and turning her back toward the house.

"What? What is it? Your father sounded like the sky was falling."

"Somebody let the air out of the Mercedes' tires and there's a dead animal in the backseat."

"Beth!" Her mother stopped in her tracks. "What's going on around here?"

"I wish I knew."

☆

Harry Simon slapped his battered fishing hat against the leg of his stained overalls. "Goddammit, Sam. What's going on around here?"

"I wish I knew, Harry."

Sam stood with his cell phone to his ear, on hold with

the county cops. He'd already told Harry not to touch the car. It was time for the big boys to investigate. With any luck, there would be fingerprints somewhere on the vehicle.

When the sheriff, Dave Weller, finally got on the line, Sam explained the situation, and Dave said he'd send a team over right away.

"What's going on out there, Sam?" the man asked.

"I wish I knew." Jesus. Sam thought as he broke the connection that he'd said those exact words a hundred times by now.

"They'll be here soon," he told Harry, who was still pacing back and forth as if he were appealing to a jury.

"You're pretty sure this is directed at Beth?" he asked.

"I don't know what else it could be, Harry." Sam shrugged helplessly.

"What about the stuff going on in town? We stopped to pick up a few things at the market, and the checker was going on and on about all the mysterious things disappearing lately. What's with that?"

"I'm pretty convinced that it doesn't have anything to do with the vandalism here at the house," Sam said.

"You're *pretty* convinced, but you're not absolutely sure." Harry was giving him his courtroom squint now. "Is that it?"

"That's it," Sam said, without divulging what he knew. He would've bet a month's pay that Kyle Ferrin was being truthful when he said he didn't have anything to do with the broken windows or the fire. Still, Sam wasn't ready to go all the way and bet the farm.

The man just didn't have a motive to vandalize the Simon house. The stealing . . . sure. He needed something more than lake water and berries to survive. But there was nothing to gain from these vicious acts. In fact, there was a lot to lose. His freedom, for one thing, along with any hope of his daughter's regard.

"Beth needs to go home with you and Linda," Sam said.

"I thought that was the plan."

"Yeah. Well, she managed to talk me out of it a while ago. She's determined to stay here. But she can't." He pointed to the car. "Not after this."

"Agreed," Harry said. "Don't worry, Sam. I'll convince her."

"Good luck," Sam answered.

☆

"Beth . . ."

"No."

"Honey . . ."

"No. No. No. I won't go, Daddy."

Beth sat back in her chair, crossed her arms, then added one more *No* just for good measure. She didn't give a damn if she was acting like a spoiled brat. She'd act like a psychotic chimp or a crazed wildebeest if she had to in order to stay at Heart Lake.

She shot a hard glare across the dinner table at Sam. How dare he sit there so cool and dispassionate after he'd consented earlier to her staying. The least he could do was speak up and offer to protect her.

Suddenly, her mother's voice sounded from the foot of the table. "Bethie, you're coming back to the city with us in the morning, and I don't want to hear another word about it."

It was unusual, if not unheard of, for Linda to insert herself into one of Harry's arguments. Even Harry at his end of the table looked slightly taken aback as Linda continued.

"And do you know why you're coming back to the city with us?" she asked. Without waiting for a reply, she answered her own question. "You're here in this house because of one thing, and one thing only, young lady. My goodwill."

She emphasized her last two words by beating her fist on the polished tabletop hard enough to make the silverware shiver at everyone's places. It wasn't at all like her mother to be so . . . so adamant. So . . . well . . . gonzo. Jeez.

"Mother . . ."

"Be quiet, Beth. I'm not done yet. You might want to consider our arrangement with this house as something like the White House, honey, where people serve at the pleasure of the president."

She paused for a sip of wine. Beth took one, too. She was fairly sure she was going to need some fortification.

"This may not be the White House, Beth, but it's *my* house, inherited from my father, and you no longer have my permission to remain in it. We're locking it up tight tomorrow morning, and no one will be here until I say they can be here."

"Except for Sam," Harry quickly reminded her.

She flung her husband an annoyed little glare. The woman was obviously on a roll and didn't want to be interrupted. "All right. Yes. Except for Sam."

Then her mother returned the full brunt of her stare to Beth. "Do I make myself clear?" she asked.

Beth sat there with her hands fisted in her lap, as angry as she had ever been in her life. More than angry, she was humiliated, especially with Sam as a witness.

It was one thing to be talked to like a six-year-old. It

was something far worse to be told, at the age of thirty-three, that all of your plans and dreams, your vision of the future, your life could be yanked from under your feet like some threadbare rug.

She couldn't even look at Sam. Her eyes were stinging with hot tears, but she'd be damned if she'd cry.

"Beth?" her mother repeated. "Is that clear?"

Swallowing hard, she tried to find her voice.

Then her mother asked again, "Is that clear, young lady?"

"Clear as a laser, Mother."

Beth pushed back from the table and stomped out of the room. If they wanted to treat her like a child, then, by God, she'd damn well act like one.

☆

"Excuse me."

Sam folded his napkin, slid it beneath the rim of his plate, and stood up.

"I had to do that, Sam," Linda said, looking up at him almost apologetically. There were tears in her eyes, and she looked older than she had only a moment earlier. "It's the only way we'll ever get her to leave. And after what happened with Shelby last year, I'm not taking any chances. I will not let my daughter get hurt. I just won't."

Linda's voice was shaking now, which it hadn't done a moment ago during her bravado performance with Beth.

From his end of the table, Harry said, "You did the right thing, Beauty. I'm sure when she thinks about it, Beth will understand. She'll cooperate. Hell, she'll be back here in a week probably once the cops catch this vandal. Right, Sam?"

"I hope so," he said.

Even as he spoke, he was edging toward the dining

room door, eager to follow Beth outside, to make sure she didn't get too far away.

"I'm going to keep an eye on her," he said. "We'll be back soon. Don't worry."

"She'll be fine, Beauty. Come on. I'll help you do the dishes."

Sam heard Harry's quiet words as he rushed through the front hall to the door. He wished he had Harry's confidence that everything would turn out fine.

Beth wasn't on the porch. He hadn't expected her to be there, actually, after witnessing the head of steam building up in her at the table. She would need to put more than a few rooms between herself and her mother after Linda's ultimatum.

He found her on the dock. A tiny figure sitting with her arms hugging her knees and her head bowed. The evening breeze was rippling the hem of her long skirt. The light from the house tinted her blond curls with a touch of gold.

God, he hated to see his Bethie looking so sad.

"What are you doing?" he asked softly. "Taking a long walk off a short pier?"

It was lame, but he'd hoped to make her smile.

She didn't.

"Bethie, sweetheart." He squatted down beside her. "Your mom didn't mean to hurt you. She just wants you to be safe."

She didn't respond, and that's when he realized she couldn't speak because she was crying. It killed him.

All he could do was gather her in his arms and hold her, rocking her slightly to the rhythm of the gentle waves around them, feeling almost like crying himself.

After a long while, she sniffed and snuffled, then raised her head.

"Okay," she said. "I've just used up my self-pity for the next fifteen or twenty years." She sniffed again. "And you know what the worst part of it is, Sam?"

"What?"

"She's right. My mother's absolutely right. It *is* her house. And I *am* here by her indulgence, or generosity, or whatever the hell she said."

"Well . . ." he murmured.

"I never really thought about that before tonight. I never considered that I'd pegged my dreams on something I couldn't depend on. It honest to God never occurred to me that she could simply take it away." She snapped her fingers. "Just like that. Poof. It's all gone."

"I don't think she meant it that way, Beth. All she wants is for you . . ."

"To be safe. I know. I know. I get the point. But that's not the point. The whole house might just as well be built on sand if it can get swept out of my grasp so easily. What's to prevent her from saying 'I don't like the way you're wearing your hair, Beth. Get out of my house.'? Or 'I really hate the color of your nail polish. Please leave.'"

"This is a little different," he said.

"No, it isn't," she snapped. "It's blackmail. Pure and simple."

"Okay. Yeah. It's blackmail," he agreed. "But in this case, it's for your own good."

She planted her hands on his chest and pushed herself out of his arms. "I'm not six years old, Sam. I don't need people telling me what's good or bad for me. Not my mother or my father. And not you. I want to make my own decisions and live my own life."

He sighed. "Well, I can't blame you for that."

Everything she said was true. Linda was resorting to

blackmail. It wasn't fair, and
thought she was in danger.

"Look," he said, "while yo
and your mother can come to s
the house. You could rent it fro
the place."

"I thought about that while
cided I don't want it."

"What?"

"I don't want it," she said crisply. "I want a place that's
all my own."

"Bethie, you love this house."

She looked over his shoulder at the brightly lit mansion.
He could see the lights reflected in her eyes.

"I do love it," she said, her voice tinged with sadness
and leftover tears, "and maybe someday it will belong to
me. But until that time, I need to find a place of my own."

While Sam was trying to wrap his head around this surprising news, Beth stood up, smoothed out her skirt, and
began walking down the middle of the dock, toward the
shore.

She paused and looked back at him. There was just
enough light for him to see a tiny smile perched on her lips.

"Oh, and Sam?"

"What?"

"I'm not going back to Chicago with them. I'm staying
right here."

☆

Twenty minutes later Beth was flinging clothes in a
suitcase while her mother sat like some sort of gargoyle on
the bed and Sam stood in the bedroom doorway glowering.

idea where her father was. Probably hiding out rriage house if he had any sense.

ou can't do this," her mother said.

"Oh, yes, I can." Beth pulled a week's worth of underwear from the top dresser drawer and tossed the garments into the suitcase.

From the moment she had decided to abandon the house and all the familial strings that went with it, something odd had happened to her. She'd started feeling . . . What? Stronger. Happier. Definitely independent. Maybe even a bit like Mary Tyler Moore, tossing her hat in the air as she proclaimed she could make it after all.

She felt great! Liberated! Free!

It was wonderful!

Brushing past Sam, the ogre in the doorway, Beth collected a few essentials from the bathroom and tossed those into her suitcase, too. If her mother glimpsed the little round wheel of birth control pills, Beth didn't care.

"You can't do this," Linda said.

"Yes, I can." She was tempted to add *And you can't stop me*, but that seemed childish.

Her mother looked at Sam. "Isn't there something you can do, Sam?"

He shook his head. "Short of duct tape or handcuffs, there's not a thing I can do, Linda."

"That's kidnapping, Mother."

"Well, it sounds like a good idea to me," her mother shot back. "I wish I had a tranquilizer gun."

"Oh, for Pete's sake. I'm an adult, Mother. I'm entitled to make my own decisions, right or wrong. And I'm going. End of story."

"And just where are you going?" her mother asked.

Good question. The decision to pack up and go hadn't

included a destination. Where indeed was she going? Beth wondered.

She turned to Sam. "Are the Kosters still renting out their little cottage?"

The tiny saltbox cabin was just a few doors away from the Mendenhall place on the north side of the lake. It had been there forever, but Emil and Ottie Koster were too old now to divide their time between their house in Mecklin and the cottage at the lake. Plus they probably needed the rental income that the lake property provided. At least that had been the case a few years ago.

Sam appeared reluctant to answer. That was nearly as good as an answer, but Beth pressed him.

"Are they, Sam?"

"Yeah, as far as I know."

"Do you know if it happens to be occupied this week?" she asked.

"I can't say for sure," he said. "But I don't think there's been anybody there for a while."

"Good." Beth zipped her suitcase. "That's where I'm going, Mother. To the Kosters' place. At least for now. If you need to reach me, I'll have my cell phone."

"This isn't a good idea, Beth. Come back to Chicago with us, if only for a few days. We'll talk about it. I know I said some harsh things about the house being mine, but we'll work something out, honey."

Linda looked as distressed as her daughter had ever seen her. Beth sat next to her and eased an arm around her mother's shoulders. They felt so fragile.

"I'm not doing this because I'm angry, Mother. Not that I wasn't at first. But this is about so much more than that. This is about me finding my own way instead of being so dependent on you and Daddy. It's probably something I should've done a long, long time ago."

Her mother looked wounded, and her voice sounded far away when she asked, "You think that we held you back, Daddy and I?"

Beth shook her head. "No. Oh, no. That's not what I mean at all, Mom. I think I held myself back, actually, for a long, long time. Coming home was always way too easy. It's just time for me to strike out on my own."

Finally, her mother managed to mount a smile. "It's not a bad decision, Bethie. I'm proud of your determination. I only wish you'd postpone it for a while, until all this vandalism stops. I'm just so worried about your safety."

Beth didn't want to go there. She was worried, too, but right now she wasn't going to let some unknown vandals stand in the way of her decision. If that meant she was foolhardy, then so be it. She hugged her mother harder, then stood up and reached for the handle of her suitcase.

"Here." Sam reached out. "Let me take that."

"No, thanks. I've got it."

She could hear him gnash his teeth as she passed him in the doorway.

☆

There was a hitch in her plans. Sam was walking ten feet behind Beth when she dropped her suitcase beside the driveway and swore.

The disabled Mercedes blocked the driveway. The Mecklin cops had fingerprinted it earlier and disposed of the dead possum, but the boys from the Gas Mart hadn't showed up to tow it away. As a result, there was no way Beth could get the Miata out of the garage.

Ha! He almost wished he'd thought of that himself.

She kicked her luggage. "Dammit."

Sam expected to be next. "I'd be happy to give you a ride to the Kosters' place."

She didn't kick him, but she did throw him a withering glare. "No, thanks. This is something I really need to do for myself."

"Aw, Beth. That's just stupid. It's dark and . . ."

"Thank you, Sam. I've got my cell phone if there's any trouble. It's not like I don't know my way around the lake."

Grasping the handle of the suitcase again, she hiked the leather strap of her handbag up her shoulder and started across the lawn to the path that led around the lake.

Funny. He always thought Shelby was the most stubborn of the Simon sisters. He couldn't have been more wrong.

He followed Beth, not close enough to annoy her but close enough to protect her if necessary.

# CHAPTER NINETEEN

When Beth awoke the next morning, she wasn't sure where she was at first. But then her Mary Tyler Moore Moment came back to her — God, what a night! — and she smiled, stretching both arms over her head. She didn't have a single regret.

By the time she and her two-ton suitcase and twenty-pound purse had arrived, Beth didn't think she could've taken one more step. Sam skulked behind her all the way, and once or twice she'd almost broken down and asked for his help, but she was glad she hadn't. It was important, foolishly or not, that she accomplish these first acts of independence alone.

She'd really lucked out when she'd arrived at the Kosters' cottage to find them there doing a bit of light maintenance on the place. Emil and Ottie Koster, both in their eighties, were thrilled to see "the little Simon girl." They welcomed her and Sam, as well, with open arms. The only truly awkward moment came when they assumed that she and Sam were married.

"We always knew you would," Ottie said, doing her best to clap her gnarled hands.

Beth had stood there stunned for a second, not knowing what to say. A mischievous part of her was tempted to hook her arm through Sam's, sigh lovingly, and wax poetic on the joys of married life. Even if she'd wanted to do that, though, she wouldn't have had time because Sam stepped forward immediately and said quite somberly, "We're just good friends, Ottie."

"Oh, well," the elderly woman said, not the least bit ruffled or dissuaded. "There's still plenty of time. Isn't that right, Emil?"

"Time for what?" her husband asked, his hand cupped to his ear.

"Time to get married."

"It's what time?"

"Oh, never mind." She dismissed him with a brusque wave of her hand and turned back toward Beth and Sam. "The old fool can't hear anymore. I don't know why I even bother to talk to him."

So much for the long-term joys of marriage, Beth had thought.

She'd written the Kosters a check for two weeks rental, bid them a loud good night, and immediately afterwards said good night to Sam, who was just then wandering around the small cottage, checking out locks on windows and doors.

"I can stay, if you want," he offered.

Beth had shaken her head. "No, thanks. Tonight I really need to be alone."

He didn't argue but kissed the top of her head then and walked out the door, calling back, "Lock this."

It had been an uneventful night. No vandals attacked.

Her phone only rang twice. The first call was from her father, just to say that he loved her and they'd see her soon. Beth was so relieved that he didn't argue with her about going to Chicago that she almost cried.

The next call, at two in the morning, was from Danny, who always conveniently forgot about the time zones that made it two hours earlier for him. As long as the chiming phone awakened her, Beth took the opportunity to respond. Just long enough to disconnect again. One of these days — and it couldn't come too soon — he just might take the hint and stop calling.

But in spite of not sleeping the whole night through, she felt rested this morning. She even felt energized, enough to bound out of bed and raise the window shade for an early-morning view of Heart Lake from this whole new perspective.

Except once she'd raised the shade, it wasn't the lake that she saw, but Sam, wrapped in a blanket, sound asleep in a chair on the cottage's small front porch. Good grief. She unlocked the window and jerked it up.

"Tell me you haven't been out there all night," she said.

He opened one eye. "Okay. I haven't been out here all night."

"Sam!" She didn't recall that he was half this irritating when they were kids. "Now tell me the truth."

The other eye opened. "Okay. I've been out here all night."

"Why?"

He was in the process of unfolding all six feet of himself from the rather small chair. "I don't know, Beth. It seemed like a good idea at the time."

"You jerk," she muttered. "I don't even have any coffee to fix for you."

"I'll fix some for you. Come over to my place."

She'd rather stay where she was, but if she didn't have her morning coffee, she'd have a throbbing headache in about two hours.

"Okay. Let me just brush my teeth and throw on some clothes."

"You don't have to," he said. He was peering in the window now, ogling her in the sleep T that didn't cover very much. "Hey, just wear that. You're the new-and-improved Beth Simon. What do you care what anybody thinks?"

"I care what I think," she said. "And I think, since you're looking at me like I'm breakfast, I better get dressed, or we'll be getting into trouble before you can even get a pot of water boiled."

"Spoilsport."

☆

Back at his place, Sam jumped in the shower to let the hot water work on the stiff muscles of his neck and the kinks in his shoulders. He used to be able to sleep anywhere — chairs, cramped bunks in the bowels of ships, floors, even on hard ground with a rock for a pillow — and rarely felt the effects the following day.

He decided he was getting old, and that decision led him immediately to another one. The decision he'd been putting off for so long. He had to get back in the military in some capacity. He had to return to what he was good at.

Maybe it was Beth's declaration of independence from her parents that somehow prompted his own decision. Hell. Maybe it was just that he'd had it playing Barney Fife in the backwoods.

While he was toweling off, he made up his mind to call Roy Shearing and take him up on his offer to participate in the Delta Force training program. Then, after he talked to Roy, he needed to talk to Beth.

"Nice ass, Sergeant Mendenhall."

He was so accustomed to living alone that he hadn't closed the bathroom door, and he'd been concentrating so hard he hadn't heard Beth arrive.

Sam turned around, grinning. "You want a piece of it, Miss Simon?"

Her gaze roamed over him appreciatively. When they were kids, Beth used to avert her eyes from his nakedness. Now he loved the boldness of her stare and her smug little grin when she saw that he wanted her.

"I want you, too," she said with a laugh, "but at the moment, I'm lusting for coffee. You will ask me again later, won't you?"

"Oh, yeah."

She started the coffee while he shaved. He pondered his face in the mirror and vowed that he wasn't going to lose this woman twice.

When he walked into the kitchen, the smell of fresh coffee was delicious, as was the sight of Beth, bent over in her short khaki shorts as she inspected the contents of his refrigerator.

"Nice ass," he said, coming up behind her.

"How can you not have at least butter, eggs, and bread in here?" she grumbled.

"There's milk."

She was opening the carton as he spoke, and crinkling her nose as she smelled it. "Oh, God, Sam." She turned the carton to check the date. "This expired over a week ago."

"That's okay. We both take our coffee black, right?"

Beth closed the door of the refrigerator and poured the sour milk down the drain. "You should take better care of yourself," she said. "Didn't you learn anything about nutrition in the Army?"

He answered while he poured coffee into two chipped mugs. "Yeah, I did, actually. But it was mostly which plants and berries were poisonous, and which bugs and grubs you should chew and which you should swallow whole. How to suck water from a cactus. That sort of stuff."

She was looking at him with a strange expression on her face. Sam couldn't tell if she was about to throw up or laugh. When she took the mug from his hand, she reached up to caress his cheek.

"When are you going to tell me about all that time in the Army?" she asked.

It was his least favorite question, so he gave her his standard reply. "Most of it's classified, honey. There's not a lot to tell."

He settled across from her at the round oak table that had been in this kitchen forever. They'd sat here as kids, playing Old Maid, Monopoly. This was where they'd shared their first beer.

Beth was staring into her coffee as if something were there she was trying to read. "Sam," she said softly.

"Hm?"

Her eyes locked onto his. "Tell me about your marriage."

He'd been wrong earlier when he chose his Army career as his least favorite subject. *This* was his least favorite subject by far. Unfortunately, it wasn't classified.

"I got drunk. I got a woman pregnant. I married her. She and the baby both died."

What his simple sentences omitted was how sad and desperate he was the night he got drunk, the way the sex that night left him almost physically sick with longing for Beth, his shame and his guilt for his contribution to Susie's death, his tiny son's death.

Across the table, Beth looked a little pale. But she pressed on. He sensed the topic was important to her.

"Did you love her, Sam?"

"No, Bethie. I didn't. Marrying her was just the right thing to do."

"How did she die?"

"There were complications with the pregnancy. Her blood pressure couldn't be stabilized. She was . . ." His throat tightened. "She was just eighteen."

"Oh, Sam. I'm so sorry."

He couldn't say it out loud. He never would. Not to Beth or anyone. But the first emotion he felt when Susie coded was relief. Maybe it was a natural reaction, considering the circumstances of the marriage, but if there was a hell, that would be the reason Sam would be going there. He'd gotten on with his life, but he'd never forgiven himself for that feeling that afternoon.

"I never meant to hurt you, Beth," he said. "I was a stupid kid, and I made a terrible mistake that cost two lives. I regret it every day."

She sipped her coffee, but never averted her eyes from his. "You did hurt me, Sam. I only wish I'd known the circumstances all those years ago." She sighed. "This will probably sound weird, but I honestly wish I could've been with you then and helped you through it. I'm sorry, too."

He felt a certain amount of closure, something he'd always longed for. And if they hadn't fully forgiven each other, he sensed that they'd at least begun. Sam lifted his coffee cup.

"Here's to a future better than our past, sweetheart," he said.

Beth smiled and clinked her mug against his. "I"ll drink to that."

She put her coffee down but continued to smile at him. "You know what I'd like to do today?"

Sam cocked his head and grinned. "Is there a mattress involved?"

"Well, that, too," she said. "But first I'd like to go back to our tree house. Bear or no bear. I don't care. I really want to see it again."

"We could do that." He didn't want to deny her any-thing, and he quickly concluded that Beth's meeting Kyle Ferrin might be helpful in bringing the older man back into his daughter's life. "Before we go to the tree house, though, I need to pick up some stuff in town."

"Works for me. I'll get some staples to fill the Kosters' bare cupboards, and I want to talk to Janet Hamlin, too."

"The real estate agent?"

"Uh-huh. I can't stay at Emil and Ottie's place indefi-nitely, and I want to find the perfect little place to turn into the new-and-improved Heart Lake Manor."

"Okay, then." He gulped his coffee and stood up. "I'll jog over to the big house, get the jeep, and pick you up in about ten minutes."

☆

Beth saw the poor Mercedes in the parking lot at the Gas Mart as they drove into Shelbyville. Sam told her they'd picked it up, and at the same time delivered a rental car for her parents to drive back to Chicago. They were pulling out of the driveway just as Sam arrived to get his jeep.

Of course, everybody in town already knew about the vandalism and about the bloody creature in the backseat. While Sam paid a visit to Blanche and his office, Beth dropped in next door at Janet Hamlin's realty agency. Janet was just a few years older than Beth. She'd taken over the agency when her parents left Michigan for the Arizona desert.

The first thing out of Janet's mouth was, "I heard about your father's car. Eeuww. What was in the back seat? A possum? A raccoon?"

"Beats me," Beth said cheerfully, then quickly changed the subject. "So, what's for sale, Janet? Any interesting waterfront property?"

"Who's looking?"

"Me."

Janet plucked off her reading glasses and dropped them on her desk. "You? Whatever for?"

*None of your business.* "Oh, I'm just looking, maybe thinking of expanding my empire. So, is anything up for sale?"

"Not at Heart Lake," she said, pulling some folders from a file. "But there's a wonderful little place at Blue Lake. Do you remember where the Eversoles used to live?"

"Vaguely."

Janet slid a photo across her desk, and Beth immediately remembered the place. It was like a little Swiss chalet. A bit on the small side, but absolutely adorable. She might even be able to afford it.

"When can I see it?" Beth asked.

"Anytime. I've got the key. Just say when."

"Well, I've got plans this afternoon . . ."

No sooner had she said that than her plans ambled through Janet's door. It was hard to ignore the fact that Janet's entire demeanor changed just then. Once again, she whipped off her reading glasses, except this time it was out of vanity rather than surprise.

"Sam! Well, if it isn't Shelbyville's finest." She actually batted her eyes, which Beth didn't even know was possible. "We've missed you lately."

Beth wondered who *we* were, but then figured it was just Janet using the royal "we" to disguise her own powerful attraction to the local, handsome, long arm of the law. The man was a hunk. No question about it.

But he was *her* hunk, dammit. And Beth didn't care if the whole town knew. She stood and walked to greet him, lifting her face for his kiss.

Without a second's hesitation, Sam lowered his head to kiss her as if he, too, didn't give a damn who witnessed it or turned them in to the gossip mill.

And for that moment, at least for Beth, the world around the two of them disappeared. It was just Sam and Beth. Beth and Sam. It felt so damn right.

"All right, you two," Janet said with a touch of irritation in her voice. "This is a real estate agency. I'm not running a dating service."

Sam lifted his head, but never took his eyes off Beth. "Let's go," he said.

She nodded. "I'll come back later to talk about that property, Janet."

"Anytime, Beth. I'm always here," the woman said, then added almost under her breath, "Not that everyone notices."

As they crossed the street to the market, Sam asked, "What property?"

"There's a cottage for sale at Blue Lake. The Eversoles' place. Remember it?"

"Yeah." His forehead furrowed. "It's not in very good shape, Beth. That place needs a lot of work."

She just smiled. If it was run-down, maybe she really could afford it. "I prefer to think of that as tender loving care, Sam."

"Yeah. Well, we'll see," he said.

"Yeah. I guess we will."

☆

Sam's mood darkened after that. He realized that all the plans he was beginning to make for himself and Beth were pretty one-sided. Hell, they were completely one-sided. She was making her own plans, and they didn't appear to include him. At any rate, she wasn't asking his advice.

But she apparently wasn't asking for her sister's advice, either, which struck Sam as a good thing since it was Shelby's advice that ripped them apart in the first place.

He wandered along behind her in the little two-aisle market, every once in a while consulting Kyle's list. Peanut butter. Saltines. Sardines. Canned salmon. The guy was definitely not a gourmet.

Last on the list was a pack of Marlboro Reds, and when Sam asked the checker for those, Beth gave him the Hairy Eyeball.

"They're for a friend," he said.

"Who?"

"You'll see."

# CHAPTER TWENTY

Deep in the woods, Beth let go of a gigantic honeysuckle branch in order to slap at a mosquito. There was a *thwap* just behind her, and Sam hissed a little curse.

"Sorry," she said, realizing she'd managed to whip him once again with foliage. "I need a machete or something. This underbrush seems a lot worse than it was before. Anyway, shouldn't you be walking in front of me?"

"I like the view from here," he said, a deep chuckle reverberating in his voice.

"What about the bear?"

"You'll meet him in a few minutes." Grinning, he took her hand and led her deeper into the woods.

Beth could only shake her head and walk along. She knew it was useless to ask Sam questions about subjects he didn't want to discuss. One of those subjects was his plan for the future. She had peppered him with questions on their drive from Shelbyville back to the lake, and he'd managed to evade them all by responding to her questions with questions of his own. She always thought that was the trick that shrinks used, but apparently the Army used the same technique.

It was frustrating. How or why Sam's plans affected her own, she wasn't willing to say, even to herself. She'd just struck out on her own, for heaven's sake, but already it seemed that her course was dependent on someone else.

Beth resented that. And yet . . .

Now that they seemed to have found each other again, how could she be happy without him? And what was this deal with the bear?

Just ahead of her, she heard the distinctive ring of Sam's cell phone. He had slipped it into a backpack, along with the items he'd picked up at the market, so now he shrugged out of the shoulder straps, unzipped the bag, and fished out the phone.

Beth gazed at him while he talked to whoever was on the other end of the line. She also peeked into the backpack. Oh, God. If this was his idea of a picnic lunch — crackers and Skippy and sardines — she was going to have to quickly reindoctrinate him to the finer points of cuisine. The man had obviously been living alone way too long judging from the sour milk in his fridge and the contents of the backpack.

"Okay. Bye."

She looked up at his face, and immediately asked, "What's wrong?"

"Something," he murmured as he chewed on his lower lip.

"Like what?"

"The Mecklin cops got a hit on the fingerprints on your father's car. A local kid by the name of Kevin Lassiter."

"Doesn't sound familiar," Beth said.

"That's probably because he's spent most of his twenty years in juvenile detention or the slammer."

"Oh, jeez. That doesn't sound good. But it's good that they know who did it, right?"

"Maybe." He still looked strangely worried for someone who'd presumably just gotten good news.

"Then what's not good about it?" she asked.

"After they got the hit on his prints," Sam said, "they went to his place to pick him up."

"And they got him?"

"Yeah." He nodded. "Sort of."

Well, that was even better news, Beth thought. They picked up the vandal. That was great news. Except . . . "What do you mean, sort of?" she asked.

"He was dead."

☆

As far as Sam could tell, Kyle and Beth were hitting it off pretty well. Once she got over the shock of who "The Bear" was and after she got past her initial standoffishness because he'd abandoned Kimmy when she was a baby, Beth actually seemed to develop a profound curiosity about his wanderings after his service in Vietnam and his reasons for not coming home.

For his part, Kyle appeared not only grateful for the company, but also for a sympathetic ear while he jabbered and ate sardines on crackers and smoked a couple of Marlboros.

Sam managed to tune out the conversation while he stood aside and went over what Sheriff Dave Weller had told him on the phone. The Mecklin cops seemed ready to close the file on Kevin Lassiter, alleged vandal and convicted hophead. Their theory was that he'd been shot in a drug deal gone bad. They were going to round up the usual suspects, naturally; but nobody seemed surprised that the guy was dead or too motivated to find the shooter who'd eliminated one of Mecklin County's ongoing problems.

"Good riddance to bad rubbish," Dave Weller had said. "But don't quote me on that, Sam."

If Kevin Lassiter truly was the vandal who'd targeted Beth, then the danger was past. But it didn't make sense to Sam that someone Beth didn't even know would make such an effort to make her life miserable. What was the point?

"Kyle?" He walked over to the campfire where he and Beth were sitting. "Let me ask you a question."

"Sure," the older man said.

Sam squatted. "On your forays around the lake and into town, did you ever run across somebody who looked like he was up to no good? There's been some vandalism going on lately, especially at the Simon place."

Kyle smiled. "That's a nice place your family's got," he said to Beth. "I knew your mother way back when. Is she still a looker?"

"She is," Beth said. "Even prettier now than when she was young."

The man nodded and seemed to go into a nostalgic reverie for a moment until Sam pulled him back.

"Have you noticed anybody like that, Kyle? Anybody suspicious?"

He ran his hand across his unshaven, grizzled chin for a moment, then said, "You know, maybe I have."

"Tell me," Sam said.

"There was a fella I saw once coming out of the trees behind the Simon house. This would've been, oh, maybe two weeks ago. Something like that. And then I saw him again a few days after that, getting into a car on the black-top, right there at the turnoff for the Simons' road."

"What'd he look like?" Dave Weller had inadvertently given Sam a brief description of Kevin Lassiter when he referred to him as "that skinny, curly-haired weasel." Sam was almost holding his breath, hoping Kyle would confirm that Kevin was the vandal.

"Well, lemme think," he said, scratching his jaw again. "He was on the young side. I'd say anywhere from thirty to thirty-five. Tall. A well-built young fella. Like he worked out a lot, you know."

"What about his hair?" Sam asked.

Kyle looked at Beth now. "About the same color as Beth's here. Not curly, though. It was long and straight. He wore it pulled back in one of those whatchacallits. Not a braid like my daughter. Loose like."

"A ponytail?" Beth asked.

"Yeah. That's it. A ponytail. I only saw him those two times."

Well, that blew the Kevin Lassiter theory all to hell, Sam thought.

"Thanks, Kyle. I'm going to see if the Mecklin cops can identify the guy from your description. I won't mention that it was you who told me."

"I appreciate that, Sam. Thanks."

☆

While Sam sauntered away to make his phone call, Beth only half listened to Kyle. Instead, she was thinking about the description of the man Kyle had seen.

Thirtyish. Well-built. A blond ponytail. It sounded like Danny.

Of course, it also sounded like quite a few young men

in this rural area, where they tended to bulk up and wear their hair long.

She thought about telling Sam, but then she decided against it. After all, she'd lived with Danny for over a year. She'd moved to San Francisco with him in the hope that they would eventually get married. Sam didn't need to hear that. She didn't want to provoke any unnecessary jealousy about her past from the man she hoped — maybe, just maybe — might be her future.

She was thinking about Kimmy, too. If she and Sam adhered to Kyle's wishes, and if Kimmy ever found out, would she blame them for not telling her the truth about her father? Or would her friend be glad that the man who'd abandoned her and her mother seemed too ashamed to make contact? Would she delight in hearing that he was homeless and suffering a pitiful fate?

"Tell me about my daughter," Kyle said at just that moment. "Do you know her pretty well? What's she like?"

"She's lovely."

"I've seen her. I know she's good-looking. But what's she *like?*"

"Well . . ." Beth wanted to be accurate. "She's a good friend. She's generous and sympathetic. The sort of person who'd drop whatever she was doing in order to help a friend. She's a very strong person, too. Her character, I mean."

"She sounds a lot like her mother," Kyle said wistfully. He stared into the little campfire, poked it with a stick for a minute, then said, "I wonder what would've happened if I'd come home all those years ago."

"Oh, Kyle." Beth's throat tightened. She knew exactly how the poor man felt. It was hard to get away from what-ifs.

She could hardly bear to think about them anymore,

hers and Sam's. And the worst what if of all was what if they didn't make it work this time?

It was a relief when Sam walked back to the fire, and said, "They're going to look for the guy you described, Kyle. Thanks."

"Sure. I'll keep an eye out for him, too."

"Great," Sam said. He held out his hand to Beth. "We should probably head back to the lake."

It was only then that she realized it was getting late. She grabbed his hand and let him whisk her to her feet. Kyle stood up, too.

"I'll be back in a day or two, Kyle," Sam said, "if you want to make another list for me."

"Yeah." He laughed sheepishly. "Could you tell all those folks I borrowed from that I didn't mean any harm?"

"You mean you want Sam to tell them your name?" Beth asked him.

"Yes, ma'am, I do. I'm about 99 percent sure that I'll stick around here permanently. Don't know where I'll live or what I'll do. But I guess all that will fall rightly into place. Things usually do."

"I think that's wonderful," Beth said. She reached out her hand and couldn't refrain from hugging him, even though he smelled like . . . well . . . a bear.

"Yeah, well . . ." Kyle demurred. "On the off chance I change my mind, don't say anything to my daughter yet. Promise me that, will you? Both of you?"

She and Sam promised, then waited while Kyle made a list. Beth looked at it and shivered before she put it in her pocket. Good grief. The man really had a thing for sardines.

☆

Once more, Sam followed Beth through the woods. He hadn't told her earlier, but the reason he chose to walk behind her wasn't simply to ogle her shapely ass, but rather to keep watch over his shoulder without causing her alarm. If anybody was going to jump them, it would be from behind, not a frontal attack.

"That's good news about Kyle planning to stick around, don't you think?" she said, with a quick glance back at him.

"I guess. How do you think Kimmy will react?"

She lifted her shoulders in a shrug. "I don't have a clue. But maybe, if she accepts the relationship, he can move in with her."

"I've been thinking about that," Sam said. "He can't keep living in the tree house, and until he finds a job, he's not going to be able to afford much. I've been thinking about offering him my cabin."

Beth stopped and turned around. "Oh, Sam. That's really generous of you. But are you sure you want to live with Kyle? Not that he's not a nice guy, but . . . Well, what if he moves in, and you can't stand him? Plus, your place is pretty small."

And here he was, Sam thought, on the brink of his news, just as he'd planned it when he brought this subject up. He drew in a deep breath, let it out slowly, and said, "There's something I need to discuss with you, Bethie."

Beth blinked, as he knew she would, and her mouth went a bit slack. Her face paled just a little. It must've been his serious, almost funereal tone of voice that suddenly unsettled her. Sam instantly regretted broaching the subject, but it seemed too late to turn back. Don't blow this, he told himself.

"What did you want to discuss?" she asked him.

"I'm considering leaving Michigan, Bethie. I've had some job offers. One in Washington D.C. A couple of others. The Army wants me back in an advisor capacity at Fort Bragg in North Carolina."

"Oh."

He just stood there and watched her lovely face as the news sank in, and her expression changed from surprised to distressed. She seemed to flinch at first, but then she worked up a ragged little smile. "Well, that's great news, Sam. I'm . . . I'm happy for you."

"Liar," he said.

She flinched again. "That's not fair."

"But it's true."

"Well, what am I supposed to say?" The color came back to her face. "Do you want me to say I'm crushed? I'm devastated."

"Yes." It was what he wanted to hear.

"Oh, Sam. How else would I feel? We just haven't had enough time . . ." Her voice drifted off. It simply escaped her.

"Well, you could always come with me." He said the words as if the notion had just occurred to him. Mr. Casual. Staff Sergeant Cool. Just a casual remark off the top of his head when what he ought to be doing was begging her on bended knee.

And if it came to that, by God, he would.

"What?" Her voice was a small, scratchy croak now. She was rubbing her upper arms, as if she were cold.

"I said you could always come with me to D.C. or North Carolina. It'd be fun."

"Fun! FUN!!"

"Well . . ."

"Do you think I walked out on my parents and my family home because I wanted to have fun?"

"I didn't mean that, Beth."

The color increased on her face. A furious red. There were blue sparks in her eyes.

Okay. This wasn't going quite the way he'd expected it to.

"What I meant was . . ."

"I don't care what you meant, Sam. You're leaving. Fine. It would've been nice if you'd given us a little more time. But, hey . . . It's your life. Do what you want. Go where you want. Just don't talk to me about it anymore. Not right now anyway."

"Beth . . ."

"Just shut up."

Saying that, she whirled around and stomped off through the underbrush, leaving Sam standing there looking the way she'd looked just a moment ago — blinking, slack-jawed, pale.

Apparently it was time for Plan B.

He wished he had one.

☆

By the time Beth neared her little rental cottage, she was practically running to keep as far ahead of Sam as she possibly could.

*You could always come with me.*

What was that? A casual invitation to a pal? A wishy-washy commitment? Or worse, a lukewarm proposal?

She was so angry she could hardly see for the hot red blur in front of her.

How could she possibly say yes to such a lame suggestion? And if she said no, was it going to be déjà vu all over again? Would Sam go south and impregnate the first Southern belle he could find just to spite her?

God. She fished her key out of her pocket, unlocked the cottage door, and locked it behind her. If Sam wanted to talk anymore, he'd have to shout through a window or break down her door.

Still fueled by anger, she stomped around the little place, checking locks, wrenching curtains closed, and finally turning off all the lights. Then, not caring whether the sun had gone down or not, whether she'd eaten or not, whether she lived or not, she flopped into bed.

Just when she'd taken the biggest, boldest step in her life . . . Just when she'd gripped her own fate by the scruff of its neck . . . Just when she'd belted out several choruses of "My Way" . . .

*You could always come with me.*

Uh-huh. Right. Sure. Why not? Why not just drop my whole life and all my plans to pick up and follow after you? Countless women have preceded me in following their menfolk. Whither thou goest and all that shit. Why should I be any different?

When her phone chimed, she answered it without a glance at the little lit ID screen. She was sure it was Sam, intent on explaining himself. Good. She was tired of screaming inside her own head. She'd yell at Sam for a while — *How could you be so insensitive? Why are you rushing this? What about my plans?* — then feel a lot better. Or a whole lot worse.

But the voice that responded after she growled hello wasn't Sam's. It was Danny.

"Hey, babe. You sound upset."

"Danny." She said his name with such deep resignation, it seemed to come from the soles of her feet.

"Aw, Beth. What's wrong? I wish I were there to take care of you."

For a second she almost forgot how this man took care of her — with his fists.

"I love you, babe," he said. "Come back to San Francisco and let me take care of you. You've had nothing but problems since you left."

"Tell me about it," she replied mournfully.

"Nobody there loves you the way I do."

Lying in bed, Beth nodded wanly. She'd never disputed his love for her. Just his method of showing it. She didn't love him anymore, if she ever did; but maybe, just maybe they could be friends.

"I'll be okay," she said.

God, she sounded pitiful, so she sat up and tried to infuse some optimism in her voice.

"Things always seem worse in the dark," she said. "It'll all look better tomorrow. So, how's Frisco? Is the sun about to set? Tell me what it looks like."

"Okay. Let me walk over to the window. Oh, wow. It's gorgeous. I wish you were here to see it, babe. There are brilliant bands of deep orange, just flecked with bits of fuchsia and . . ."

While Danny described the colors of the sky as only a painter could, Beth could only think it was a measure of her own desperation that she was actually having a conversation with her ex-boyfriend. And after about ten minutes, she said, "It's been good talking to you, Danny" just before she clicked off. It was also a measure of how angry she was at Sam.

Not wanting to just lie in bed and fume anymore, Beth got up and turned on the Kosters' small television. Thank god they had cable, she thought as she surfed across the channels.

Old movies. Bonanza. News. More news. Infomercials.

Then a weather map caught her eye. It depicted big, blue raindrops all down the West Coast from Washington state to the Mexican border. The weatherman pointed to the pictures, and intoned, "Out in San Francisco, they haven't seen the sun for five days."

She stared at the screen, bewildered. Why in the world would Danny lie about something as innocuous as a sunset?

It just didn't make any sense.

# CHAPTER TWENTY-ONE

It didn't make sense at all.

Unless . . .

Oh, God.

Beth grabbed her phone and punched in Sam's number. "Can you come over?" she asked as soon as he picked up. She hadn't been aware of the depth of her own anxiety until she heard the tremble in her voice.

It seemed as if he knocked on her door a mere two seconds later. Oh, Lord. He hadn't been sleeping in the chair on her patio again, had he?

He'd hardly crossed the threshold before he pulled her into his arms and held her so tightly it hurt.

"I will not lose you a second time, Beth. I swear to God. I'll do whatever I have to do. If you need more time, you've got it. If you want to stay here, I'll stay here. Whatever you want, Bethie."

Well, so much for yelling at him or wringing an apology out of him. Beth almost laughed. She hugged him back as hard as she could.

"I don't want to lose you either, Sam. We have to work this out somehow. We just have to."

"God, I hope so, baby."

She stood there a moment, wholly content in his hard, all-encompassing embrace, wishing the rest of the world would just disappear for the next fifty or sixty years and leave them here, holding each other like this. She wished they were the only two people on the planet. Only they weren't. And then she remembered why she'd called him.

"Sam, I think I know who the vandal is."

He tipped his head back to look at her face. "Who?" he asked.

"I think it's my ex-boyfriend, Danny Eiler."

"Tell me why you suspect him."

Sam led her to the sofa and sat beside her, holding her hand, listening intently as she told him about Danny's resemblance to the man Kyle had described and the sunset in San Francisco episode that had just taken place.

"He said he was calling you from San Francisco?"

She nodded. "He's been calling me ever since I left a couple weeks ago. The area code shows up on caller ID. So, of course, I assumed that's where he was calling from."

"He could be anywhere, Beth, and his number would still show up as the same."

"It just never occurred to me. Plus he was always giving me weather reports and telling me how beautiful the bay looked and how the sun was shining on the bridge. Stuff like that." She slapped her hand on the sofa cushion. "Man, I guess I fell for that like a stupid ton of bricks."

"You still don't know that he's here in Shelbyville, Beth."

"Yes, I do. I can feel him."

She didn't appreciate the fact that Sam made a small, dismissive cluck with his tongue.

"I'm not kidding, Sam. And, unfortunately, neither is Danny. He's always said he'd do anything to get me to come back to him. Maybe he thinks scaring me away from Michigan will do it. I don't know what the hell he thinks, actually. He's just crazy. He doesn't have much self-control. At least not with me."

Sam was quiet for a moment, then he asked, "Is that why you left him?"

Something in his voice was so sad. Beth imagined her own voice had been tinged the same way, with an identical sadness, when she'd inquired about his marriage. How she hated even saying Danny's name to the man sitting beside her.

Why did she leave him? Why did she leave every man she'd been with in the past sixteen years? Because he wasn't Sam.

"I left him because he hit me," she said.

Sam's grip on her hand tightened significantly. He breathed a rough curse. "Okay. Here's what we're going to do. I'm going to call Dave Weller, the sheriff in Mecklin, and have him put some of his guys on this. Do you have a photo of this asshole?"

She shook her head. "No, but he was around here for nearly a year, helping me renovate the house. Plenty of people knew him."

"Good. That'll help. First thing tomorrow I'll snoop around town and ask some questions. I want you to call Kimmy and have her come over and stay here with you while I'm gone. Will you do that?"

Beth nodded again. When she'd imagined the vandal was just some unknown troublemaker, it had been easy to resist

Sam's demands. Now that the vandal might be Danny, she was terrified. Who knew to what lengths he might go in order to keep her from being with anybody else?

"You need to be careful, too, Sam. Really. When I said Danny is crazy, I didn't mean goofy or incompetent crazy. I meant mean and vicious crazy."

"Don't worry about me," he said.

Her phone rang just then, and when Beth started to get up to answer it, Sam pulled her back. "Let me get it. Where's your phone?"

She pointed toward the bedroom. "It's on the table beside the bed."

Following him, she couldn't help but wish that they were rushing into her bedroom for a completely different reason. Sam grabbed the phone and looked at the Caller ID. He scowled as he hit the answer button.

"Hello." His voice sounded deeper by at least an octave. Deeper and dangerous. "Who is this?" Finally, he clicked off. "That was him. He hung up without saying anything."

"Coward," Beth muttered. That didn't seem satisfactory, so she added "Asshole" under her breath.

"Grab what you need for tonight, Bethie. I want you to stay at my place. The locks are better, and you'll be safer there. Come on. Let's go."

It took her all of a minute to gather up a few things. She felt safer already, in the curve of Sam's arm as they walked to his cabin.

☆

After alerting the county cops, Sam did what he usually did to work off tension. He cleaned his gun. For a while, the rote mechanics of the effort distracted him from the rage he felt for anyone who would hit or in any way hurt his Beth.

He wondered if Shelby had known about the situation last year when she stayed at the lake, and, if so, why she didn't tell him that Beth was in trouble. Hell. Maybe she did try to tell him, and he'd just ignored her because of his longtime grudge against her.

Maybe it didn't matter. He knew about the abuse now, and that meant he had to do something about it. He hoped he got the opportunity. And sooner rather than later.

Beth came up behind him and draped her arms around his neck. "I'm afraid of guns," she said.

"Only because you don't know how to use them. I'll teach you one of these days." He tilted his head to touch her arm with his cheek. "Did you call Kimmy?"

"Yes. She's happy to come spend some time with me. She said she'd even clean your cabin while she was here. For free!"

"She doesn't have to do that."

"I know. I think she just feels more comfortable when she's busy. Anyway, I told her we'd pick her up at eight tomorrow morning. Is that okay?"

"Works for me," he said. "We'll pick her up, then I'll drop the two of you off here. After that, I'll go into town and see what I can find out about Danny." Just saying the creep's name left a sour taste in his mouth.

"What do you think we should do about Kimmy and Kyle?" she asked. "Should I tell her?"

"Dunno. That's a tough call. What if it were your father, coming back after all these years? Would you want to know?"

"Absolutely. No question about it. It's just not fair, having facts withheld. My god, Sam. If I'd known about your letters . . ." She exhaled a sigh that seemed full of both frustration and regret. "If I had read your letters . . . Well, who knows what might've happened with us?"

Sam put down the oily cloth he'd been using to clean his weapon. He reached up to clasp her arms. "Well, baby, either we'd have six kids by now, or you'd have filed for divorce at the age of eighteen or nineteen. I don't suppose we'll ever know."

"No. You're probably right. When I was seventeen, all I knew how to do was bake chocolate-chip cookies." She laughed. "You probably would've gotten kicked out of the Army for being overweight."

Sam turned in his chair and pulled her onto his lap. "You know what I think?" he whispered against her ear.

"What?"

"I think we would've had some rough spots, no doubt about it, but in spite of them, I think we would've lived happily ever after."

"And now?" she asked him.

"I think the very same thing. I think if we manage to get this right, we'll live happily ever after. In spite of some rough spots."

"Sort of our own postponed fairy tale."

"Sort of," he said. "You know, if we'd gotten married back then, I never would have gone into Special Ops because I'd have been too worried about the effect on you."

"Then what would you have done instead?"

"I don't know. The main reason I enlisted was to finance a college education after my duty ended. Something I had in the back of my brain way back then was going to law school after the Army, and maybe, if I was very lucky, setting up shop in your father's firm."

Beth gasped. "I never knew that."

"Well, it seemed like a pipe dream at the time, so I guess I never mentioned it."

"I wish you had, Sam."

"Actually, I'm glad it didn't happen. I never would have made a good attorney."

"Why?"

"I don't think I have the patience. I don't know. Maybe it was the Army training that beat the patience out of me. But it seemed a whole lot more effective in the end to shoot the bad guys instead of plea-bargaining them."

She laughed nervously. "That's not why you're cleaning the gun, is it?"

"No." His response was probably too adamant because Beth immediately tried to escape his lap. He pulled her back, and said, "No. That's not why I'm cleaning the gun. That's just an old habit. Something I do to relax."

She wasn't buying his excuse apparently because the next words out of her mouth were, "But would you use it on somebody? I mean, if you had the chance?"

"If I had the chance?" Jesus. What did she think of him? That he was a trained, but barely restrained assassin? "I'm a civilian now. I'd only use my gun in self-defense or to defend someone else. That's the law, Beth."

"I know that. I was just curious about a carryover effect from the military, where killing is an occupation."

"Defense is an occupation," he said. "Killing is a last resort."

She studied his face intently, then asked, "Did you?"

"Did I ever kill anyone?"

She nodded.

"Yes."

"But you'll never tell me about it, will you?"

"No, I won't. That's not a part of me, of my past, that I

can share with you." He was about to fall back on his old, reliable Anyway-it's-classified excuse, but Beth deserved more.

"I was a good soldier, Bethie. I helped a lot of people. I saved a lot of lives. But in order to do that, I took some lives when it was necessary, when there was no other way to accomplish a task."

"Does it bother you, looking back, remembering?" she asked.

"I'm proud that I saved some lives. I'm not proud of taking them, but, no, it doesn't bother me. I don't have any regrets or remorse. I don't feel guilty. Does that bother you?"

She shook her head. "No. I'm proud of everything you've done, Sam." She laughed softly, wrapping her arms around him, nuzzling her face into his neck. "Even the things I don't know about. You risked your life for the sake of others. God knows you have the scars to prove it. That's a damned fine thing, in my book. In anybody's book."

"Well, then . . ." He grinned. "How about letting me finish up with this firearm, and then how would you feel about going to bed with a trained assassin?"

"Mm." She snagged his earlobe with her teeth. "Are you going to do kinky things to me?"

He laughed. "They didn't cover that in assassin school, I'm afraid."

"Damn."

"They did, however, teach me how to improvise."

☆

The next morning, after they picked up Kimmy and Sam left the two of them at his cabin with strict instructions to stay there, Beth immediately started feeling guilty for concealing the truth from her friend.

Kimmy had taken one look at Sam's little kitchen and immediately rolled up her sleeves and grabbed a can of cleanser, muttering about men, pigs, and the general state of the male-dominated world.

Beth sat at the cluttered kitchen table, sipping some of the nasty coffee Sam had fixed at dawn. "That's a bit harsh, isn't it?" she asked. "I like men." Actually, she liked one man in particular. Sam. Actually, she loved him.

Kimmy was wringing out a sponge in the sink, looking like she wished it were somebody's neck. "Harsh? I don't think so. I don't know, Beth. Maybe it's because I didn't have a father. Men just seem like alien beings to me."

Beth's guilt meter rose about a hundred degrees. It just wasn't right, withholding this information from Kimmy. Not when her father was a mile or two away right then. Not when he might make such an important difference in her life.

How to begin?

"Kimmy, if I knew something about your father, would you want me to tell you?"

Her hands seemed to freeze on the damp sponge. "What do you mean? What do you know?"

"Well . . ." Now that she'd begun, Beth wasn't quite so sure it was the right thing to do.

"If you know something . . . If you know anything, Beth Simon, you tell me, and you tell me now." Kimmy yanked out a chair and planted herself beside Beth. "The truth. Good or bad. I need to hear it. I'm entitled to the truth."

"Yes, you are." She sucked in a breath, and began. "I know where he is. Your father."

☆

In Shelbyville, when you wanted to know things, there was no place better than the post office. As soon as Sam walked in, Thelma glared a few daggers at him.

"Have you found my flag, sonny?"

"No, but I'm working on it, Thelma."

Her response was a snort.

Sam leaned against her counter. "Let me ask you something. What do you know about a man named Danny Eiler?"

"Plenty." She crossed her arms and tilted her head. "What do you want to know?"

"For starters," he said, "everything."

"Well, let's see. He was a long-haired, shifty-eyed son of a bitch. Pardon my French."

"How so?"

"For one thing, he used to come in and pick up Beth Simon's mail, and before he was out the door he'd have gone through it. I used to see him sit in his car out there, reading letters that had been addressed to her. I called him on it, but he denied it, of course."

"Did you ever tell Beth?"

"Durn tootin'. She said she'd talk to him about it, but I doubt she ever did. If you ask me, she was afraid of him."

"Does he have any family around here?"

"None that I know of. He just showed up a couple years ago when Beth advertised for a painter. If you ask me, he wasn't even a good one. I mean, who paints a house gray and blue and purple and gold? Old Orvis Shelby must be spinning in his grave."

"When was the last time you saw him?"

"Orvis?"

"No. Danny."

"Oh. I guess that would've been just before they left for California. I haven't seen him since then, thank heaven."

Sam was hoping the postmistress had seen him skulking around town lately. That would've made his job a lot easier. Hell, even Barney Fife caught a break once in a while.

"You're not saying you think Danny's the culprit who's been taking things, are you, Sam? I wouldn't put it past him."

Sooner or later, he was going to have to out Kyle Ferrin. But this wasn't the time.

"I'm just following my nose, Thelma. Thanks for the information."

As he walked out the door, she called, "Well, I hope you and your nose find my flag, Constable."

Sam stood out on the sidewalk for a moment, trying to decide what to do next. It might be a good idea to drive over to Mecklin and see what, if anything, they'd turned up in the death of Kevin Lassiter. He wondered if he shook that tree if Danny Eiler might fall out. At least it was worth a try.

He opened the door of his jeep and was angling himself into the driver's seat when a rifle shot cracked. All of Sam's senses went on alert. His adrenaline kicked in so hard that it took him a few seconds to realize he'd been hit.

# CHAPTER TWENTY-TWO

"Kimmy, this is not a good idea," Beth shouted through the front door of Sam's place at the woman who'd just exited like a bat out of hell.

Dammit. When she'd told Kimmy the truth about her father and his current whereabouts, she expected her friend to take some time to mull over the situation. Did she truly want to meet him? What would the consequences be? Maybe even what should she wear?

The last thing Beth expected was for her friend to jump up from the table with her hair on fire and demand to be taken right this minute to the tree house.

Shit.

Beth didn't even have shoes on when Kimmy rushed out. By the time she shoved her bare feet into her sneakers and went out the door, the woman was pacing back and forth in Sam's little backyard.

"Before we go, I'm calling Sam," she said, trotting down the porch steps. "And if he says don't go, then we're not going. I mean it, Kimmy."

"I'm going. I don't care what Sam says. I mean it, too, Beth."

"You don't even know how to get there."

"I'll find it if it takes me a whole damn week."

As she began punching in Sam's cell number, Beth wondered if she could knock Kimmy down and sit on her until Sam arrived. It was silly even to call him because she already knew what he was going to say. A big fat no.

His phone rang a couple of times before his voice mail kicked in. *We're sorry. The caller has turned off his phone. Please leave a message at the tone.*

That was odd, she thought. Then she decided against leaving a message that could only sound like hysterical ravings. She'd try to call him later, and hoped like hell he didn't come back to his place before she and Kimmy returned.

"Will you come *on!*" Kimmy yelled from the edge of the woods behind Sam's property.

"Okay. Okay."

Oh, God. She was going to be in such deep shit. In doo-doo up to her armpits. With Sam. With Kyle Ferrin. Sam would be furious if he discovered she left his cabin. And who knew what Kyle would do when she showed up with his daughter in an hour or so?

The only good thing about it, Beth supposed, was that the prospect of getting into trouble with Sam and Kyle certainly took her mind off her trouble with that loser, Danny.

☆

Thelma came out of the post office as fast as her ancient legs would carry her. Sam yelled at her to go back inside.

He was crouching down, using the jeep as cover, bleeding all over the damned sidewalk.

"Thelma, get the hell back inside," he yelled again.

"I will not." She looked to her right, and waved like someone flagging down a ship. "Blanche! Yoo-hoo! Hurry. Sam's been hurt."

Suddenly people were coming out of doors all up and down Main Street. Sam bit off a curse as he stood up, shouting.

"Everybody back inside. There might be a sniper. You're all in danger. Take cover. Now."

Thank God people scurried back through their doors, with the exception of Thelma and Blanche, who ganged up on him, one grasping his good arm, the other prodding his back as they hustled him into the post office.

"I've got a first-aid kit in back," Thelma said.

"Let's all go in back, away from these windows," Sam said.

Even as he spoke, though, he had a strong feeling that the bullet was personal, meant for him alone, and he doubted there was a sniper out there, waiting to pick off more residents of the town.

"Well, come on," Thelma told him. "You're bleeding all over my clean floor, Sam."

"I can't help it, Thelma."

Once in the back room, Sam sat on a sorting table like a piece of priority mail while the two women proceeded to work on him as efficiently as any medics he'd ever seen in the field. Blanche ripped off the sleeve of his shirt to expose the wound, which wasn't as bad as he'd anticipated. The bullet had simply gouged out a long chunk of flesh in his upper arm. It hadn't penetrated the muscle.

"This might sting," Thelma said as she slapped a square of soaked gauze on him.

Sam nearly bit through his lip. "Christ, Thelma. At least you could give a guy a bullet to bite on before you do that."

"Wimp," the postmistress muttered as she applied another square of gauze and began to wind more around his arm. "This'll do until you get to an emergency room."

He wished he had time. Sam winced as he reached for the phone in his back pocket. He didn't remember turning it off, dammit. Maybe he'd sat on it wrong.

As soon as he punched the button to activate it, the phone began to ring.

"Sam, it's Gus. Larry and I jumped in my truck and followed that shooter. We're right behind him now on Eighteen Mile Road."

That's all he needed, Sam thought. Two yahoos playing cowboy. "Don't get too close, Gus. You hear me? I'll be there in two minutes."

Sam was already off the table. He could hardly hear Gus for the clucking of Blanche and Thelma.

"You hear me, Gus?"

"I hear you."

"Did you get a look at him?"

"Yeah. Long-haired guy. Big. Maybe six-two."

"Could it be Danny Eiler?" Sam asked.

"Damn. I never thought of that. It sure could be. Oh, wait. The bastard's turning now onto the old gravel pit road."

. . . which dead-ended about a quarter of a mile from the tree house, Sam recalled. What the hell was this guy up to?

"Pull over, Gus. Don't follow him in. I'm coming."

"Okay, Sam. We'll sit here and get him if he comes out."

Great. A sniper. Two cowboys. And poor ol' Barney Fife without enough time to get back to his place for a weapon.

"You don't happen to have a firearm with you, do you, Gus?"

"Got my old deer rifle right behind me on the rack."

"I'm going to need that. You and Larry stay right there."

"Roger that, Sam."

Oh, brother.

He ran out of the post office with the two old women right on his heels. He had to push his way through the little crowd that had gathered outside to get to his jeep.

As he headed west out of town, he remembered chasing after Beth in her speeding Miata. It seemed like a hundred years ago. With one hand on the wheel now, he thumbed her number into his phone.

He was torn between proceeding directly to his place where Beth was holed up with Kimmy, or pursuing Danny. At least the guy wasn't headed for Heart Lake. Right now Sam was grateful for any good news.

Beth finally answered her phone, only to tell him "Just a minute, Sam" and then call out, "Kimmy. Wait. Hold up. Sam's on the phone."

Wait? Hold up? Those weren't things you said to somebody who was inside a small cabin with you.

"Beth, where are you?" he demanded.

"Well . . ."

"Where? Tell me, for God's sake."

"Well . . . You're probably not going to like this, but we're on our way to the tree house. I told Kimmy about Kyle, and she's desperate to meet him. I couldn't stop her."

"Go back!" he shouted into the phone.

"What?"

"Go back!"

"We're almost there, Sam. It wouldn't make any sense to . . . Oh, no. Kimmy! Oh, my God . . ."

"Beth!"

Their connection was broken.

☆

Danny had come out of nowhere to wrap one arm around Kimmy's neck while the other held a gun to her head. He ordered Beth to drop the phone or he'd shoot her friend.

She didn't drop it. She threw it at him. My God. He really was here in Michigan! And right now he looked so crazed that she almost believed he'd do what he threatened.

"Let her go, Danny. For God's sake. She didn't do anything to you."

"Shut up, Beth."

"Let her go."

"I told you to shut up."

Kimmy's face had gone chalk white. Her eyes were huge and terrified. She looked as if she were going to faint.

"It'll be okay, Kimmy," Beth told her. "Trust me, sweetie. I'll make it okay."

Kimmy tried to speak, but Danny's arm was choking her.

"Stop it. Let her go. You're hurting her."

"Shut up, Beth," Danny yelled again. "I'll hurt her worse if you don't keep your mouth shut. I can do it, too. And I've got nothing to lose since I already killed that doper who left his fingerprints all over your father's car. And last but not least, your boyfriend. He's dead, Beth. I killed him. What do you think of that?"

"No! That's not true. I was just talking to him." Beth searched the ground for a rock or a stick she could throw at him.

"Well, I don't know how he could've used a phone, babe. Unless he was calling 911. I shot him, and I saw him go down. I saw the blood."

It wasn't true, was it? All of a sudden Beth felt disoriented and confused. Hadn't she just been talking to Sam? Or was that longer ago than it seemed? Her head was buzzing, and her stomach was turning. The whole world felt like it was turning upside down. Suddenly nothing made sense.

Danny looked rabid. His hair and clothes were dirty. Even though she was several feet away, Beth could see that his pupils were dilated. There was white foamy spittle in the corners of his mouth. He yanked his arm from around Kimmy's neck, then grabbed her braid, wrenching her head to the side, still pointing the pistol at her temple. Kimmy screamed in pain.

"Oh, don't," Beth pleaded. "Stop it, Danny. You're hurting her."

"Read my lips, Beth. I. Don't. Care."

"What do you want?"

"What do I want? That's simple. You. I want you. That's why I followed you from California. That's why I bugged your cell phone. It's why I know you've been such a deceitful, disloyal bitch."

"I don't belong to you," she said. "You have no right . . ."

"Shut up," he screamed. "You do belong to me. You just don't know it yet. I thought you'd understand that after all the problems you had here. The fire. The windows. I thought you'd understand that you belonged back with me."

"Oh, Danny." She didn't know what else to say. Before he'd been possessive and obsessed. Now he just seemed crazy.

"I want you to walk in front of me," he said. "You do what I tell you. Come on. This way." He angled his head in the direction of the tree house. "If you try to run, or do anything stupid, I'll kill this woman. I promise you. I'll kill her. It'll be your fault."

Whether he was insane or strung out on drugs or both, she utterly believed him, so on shaky legs, Beth started in the direction Danny had indicated. She took one step. Then two.

She kept her feet moving forward by telling herself Sam's not dead. Sam's not dead. If he were dead, I'd know it. I'd feel it in my heart. Dear God, don't let Sam be dead.

"Please don't do this," she said when she was abreast of Danny, trying so hard to keep the fear and panic out of her voice. She had to be strong. If she managed to sound strong somehow, maybe he'd back off. Or if she could convince him she still cared about him. "I'll do whatever you want, Danny. Whatever you say. Just let Kimmy go."

He stared at her, wet-mouthed, wild-eyed. A crazed beast. He even sounded like an animal. "You have no idea how much I love you, do you? You have absolutely no fucking idea."

"I do," she said, hoping to calm him. "I didn't know before, but now I do. I love you, too, Danny. I'm sure we can work this out."

"You love me. That's a joke. What a goddamn lie."

"I'm not lying. I do love you. Let Kimmy go, and I'll prove it."

"You belong to me, Beth. Goddammit. You're mine. Nobody else's."

"Okay. Well, we'll work this out." She held out her hands in supplication. "Let her go, Danny. I'll go back to California with you, if that's what you want. Is that what you want?"

"I'll tell you what I want. Just walk. Just start walking. Move!"

☆

Sam hit the brakes so hard behind Gus's pickup that he almost went through the windshield of his jeep.

"Eiler's still down the road," Gus said. "At least he hasn't come back out here. He's driving an old white Dodge."

"Here you go, Sam." Larry handed him the rifle. "It's loaded."

Sam checked the battered old Remington just to be sure. "What's it good for?" he asked.

"Oh, 'bout seventy-five yards, give or take," Larry said.

"Okay. You two stay here," Sam told them.

He debated a second whether to take the jeep. He'd never been fast, even during his best years, and now the metal plates and screws in his leg had slowed him even more. But then he decided that the element of surprise was probably more important than speed. God, he hoped so, as he sprinted down the gravel pit road toward the woods.

☆

When they reached the tree house, Danny seemed a bit confused, as if he didn't quite know what to do next. He'd stopped holding Kimmy by her braid and was now jamming his gun into her ribs, forcing her ahead of him as he circled Kyle's campsite.

"Who's that old guy who was staying here?" he asked.

Kimmy didn't answer, so Beth volunteered. Anything not to anger their captor. Anything to give her time to figure out how to get away from him.

"He's Kimmy's father," she said. "We were on our way to see him."

"Well, you're too late. He tried to stop me back there in the woods. Only I stopped him." He gave a sick little chuckle, jammed the barrel of his gun harder into Kimmy's side, and said, "Sorry about that."

Poor Kimmy dropped to her knees, weeping. When Beth started forward, Danny turned his weapon on her.

"Sit down," he said.

"But I . . ."

"Sit down."

She did, as close to Kyle's campfire as she could get. Maybe if there were still some hot coals beneath the ashes, she could figure out a way to make Danny drop the gun. She wondered what Sam would do in this situation, and her throat seized up and tears stung her eyes.

He wasn't dead. She wouldn't let him be dead. How could she live the rest of her life without him?

Danny sat down beside her, so close it made her flesh crawl. When she started to edge away, he snarled like a rabid dog.

"You move when I tell you to move. You got that?"

She nodded. For the first time since she'd laid eyes on him today, Beth realized to her horror how this was all going to end. Either he would kill her, or she would kill him.

There was no other way.

☆

Sam swore under his breath. Until that son of a bitch moved far enough away from Beth and Kimmy, there was no way he could get a safe shot off, especially with a weapon he'd never fired before.

There wasn't room for error.

He'd just have to wait.

Ignoring the pain in his arm. Stilling the panic that tried to ripple through his chest. Breathing evenly as he'd been trained to do. Focusing. Keeping his target in his sights.

Just then, off to his left, he heard something. A rustle of tree branches. The breaking of twigs. They were human sounds.

He took his eye off Danny just long enough to see Kyle Ferrin staggering through the trees.

It was too late to stop him.

☆

Kyle blundered out of the woods like a bloodied wounded bear, growling as he came.

Danny leapt to his feet, firing.

And Kyle kept coming.

Beth scrambled out of his way, while Kimmy simply stared, frozen in place.

Danny stepped back and fired again. Two. Three times. All point-blank.

With one last bloody lunge, Kyle fell at his feet.

One more shot rang out.

Danny dropped his gun and toppled backward, his crazed eyes still staring at Beth, but now there was a bullet hole between them.

And then, for just a moment, the world went absolutely still.

# CHAPTER TWENTY-THREE

The next hour was a blur for Beth. A blur of blood, bodies both alive and dead, voices that seemed to come from far away, and Sam. Always Sam. Beth couldn't, wouldn't let him out of her sight.

It was only later, in the emergency room in Mecklin, that the blur began to dissolve, and her numbness at last gave way to tears. They gave her a pill; she didn't even know what it was for, but obediently swallowed it if it would make her stop crying.

She wouldn't let go of Sam's hand, so she was forced to turn her head when a doctor stitched up his arm.

Finally, Sam said, "Let's get out of here."

"Where's Kimmy?"

"She's under sedation," he said. "She was in pretty rough shape, so they're going to keep her here at least twenty-four hours." He took her face in both hands. "How are you?"

It was probably the hundredth time he'd asked her, and each time she had replied "I'm okay," but this time she really meant it.

"Are you okay enough to go back to the tree house for a minute? I want to get Kyle's personal effects before they close down the crime scene, and the place gets trashed by a lot of curious ghouls."

"I can do that," she said. "Let's go."

He looked at her with shining eyes. Beth read pride in them, and admiration, and a warmth that almost seemed to flow into her own body. He smiled, and whispered, "You're a tough cookie, cookie."

Beth smiled back. The mere act of doing that seemed to distance her a bit more from the horrible events of the morning. "I feel more like a crumbled cookie, to tell you the truth."

Crumbled or not, as they drove back to Heart Lake, Beth felt fierce and strong about one thing. She was going to spend the rest of her life with Sam. The clarity of this notion, its utter inevitability, had struck her while he'd been holding her hand in the emergency room.

She thought of all the missteps she'd taken in her life, all the bad decisions and misguided affections, all the damn failures, and realized that rather than drag her down, they had ultimately led her back to the love of her life. Not that she excused herself, especially for her disastrous relationship with Danny, but she took responsibility for those mistakes and blessed them at the same time because they had brought her home.

*Whither thou goest . . .*

It suddenly made perfect sense.

☆

Sam was glad they'd come back to the tree house as soon as they did because already there were a dozen curious onlookers loitering just beyond the yellow crime scene tape. Once the county cops were gone, the tape wasn't going to deter anybody.

With Bethie's hand still tucked warmly into his, he sought out the sheriff.

"Dave, mind if I go up in the tree house and get some of Kyle Ferrin's personal effects before this place gets torn up? I'd like his daughter to have as much of his stuff as possible."

"I need to ask you some questions about that, Sam. You and Miss Simon, here."

"Beth's pretty wrung out, Dave. Can we put that off until tomorrow?"

The sheriff gave him one of those I'm-in-charge-here-but-I'm-a-reasonable-man looks. "Yeah. Be at the station by nine o'clock. And I want to see whatever you're taking from there." He pointed to the tree house.

"You got it. Thanks, Dave."

Sam gave Beth a boost up the ladder, and bent to follow her through the door they'd put there almost twenty years before.

"Oh, Sam! Oh, my God," she breathed. "I know this place by heart."

While he searched through Kyle's things — sadly, not much — Beth revisited their past.

"Here's the old linoleum we took out of the Brecht cottage before they tore it down. Oh, and look at this! I can't believe it's still here, Sam. The quilt my mother was going to toss, so we brought it here."

"Hard to believe it after all these years," he said, opening a battered shoe box he was sure had belonged to Kyle.

"Here's our honeymoon jar," she exclaimed. "Look at this!" She shook the glass jar, and they both heard the coins they'd deposited from a summer of making love. It had been Beth's idea — to save for their eventual honeymoon.

Sam couldn't help but laugh. "That and a couple hundred dollars would get us as far as Detroit."

"We were going to go to Spain. Remember?"

He remembered. "Take a look at these, Beth." He handed her the dilapidated shoe box.

"What are they?"

"Looks like all the letters Kimmy's mother wrote to Kyle when he was in Vietnam. There are dozens of them."

Beth thumbed through the envelopes. "I hope these will give poor Kimmy some kind of solace. Poor Kyle. He was trying to save us, Sam."

"I know. I wish I could've stopped that son of a bitch, but I didn't have a clear shot until it was too late."

She sighed, putting the top on the box. "Well, maybe it's what Kyle wanted in a weird way. To be a hero to his daughter instead of a derelict dad. It's so sad."

Sam reached out and pulled her against him, and they just sat there in silence for a few minutes. It occurred to him to suggest that they use their honeymoon jar in the near future. But he was too much of a coward.

What if she said no?

☆

"Let's go home," Sam said, after the police had cleared all the items he wanted to take, including, among other things, Thelma's precious flag.

Beth assumed they were going back to his cabin, so when he bypassed the road to the north side of Heart Lake, she asked, "Where are we going?"

"Home," he said, turning his poor old jeep onto the road that led to her house. "You'll be safe here now, sweetheart. It's all over."

The house had never looked so good to her as they walked up the lawn. Beth even managed to blot out the memory of Danny on a scaffold, putting final touches to the trim, just as she tried to blot out her last view of him as he fell with Sam's bullet in his skull. She had cared for him once. Maybe, she hoped, she'd feel bad about his death someday.

Sam still had the key her parents had given him, so there was no problem getting in. The familiar fragrance of the house — part age, part cool shade, part eucalyptus in huge porcelain vases — nearly overwhelmed her.

It wasn't much after noon, but to Beth it suddenly felt like midnight.

"I'm exhausted," she said. "I think I could sleep for a year."

"Sounds good to me."

Almost before she knew it, Sam had picked her up and was carrying her up the staircase.

"Which room, my lady?" he asked.

Without even thinking, Beth answered, "My old room. Oh, Sam. I wish we could turn back the clock and be kids again. I wish we could have all those years we lost. What an awful waste."

His arms tightened around her, but he didn't say anything. Beth couldn't read his expression, other than a weariness not unlike her own. His silence worried her, but she reminded herself that Sam had shot a man to death only hours before. In light of that, she shouldn't be surprised that he didn't feel like reveling in their good old days right now.

She didn't either, come to think of it. She longed to talk about their future rather than their past. Maybe after they both got some sleep . . .

Her old bedroom was dark because the windows were still boarded up. Beth was almost glad she hadn't had them fixed yet. This midday darkness was exactly what she wanted, what she needed. Sam put her gently on the bed. Oh, it felt so good. Now if only she could really relax. If only she could turn off the thoughts rampaging through her head.

"I'll be right back," Sam said.

She was so tempted to reach for his hand and beg him not to leave her, but she refrained, not wanting to seem like a total wuss. Sam deserved better from a mate.

With a deep sigh, she closed her eyes and invited sleep to cleanse her brain, if only for a while. In the adjacent bathroom, she heard water running in the big claw-footed tub, and decided that a bath was probably Sam's way to unwind. It sounded like a wonderful idea, actually.

A few minutes later Sam came back into the bedroom, slid his arms beneath her knees and her back, and picked her up.

"What are you doing?" she asked.

"Not me. You. You're taking a bubble bath."

He undressed her in the bathroom, not like a lover so much as a mother gently undressing a sleepy child. Then he picked her up again and lowered her through the gardenia-scented bubbles and into the deep warmth of the water.

All she could do was moan with pleasure.

"Too hot?" he asked.

"It's just perfect. Thank you, Sam."

He squatted down beside the tub, reached out and tucked a curl behind her ear. "Want me to stay or leave you here to relax?"

"Stay."

"Okay." He settled on the floor.

"Does that bother your leg?" she asked when he looked uncomfortable.

"Just a little."

Beth's eyes widened. "Sam Mendenhall, I think that's the first time in our whole lives that I've ever heard you admit to even slight discomfort. My God. We must be getting old."

He grinned. "I am. But you're still the same. Did you know that every time I saw this tub, I always imagined this. You, leaning back like that, your hair getting all damp and corkscrewed." He dipped his fingers into the bubbles. "All these bubbles just barely covering you."

Beth smiled languidly. "Come on in."

"I'll just watch. This time, anyway. We'll have to get a bigger tub."

"You're right."

She closed her eyes, breathing in the rising steam, reveling in this moment.

"I love you, Sam." It seemed so natural, saying that. So absolutely right.

"I love you, too, Bethie. I always have."

"Say it again, Sam. Those are the most beautiful words in the world."

"I love you, Beth."

She sighed and opened one eye. "What do you think we ought to do about it?"

"Marriage sounds pretty good to me. How about you?"

"It sounds good to me, too." She laughed. "Is that an official proposal?"

"No." He winced slightly as he got up on his knees. "But this is. Will you marry me, Beth?"

"Yes. Yes and yes again. If I had a thousand lifetimes, a million, I'd marry you in every one of them."

Sam smiled. "And maybe by the millionth, we'd learn how to get it right the first time."

☆

Beth and Sam sat with Kimmy during Kyle's funeral. The little church in Shelbyville was crowded. It hadn't taken long for word to get out that Kyle had not only saved the lives of Beth and Kimmy, but that he was the phantom thief. Nobody held it against him. Quite the opposite. Blanche had provided the flowers for the service from her own garden, and Thelma's flag was draped ceremonially over the casket.

When the pastor finished his eulogy, Kimmy whispered to Beth, "He's finally home. I wish he'd come back sooner. Look how many people cared about him."

Six men from the VFW carried his coffin from the church to the little cemetery next door. One of them folded the flag and presented it to Kimmy. A bugler from the high school band played "Taps."

Beth had been so worried about her friend and how she'd cope with finding and losing her father so tragically. For the past few days, it seemed all Kimmy could do was cry.

Kimmy hugged the folded flag to her chest as they walked out of the cemetery. By the time they reached Beth's car, she had dried her tears and was even wearing a little smile.

"That's better," Sam said.

"I'll be fine," she said. "Thanks for bringing me those letters, Sam. They helped. He loved me. He wrote it over and over again."

Beth pointed to the flag. "That was nice of Thelma."

Kimmy laughed. It was so good to hear.

"What's so funny?" Beth asked her.

"I'm going to have to hide this. I just know the old bat's going to want it back."

☆

They drove back to the big old house at Heart Lake, where the U-Haul trailer Sam had packed waited in the driveway. While he hooked it up to the Miata, Beth and Kimmy walked up to the house.

"I'll miss you two," Kimmy said. "I'll take good care of your house while you're gone. I promise."

"I know you will. That's why I asked you to stay and keep an eye on it. And we'll be back in a year or two. Sam just needs to do something he's really good at for a while."

Kimmy cocked her head. "What about you, pal?"

"Well, I'm really good at this." She spread her arms toward the house. "So we're going to find an old wreck of a house in North Carolina, near the base, and I'm going to turn it into the best little bed-and-breakfast in the state."

"Bethie? You ready?" Sam called. "I promised your mother we'd be there by five."

"When's the wedding?" Kimmy asked.

"Seven tonight. I just hope I can keep the groom from strangling my matron of honor."

"Shelby."

"Who else?"

# ABOUT THE AUTHOR

Mary McBride has been writing romance, both historical and contemporary, for a dozen years. She lives in St. Louis, Missouri, with her husband and two sons.

She loves to hear from readers, so please visit her Web site at MaryMcBride.net or write to her c/o P.O. Box 411202, St. Louis, MO 63141.

# THE EDITOR'S DIARY

*Dear Reader,*

Love at first sight is nice. But love the second time around is even sweeter—especially if it's with the same person. From a blissful return to young love to a second chance at life, come see how two is better than one is these new Warner Forever titles this December.

Ever daydream about what happened to your childhood sweetheart? Well, wipe the sleep from your eyes as we present **Mary McBride**'s latest **SAY IT AGAIN, SAM**, a romp bound to jump-start your heart and spice up your fantasies. *Bookpage* called her last book "sparkling" and "irresistible" so prepare to be dazzled. Weird things have been happening at Heart Lake. Strange things are being stolen—a trophy in a high school collection and even tuna fish from a local market—and everybody is jumpy. So Sam Mendenhall, former Delta Force operator, is called in to keep the peace. Little does he know that the chaos is just beginning as Beth Simon, his childhood sweetheart, is back in town. They were the perfect couple years ago . . . until Sam proposed, Beth refused, and Sam married someone else. Now single and hot on the trail of the person behind the mysterious thefts, he can't resist when the spark between them ignites, leading them to the little cabin in the woods where they fell in love years ago.

What would you do if your Navy SEAL husband who is presumed dead suddenly reappears, but with absolutely no memory of you, your daughter, or the life you shared? Helen Renault from **Marliss Melton**'s **FORGET ME**

**NOT** has no idea what to do. She was just standing on her own two feet at last—and proud of it—when Gabe returns. Though she cares for him, they married young and for all the wrong reasons. But as she nurses him back to health from both his physical and mental trauma, she can't help but see he is a very different man now. Gone is the distant, secretive husband he once was. This new Gabe is a man she could finally fall in love with. But as his memory returns, bit by bit, a governmental cover-up is exposed, putting all three lives in danger . . . and jeopardizing their second chance at love. I hope you don't have other plans for today because, as *New York Times* bestselling author Lisa Jackson says, "FORGET ME NOT will pull you in and never let you go."

To find out more about Warner Forever, these December titles, and the author, visit us at www.warnerforever.com.

With warmest wishes,

*Karen Kosztolnyik*

Karen Kosztolnyik, Senior Editor

P.S. The New Year is just around the corner and here are two little resolutions you can't help but keep. **Kathryn Caskie** pens the witty and charming story of a lady's maid whose tingle cream—and her romance with a Scottish marquis—sets the ton abuzz in **LADY IN WAITING**; and **Shari Anton** delivers the spellbinding and sensual tale of a widow who hires a mercenary to keep her daughter and her village safe, only to pay with her heart in **AT HER SERVICE**.